DEFENDERS O...

SPEARS
AND
SHADOWS

S. C. GRAYSON

SPEARS AND SHADOWS

S. C. GRAYSON

CITY OWL
PRESS

SPEARS AND SHADOWS
Defenders of the Light, Book 1

CITY OWL PRESS
www.cityowlpress.com

Cover Design by MiblArt. All stock photos licensed appropriately.

Edited by Lisa Green.

For information on subsidiary rights, please contact the publisher at info@cityowlpress.com.

Print Edition ISBN: 978-1-64898-182-1

Digital Edition ISBN: 978-1-64898-181-4

Printed in the United States of America

For Rhys.
Through the darkest night.

PRAISE FOR S. C. GRAYSON

"Filled with romance and action, *Spears and Shadows* is a promising introduction to a world where everlasting love and the ongoing fight between Good and Evil abound! Where sorcerers are disguised as professors, where the girl participates in her own protection, and where love transcends the restrictions of time. Main characters are relatable and likeable while secondary characters provide subtle side stories. This new world being crafted by S. C. Grayson promises to be an interesting and intriguing world into which readers will gladly want to escape." – *InD'tale Magazine*

"The perfect balance of action, mystery, fantasy, and deliciously sweet romance, *Chaos and Crowns* was an unputdownable adventure 'til the very end. I adore Grayson's whip-smart heroines and powerful cinnamon roll heroes!" – *Lily Riley, author of The Assassin and the Libertine*

"The twists and turns come fast and furious in this rapid paced novel, Beauty and the Blade. The character development is great as their perspectives are challenged and they learn more about each other. The supporting characters are funny, charming, and also serve to help Contessa and Nathaniel in their growth and development. Filled with intrigue and skilled fighting, this fantasy is sure to have hearts pumping and blood racing. The next in this series can't come soon enough!" – *InD'tale Magazine*

"S.C. Grayson has written a fantastic debut fantasy romance with *Spears and Shadows*! Adam is one of my favorite heroes I've read so far this year. He's the perfect balance of this strong mysterious fighter, but also dedicated and smart (he's a professor!) and sweet.

Talk about swoon worthy! Nora a fantastic main character! You'll be rooting for her the whole time, and feel with her through all of the ups and downs of navigating this new magical world." – *E. E. Hornburg, author of The Night's Chosen*

"Peaky Blinders meets Bridgerton in this lush reimagining of *Beauty and the Beast* with an endearing cast of characters, subtle magic, and a deliciously agonizing slow burn romance. From the very first chapter we're transported for an alternate historical version of London filled with the subtle magic wielded by the Talented. The descriptions and dialogue fit so well and painted lush pictures in my mind the entire time I read. The use of subtle magic and the way it affects the characters and society as a whole is brilliant, and so refreshing. This book was absolutely everything I wanted it to be and more." – *Megan Van Dyke, author of Second Star to the Left*

1

THE BLISTERS ON NORA'S FEET THROBBED IN TIME WITH THE amplified base pounding out of the speakers above the crowded bar. Colored lights cut through hazy air, and the song blasting through the room was by some pop star whose name Nora should probably know but couldn't call to mind.

She took a sip of the drink her sister had ordered for her and grimaced when she found it was fruity and cloyingly sweet. It appeared the bar's only saving grace was their hot wings, which Odelle had ordered for Nora.

Now Odelle raised her glass to her sister in a toast. "Cheers to the youngest department head in Chicago Field Museum history."

Nora raised the chicken wing in her hand and bumped it against the rim of Odelle's martini glass, even as she countered, "Well, I'm not officially department head yet."

"It's only a matter of time, just take the damn compliment," Odelle retorted, shaking her head so the neon lights reflected off her sleek platinum bob. "You nailed your presentation and got funding for your project restoring those weapons from ancient Greece. Although, maybe I should get some of the credit too. I bet those dull old fogeys at the museum would have given you the funding for your project no matter what you said, as long as you stood up there wearing the outfit I selected."

"I'm sure you're right, *zaika*," Nora commented, intentionally not bringing up the myriad of blisters caused by the heels her sister had picked out. "The museum board decides what departments get funding solely based on how much they want to sleep with the person presenting the pitch. Now I understand why the paleontology department always gets all the money. I mean, have you seen Bert?"

Odelle snorted in an unladylike manner. "Of course, big gray tufts of ear hair have always been my greatest turn-on."

Nora smiled as she polished off the wing in her hand and licked the sauce from between her fingers.

"In all seriousness, though, thank you for your help with the presentation. Getting to restore these artifacts all but guarantees I'll get that department head promotion I've been gunning for. I mean seriously, Leo keeps trash-talking me to the board, saying I'm too young for the position, but he hasn't made any contributions this big since he ran that mummy through an MRI machine almost five years ago!"

"Okay, okay," Odelle cut in. "Now is not the time to start in on all the drama. If I let you vent about department politics, I'll be here until I have grey ear tufts of my own."

Nora bit back her retort, knowing her sister had listened to her go on about the dramas of academia enough in the past. Besides, she had promised her sister that tonight would be a celebration, and she wouldn't spend the entire time talking about work, as much as she would prefer to be thinking about work these days. Instead, she asked, "Did you have to wear the tall prosthetics plus the shoes? Isn't that a touch redundant?"

Tonight, Odelle had chosen to wear the pair of sculpted prosthetic legs that made her six feet tall, then proceeded to add a pair of killer heels to the ensemble. The finished product had the effect of making Odelle look like a veritable Amazon.

"What's the point of having feet made of carbon fiber if I don't take advantage of it by wearing fantastic shoes? Besides, I like feeling as if I could eat men alive."

Nora nodded over her drink. "Speaking of which, that one over there looks as if he wouldn't mind being eaten alive."

Odelle glanced over her shoulder at the tanned Ken doll of a man who eyed her from a few feet away. Seeing her looking, he approached and slid himself onto the empty bar stool next to them.

Nora smiled and took another sip of her drink, suppressing a grimace again at the overpowering sweetness as Odelle struck up a conversation. Nora caught the bartender's eye and waved him over to order herself a dirty martini as her sister continued to flirt.

Just as the bartender arrived with her drink, Nora's phone vibrated in her back pocket. She fished it out of her jeans and frowned at the illuminated screen.

Even as she read the message from the emergency notification system at work, her phone buzzed in her hand again, with several new texts popping up on the screen from coworkers. They immediately began arguing about whose job it was to go in and check on things. Nora didn't hesitate before typing a message of her own.

As soon as it was sent, she turned back to Odelle to explain that she had to leave, but her sister was still otherwise occupied. Odelle had leaned in towards her admirer and he was reaching out to put a hand on her knee, just below the hem of her short black dress. He clearly hadn't noticed that she had hinges instead of knees in the dim light of the bar, too distracted by Odelle's coy smile. Nora smirked despite herself when the man jumped as his hand encountered cool carbon fiber instead of warm skin. He raised his eyebrows a fraction, but Odelle gave him a wicked grin and continued their conversation.

Nora tapped Odelle on the shoulder to get her attention.

"Hey *zaika*, I have to go. There is a security breach at work, and I need to go deal with it," Nora explained, already slipping on her leather jacket.

"Girl, you do not know how to take a break. It's supposed to be your night off!"

"Comes with the territory of getting promoted," Nora countered as she grabbed a few crumpled bills out of her purse and put them on the bar. "I've got to show people I can handle the responsibilities. You stay and enjoy yourself. It looks like you aren't quite done breaking that poor man's heart."

Indeed, Odelle's admirer was obviously appreciating the fit of Odelle's dress as the women spoke.

"Oh, I'm not," Odelle admitted, "but he can wait. I'm coming to the museum with you to make sure you don't stay too late."

Odelle fished a pen out of her purse and grabbed the man's wrist. His brows drew together in puzzlement before he smirked at the realization that she was scribbling her number on the back of his hand. Nora sighed. If she knew Odelle, she would lead this man on for the next two weeks before realizing he didn't have the brains to keep up with her, then she'd leave him hanging.

"All right, let's get out of here," Odelle said as she grabbed Nora's elbow to start weaving towards the exit. Just before they slipped into the crowd, Odelle looked over her shoulder and shot a wink at the enamored man whose gaze still followed them.

Nora chuckled as they pushed towards the door.

"That poor man. He's not going to know what hit him."

As the cab pulled up outside the museum, Nora's stomach clenched with unease. Red and blue flashing lights filtered in through the car windows. She threw open the door and pushed her way into the chilly air as Odelle handled paying the driver.

Wrapping her scarf around her neck to combat the cold night air, Nora made her way over to the nearest squad car.

"Excuse me, sir?" Nora asked. "What's going on here? I work at the museum and I got an alert about a security breach."

The police officer looked rather uninterested as he answered. "A bunch of security alarms went off in an office on the lower level, called in the emergency services automatically. We've searched the whole area, but there's nobody around." The officer shrugged as he continued. "Must have been a glitch in the system."

"Well, I work in an office on the lower level. Can I at least go in and make sure that nothing was damaged or stolen? We store a lot of priceless artifacts down there."

"That would be perfect, actually." The officer's tone turned grateful. "We need somebody to confirm that nothing was taken before we can leave the scene. You can go inside and take stock."

Nora dug through her purse for her office keys as she wove her way through the parked squad cars to the main entrance. Before she could make it to the bottom of the museum steps, Odelle strode up behind her and grabbed her arm.

"What are you doing?"

"Going inside to make sure nothing was damaged, of course."

Odelle looked at her like she had grown a third arm. "You can't go in there. What if the burglar is still inside?"

"Um, yes I can," Nora said, turning and continuing her march up the steps. "Besides, the police said they swept the area and it was empty."

Odelle continued to follow her. "Well, then I'm coming with you."

Nora sighed but did not slow her walking. "You're just coming with so you can be the first reporter on the scene. Get the inside scoop on any big news before anybody else gets wind of it."

"Well, maybe," Odelle admitted, not sounding the least bit contrite. "But somebody also has to protect you. You may specialize in ancient weaponry, but you would be useless in actual combat."

"And you plan on fighting off a burglar in those shoes?"

Odelle seemed unconcerned. "If Wonder Woman can figure it out, then so can I."

Nora chuckled as she led them into the darkened museum.

"You know," she commented as they passed the looming Tyrannosaurus Rex in the main entrance, which looked haunting in the dim lighting, "I've always wanted to come in here at night. See if the dinosaurs and mummies come alive when we aren't looking."

"Stop joking around," Odelle scolded her without venom, the click of her heels echoing as they made their way down the steps to the basement. "This is a crime scene."

"It's not a crime scene; it's just the scene of a glitch in the security system."

As they reached the bottom of the stairs, Nora grew warm and was forced to loosen the scarf around her neck. Even then, a bead of moisture trickled down the small of her back.

As if she had heard her thoughts, Odelle asked, "Is it just me or is it really hot down here?"

"It's not just you." Nora unzipped her jacket.

"Maybe there's some sort of problem with the boiler. That might have tripped the security system."

"Is that even possible?" Nora asked as they reached the door to her office. Just as she moved to unlock it, a slight shuffle at the other end of the hallway grabbed her attention.

She whirled towards the sound, eyes straining to see any movement in the darkness. Just as she was about to turn back to her office door, scolding herself for being skittish, a dark shape shifted, moving towards the loading docks.

Nora froze once more, her hand snaking out to grab Odelle's wrist. Understanding the unspoken message, she remained silent. There was a tense moment where both the intruder and Nora seemed to acknowledge their awareness of the other's presence. The hot air was preternaturally still, as if the whole world was watching to see who would break the silence first.

Then, the intruder bolted. Nora took off after him without a second thought, dashing down the hallway, all the blisters on her feet forgotten in the adrenaline of the moment. She barreled after him, combat boots pounding against the concrete floor. He was heading toward the loading docks, where there was a back door he could use as an escape.

The figure was tall and lean, with long legs that allowed him to run faster than Nora, but her familiarity with the basement hallways allowed her to keep up. She skidded around several corners, trying to keep him in her line of sight. The intruder crashed out through the back door, Nora following behind. In the open ground of the moonlit back alley, the man was able to gain speed, and it became clear she wasn't going to be able to catch up.

Before she could think through the stupidity of her actions, Nora shouted, "Stop!" The word came out a little breathless from her sprint.

To her eternal surprise, the man froze, and Nora was taken off guard enough that she skidded to a halt behind him, the soles of her boots scraping against the asphalt. The man's shoulders were tense, as if he were fighting some internal battle. He turned his head as if to look behind him but stopped halfway. The moment stretched on, but Nora remained frozen, unsure of what to do now that she was no longer chasing the man.

As suddenly as he had stopped, the man took off again at a breakneck speed. Nora was about to bolt after him once more when Odelle flew through the door behind her and grabbed her arm, halting her.

"*Zolotse*, are you crazy?" Odelle's voice was breathless, too, but Nora hardly registered it as she watched the man's lanky figure disappear around the corner and into the night.

Odelle stepped in front of her, getting her attention.

"You just bolted away from me! What's gotten into you?"

"The man...didn't you see him?"

Odelle's eyes narrowed, and she looked towards the end of the alley where Nora was gesturing. "A man?"

Nora nodded.

"Nora...I didn't see anything."

Nora's mouth fell open.

"It was probably just too dark for you to see, but I swear there was a man. He ran out here!"

Odelle shook the arm she was still holding. "And you ran after him? He could have had a gun... He could have hurt you!"

Nora had the sense to look contrite. "I didn't even think of that."

Odelle clapped a hand to her forehead. "Why am I not surprised by that answer? Come on, let's go find the cops. Maybe they can still catch him."

NORA DID HER BEST TO GIVE THE POLICE A DESCRIPTION OF THE MAN, but she had only seen him from the back, and it had been dark. The officer listened to her story, but Nora got the distinct impression that he had pinned her as a frightened female whose nerves had gotten the better of her. The police informed her they would continue to monitor the area, but the monotone in which he said it convinced Nora he was just repeating the approved party line for her benefit. He made a point of telling her before she left that she should in fact run away from imaginary burglars and not towards them. Odelle looked at her meaningfully, clearly intimating an *I told you so* before dragging her off to hail a cab.

Odelle chattered in the cab about how Nora owed her a proper night out and speculated aloud about the man she had met at the bar. Nora nodded along, too tired to protest, her mind replaying the moment in the back alley on repeat. It seemed impossible that she had imagined him, but Odelle was observant, and it wasn't like her to miss things. Still, she couldn't help picturing the tense set of the man's shoulders before he had bolted. Nora told herself that her heart only hammered at the image from the adrenaline of the chase, but something in her was drawn to the stranger. She forced herself not to think about who the man might be or where she could find him as she fell into bed.

2

NORA MARCHED DOWN THE HALLWAY AT WORK, AN HOUR LATER THAN she normally liked to arrive at the office. She clutched a full cup of black coffee in one hand and felt vindicated by her usual insistence on not going out on a weeknight.

When she reached the door to the basement office, she paused with her hand on the knob, looking down the hall to where she'd spotted the strange man the night before. In the bright florescent lights and the hustle and bustle of her coworkers arriving, it was easy to believe she had imagined him. Still, the image of him frozen in the alley stuck in her mind.

Shaking her head, she pushed into her office to face her workday.

HER MORNING AT THE OFFICE ENDED UP KEEPING NORA BUSY ENOUGH that she didn't have time to ponder the incident beyond a cursory assurance to her officemates that the security breach had been dealt with. Despite feeling exhausted after an eventful night, Nora threw herself into finishing the projects still on her workbench and completing her inventory of all the weapons and artifacts being restored by her team. She needed to prioritize the restoration of the classical Greek sword and spear due to arrive the following week.

She was torn away from the task of cleaning a twelfth century *Zweihänder* by a friendly voice.

"Nora, are you going to take a lunch break, or just keep ploughing through like there is no tomorrow?"

Nora's coworker, Mandy, stood propped against the edge of her workbench. Her arms were folded but her thin dark eyes were full of kindness.

"You should definitely take a lunch break," Mandy continued. "You look like you've been run over by a dump truck."

"Thank you, Mandy," Nora said drily. "But haven't you heard? It's all the rage. Everybody is trying to look like they just crawled out of a dumpster." She began pulling off the gloves she'd donned to clean the sword and shoved some escaped curls from her face.

Mandy let out a giggle. "No, I just meant that you seem like you could use a break. Seriously, you were looking really glazed over. You feeling all right?"

Nora shrugged. "I'm fine, just had to come in late last night to deal with that security alert. Didn't end up getting very much sleep."

Mandy frowned. "I was hoping you were going to tell me you had a wild night on the town—or maybe that you went on a date last night."

"Well, I was actually out celebrating with my sister before work interrupted."

"Odelle finally manages to drag you out for some laughs and, the first chance you get, you run back to the office." Mandy pursed her lips in disapproval. "Can you ever enjoy yourself?"

"I was enjoying myself, but I'll never pass up an opportunity to get ahead and make a good impression."

"Get ahead? Nora, you have the promotion in the bag. You don't have to solve every single problem for everybody."

Nora shrugged and tugged at the hem of her chunky sweater. "I've been passed up for opportunities for stupid political reasons before."

Mandy gave a long-suffering sigh. "They aren't going to pass you up for a promotion for taking a lunch break. Now go and take your time. I'll hold down the fort around here."

Nora gave Mandy a mock salute before pushing her way out of the cramped basement office. She made her way down the narrow hallway to the stairs and climbed up into the museum proper, considering making her way to the cafeteria. It was Tuesday, which meant they'd be serving tacos, and melty queso sounded fantastic to Nora in her exhausted and irritable state.

As she wove through the crowds of visitors milling about, it struck Nora that she hadn't spent any time in the exhibits while they were open to the public in weeks. She momentarily let herself drift with the crowd towards the section under the banner reading Ancient Arms and Armaments. She made her way past the familiar cases filled with all manner of arrowheads, daggers, and antique revolvers until she found herself propped in a doorway across from the case containing artifacts originating from Greek and Roman empires.

As Nora observed the people milling through the exhibit, her attention caught on a tall man paused in front of the case containing the hoplite armor. He had been standing in front of it for longer than was typical for the casual museum patron, and the crowds were forced to part and flow around him as if he were a boulder in a stream. Nora pushed off the doorway she had been leaning on and took a step closer to the man. She told herself she was doing her job as a museum worker by answering patron's questions about artifacts, but something in the set of his shoulders drew her in.

As she stepped up next to him, she commented, "It's a fascinating collection, isn't it?"

Apparently, her attempt at a casual conversation starter was off base because he started violently. He jumped backwards, and his hands flew to his bag as if prepared to draw a weapon of his own. Before Nora could apologize for startling him, however, his wide russet eyes softened and the tension in his stance faded.

"I was not expecting you," the man said, as he smoothed the lapels of his blazer.

"I'm sorry for surprising you," Nora apologized, tilting her head up to meet his eyes, something she wasn't accustomed to given her stature. "I promise I don't make a habit of sneaking up on unsuspecting museum patrons. This is a one-time thing."

The man's eyes narrowed behind his round glasses. "Museum patrons? Do you work here?"

"I'm one of the weapons experts."

"Do you happen to be Nora?"

It was Nora's turn to be startled, and she shifted from foot to foot as she responded. "Yes. Have we met?"

Perhaps he was a benefactor she had spoken to at a museum fundraiser, but it seemed unlikely. Nora would remember somebody with a jawline as sharp his.

He shook his head, making the curls on his forehead flop back and forth.

"No, but I can't believe my luck in running into you."

Nora was saved from struggling to form an adequate response when the man barreled on to explain himself.

"You see, I've been doing some extensive research on weaponry from this era, and I kept coming across your name. I came here today to continue my research, but I never considered I might get lucky enough to actually meet you."

Nora's mind warred with itself on whether she should be flattered or unsettled, so the only thing she could think to say was, "Well, here I am."

"Here you are indeed."

In the silence following his odd statement, the battle between unease and flattery intensified until her stomach fluttered. The warm color of his eyes was pushing her towards flattered, but Nora reminded herself that she was at work. Distracting herself, she asked, "So what exactly did you come here to study?"

The man tore his gaze away from her and turned back to the case of hoplite armor,

"You see, I'm a literature professor at Northwestern University here in the city. I focus on classics with a particular emphasis on the works of ancient Greece. I had read in the paper about the new weapons that would be arriving here, and I was curious if your team would be interested in a sort of...professional collaboration for the sake of research?"

Nora chewed at her perpetually chapped bottom lip as she considered. A partnership in academia could be valuable to her research, but it hadn't been remotely what she'd expected when she'd decided to approach a museum visitor on a whim.

"Do you have a business card?" she hedged.

The man rifled in his weathered leather messenger bag and surfaced with a card, which he offered to Nora.

"Dr. Adam Scott," she read aloud.

"At your service," he responded with an inclination of his head. For all his forwardness, he was decidedly charming.

Nora dug into her own crammed purse. It took her a few moments, but she located one of her own business cards and offered it to Adam.

He peered down at it and commented, "Zvezda. That's an interesting last name."

"It's Russian. Constantly getting mispronounced."

"Nora, I'd love to grab some tea together and discuss how we might be able to assist one another with our research." He nodded towards a small café at the end of the gallery.

Nora shook her head. "I only came up here to grab some lunch, and I have to be getting back down to the office soon. You can email me, though."

"In that case, I look forward to seeing you soon." He offered her his hand to shake and Nora took it after the slightest of hesitations, finding his skin warm and rough under her palm. The back of her neck tingled.

"It was a pleasure to meet you Adam," she responded, releasing his hand and taking a step back.

"The pleasure was all mine, Nora."

Nora turned to walk away, but as she retreated, she felt his gaze trained on her for an inordinately long time. When she reached the bottom of the stairs that headed up towards the cafeteria, she glanced behind her, only to find he had turned back to the case of armor. He looked at the Corinthian helmet with bold red plumage with rapt attention, just as he had when she'd first approached him. She shook her head at the oddity of it all before marching up the stairs in pursuit of some tacos.

DESPITE MANDY HAVING ENCOURAGED HER TO TAKE HER TIME DURING lunch, Nora found herself back at her desk with her tacos. After her unusual interaction in the museum, she had opted to eat in the far less populated office, taking the opportunity to catch up on some related research.

She browsed through articles pulled up on her phone and tried —but failed—not to get sour cream on the screen as she scrolled. She had just started in on an article detailing the use of DNA sequencing from animal hides to determine the geographical origins of shields in Africa when the phone vibrated in her hand with an incoming call.

Her heart stuttered in her chest at the name on the caller ID before her brows knit together in confusion. *Drew Coleman.*

Her thumb hovered over the ignore button, but she didn't press it. They hadn't spoken since breaking things off months ago; it seemed odd that he would call her in the middle of the workday— unless it was something urgent.

She answered the call and pressed the phone to her ear.

"Hello?"

"Nora?" came the gruff response.

"What's wrong, Drew?" she asked, anxiety making her lunch sit uneasily in her belly.

Drew's puzzled voice came through the receiver. "Wrong? How do you mean?"

"You're calling me in the middle of the day after we haven't spoken in months. I figure something has happened." Nora leaned back in her desk chair and began picking at her sweater as she spoke.

"Oh, no. Nothing has happened. Nothing bad, at least."

Drew paused, and his breath crackled through the receiver as he sighed.

"I just saw the article in the newspaper about the project you are going to be spearheading and I wanted to call and congratulate you. I know that must mean that promotion you wanted isn't far behind."

"Oh, right. Thanks. It was nice of you to call," Nora hedged.

The line went quiet and Nora swiveled her desk chair back and forth, unsure where to go from here. It seemed the world had conspired to fire awkward conversations at her when she was already tired and just trying to survive her day at the office. She was on the verge of telling him she had to get back to work when his soft voice interrupted her train of thought.

"Nora? I miss you."

It was Nora's turn to sigh and close her eyes.

"I miss you, too, Drew. But it doesn't change anything."

"Not like that. I want kids, you don't. Breaking up was for the best," Drew stumbled on, the words falling out of his mouth, "but you're my best friend."

Nora squeezed her eyes shut even more tightly and pinched the bridge of her nose.

There was a pause, followed by a soft *whump* that sounded like

Drew falling back onto a bed. "I just... I had to call. Last night at the hospital was rough. A bus wrecked and we had to treat half a dozen critical injuries. It left me so...drained. I needed a friend, and you know me better than anyone. I don't want to lose that just because we aren't dating anymore."

Nora chewed her bottom lip. "Well, I can still be your friend."

"I'd like that." Nora heard the relief in Drew's tone. "Do you think you might come back to the pool league again? I promise not to make it awkward for you. I'd like to be able to talk to you again."

"Are you sure you're ready to have me kick your ass at pool again? Haven't you been enjoying winning for the past few months?" Nora teased to lighten the mood.

Drew scoffed on the other end. "I think you'll find I've learned some new tricks in the past few months. Might be able to give you a run for your money now."

Nora chuckled before silence fell again.

"In all seriousness, though," Drew continued. "It would be great to see you. I'm determined to make this breakup less awkward than my breakup with Jason. I had to run out of the library whenever he entered for a straight year."

"I don't think it will be hard for me to behave better than Jason."

"Good, then I'll see you there soon. Tell Odelle and Irina I say hello, okay?"

"Of course. It was good to hear from you, Drew," Nora said before hanging up the phone.

She turned back to her half-eaten plate of tacos. She was glad she had indulged and gotten queso. Even though that conversation had gone better than she could have hoped, she deserved a treat for all the curve balls life had been throwing at her in the past twenty-four hours.

THE REST OF THE WEEK AT WORK LEFT NORA WITH VERY LITTLE TIME to worry about her personal life. On Thursday, the crates arrived from the excavation in Greece and it was as if somebody had thrown a hornet's nest into the basement workspace. Nora and her team were in a state of constant motion, cracking open crates, tagging and identifying pieces, and chipping away layers of protective plaster. The carefully climate-controlled air was filled with dust and conversation as the team devised a plan for organizing and processing all the pieces in the large shipment.

On Friday morning, Nora finally had time to unearth the two weapons that she was most looking forward to working with. Unpackaging a shipping crate, she found a heavy bundle, meticulously wrapped in layers of cotton, and Mandy helped her move it to the table. Nora slipped on her mask to guard the artifact from the humidity of her breath and began unwrapping the bundle. It was a surprise to find the sword packaged like this. She was used to having discoveries arrive on her bench still entrenched in a block of earth, which she would have to spend hours chipping away at, bit by bit. Instead, as she continued to unwrap the sword, she caught glimpses of pure bronze.

Nora stifled a gasp as the last of the wrappings fell away. On her workbench lay a flawless blade, looking as if it had been made a few years prior instead of over two millennia ago. Mandy peered over her shoulder and let out a low whistle.

The sword was just under two feet long, a type known as a Xiphos, with two curved edges that made it ideal for slashing in close range combat. This Xiphos was of exquisite craftsmanship and, by Nora's observation, still sharp. Running down the length of the blade was an inscription in a language she did not recognize. She would have to make a copy of it after she got the blade cleaned off. Not that there was much to clean.

There appeared to be very little corrosion on the leaf-shaped blade, probably due to its construction from bronze instead of iron. Still, even for a sword made of an enduring material, its preservation was remarkable. Nora peered at it, snatching up her magnifier to get a closer look at the inscription. While she could make out the etchings, she could not decipher them at all. Even the alphabet used was one Nora didn't recognize.

Nora straightened from her inspection to find Mandy with one hip propped on the workbench, still watching her work.

"Any idea on this inscription?" Nora asked. "I don't have a clue what alphabet this even is."

Mandy shook her head, a few loose pieces of sleek hair falling across her face. "If you can't figure it out, then nobody in this office is going to stand a chance. The report from the field said that nobody on the dig recognized the language either."

Nora hummed in response and glanced back at the blade, itching to uncover its secrets and already mentally running through professionals in her contact list who might be familiar with the ancient language.

A drawl behind her snapped her from her reverie.

"I wonder what the board will think when you have to admit you can't translate that inscription."

Nora turned on her heel to find Leo looking down his nose at her with the same expression she pictured pinned to the dart board when she was persuaded to play a few rounds at pool night. Mandy rolled her eyes over his shoulder and Nora folded her arms.

"I'm too busy wondering if I'll get an office all to myself when I do translate it," Nora retorted.

Leo's face purpled, and Nora resisted the urge to punctuate her statement with a rude hand gesture, remembering they were in a shared workspace. Still, all the workers around her kept their heads dutifully down, nobody willing to insert themselves into the workplace's most notorious rivalry.

"People whose dissertations were published in the last decade don't get private offices," Leo sneered.

"We'll see. Why don't you just run along and play with your arrowheads and leave the translating to me?"

Leo scowled but turned and headed back to his own workbench.

"Ugh," Nora groaned to Mandy once he was gone. "Why does he have to be such an insufferable fungus waffle, even in my moment of victory?"

Mandy waved her hand dismissively.

"He's just jealous, and he can't accept that you were clever enough to beat him out for the promotion when he thought he was sure to get it on pure seniority. Don't let him distract you."

Nora tried to take her advice. She and Mandy spent the rest of the morning trying to copy down the engraving as best they could while searching for a linguist who might be able to translate it for them. They didn't make much progress. Nora found herself frustrated by the dead end and was anxious to move on to the next weapon to see if they might have more luck there.

Nora went through a similar process as with the sword, unpackaging it from the box. However, when she and Mandy went to move the long, slim bundle to the table, they almost dropped the weapon in surprise. It was heavy, far heavier than a spear of this size should be.

"What the heck?" Mandy said once they had hefted the bundle onto the workbench. "Have I been skipping too many Pilates classes or is that thing mammoth?"

"It's definitely not just you."

Nora hurried to put on her gloves and mask, wondering what could be making this spear so heavy. The heaviest weapons of these dimensions were usually only four pounds, but this had to be at least three times that weight.

As she pulled back the protective wrappings, it became apparent why they had been surprised by the weight. Traditional spears from this age, called dories were composed of long ash handles with iron blades at one end and counterbalancing spikes at the other. The spear lying on Nora's bench, however, was made entirely of bronze. It was six feet long, and everything from its burnished handle to the leaf-shaped blade at its tip was crafted of solid metal. Nora's heart pounded in her chest as she leaned in to examine the lethal looking spearhead the size of her hand.

Mandy's voice came from over her shoulder. "Why would somebody make a spear completely out of bronze? Maybe it was for ceremonial purposes?"

Nora scrunched up her face. "You know I hate saying things were used for ceremonial purposes. It's like admitting we don't really know what they were for."

"What about that artifact that was brought over a few months ago that you said was used for ceremonial purposes in an ancient fertility ritual?"

Nora snorted. "That was just because I couldn't say the words *ancient dildo* to my boss with a straight face."

"I can't fault you there," Mandy commented drily as Nora snatched up her magnifier to take a closer look.

"I don't think it was ceremonial anyways. There are distinctive scratch marks up here by the blade. This thing has seen combat."

Mandy swore under her breath. "What kind of animal would have fought with a weapon like that? Can you imagine carrying that behemoth into battle? A dory is supposed to be a one-handed weapon, but that thing would be heavy to use alongside a shield."

Nora pondered the question even though Mandy meant it to be rhetorical. As she looked at the weapon, she discovered slight wear marks on the handle. They must have been the points where the wielder put their hands when fighting. Gingerly, Nora lay one of her gloved hands on the thick shaft over one of the indentations and the hair stood up on the back of her neck. She instantly envisioned somebody carrying this weapon into battle—a Greek hoplite in traditional armor, standing tall and sporting a helmet topped with a dramatic red plume.

Mandy's cheery voice interrupted her vision. "At least crafting it completely of bronze made it resistant to corrosion. Wood decomposes so quickly and all that. We should be able to learn a lot from this."

Nora nodded her agreement as she opened her toolkit to get to work.

Nora was the last one to leave the office. She had lost track of time, as enraptured as she was by her new finds, and didn't move to pack up her things until Mandy closed the door behind her.

The clock indicated it was well past rush hour, and the next bus home wouldn't be arriving for another forty minutes. Nora slid into her desk chair and tapped on her laptop until the screen brightened, pulling up her inbox.

Her eyebrows shot up when she looked at the first email. The subject line read, *Meet me for coffee?* and the sender was a.scott@nu.edu.

When she opened it to skim through, she found it was indeed from the man she had encountered on Tuesday, and he was asking her if she would like to meet to discuss their possible collaboration further. He named a café not far from the lakefront as well as a time — tomorrow afternoon. Nora's eyebrows crept higher at his suggestion of a work meeting over the weekend. He must be desperate for her expertise on whatever his project was.

She was about to type out a reply putting him off, and even considered just shutting her laptop and ignoring him altogether when the email signature below his name caught her eye.

Professor of Literature and Ancient Languages

A professor of ancient languages sounded like just what Nora needed to help decipher the inscription on the sword, and if he couldn't do the job himself, then he might know somebody who could.

She tapped a response, agreeing to the meeting before moving on to the rest of her inbox. She hadn't finished reading the departmental memo that was next in her queue before Adam's reply popped into her inbox, telling her he was eager for their meeting.

His quick reply was unexpected at this time on a Friday night, but she pushed the thought from her head in favor of considering what she should pick up for dinner from the Indian deli down the street on her way home.

NORA FOUND THE FRENCH CAFÉ THAT ADAM DIRECTED HER TO AND pushed open the door. The corner of her lips pulled up at the sight that greeted her. This was her type of place. Small, circular tables filled the cozy space, and the lamps filled the room with a warm glow that contrasted nicely with the muted gray colors of the fall day outside. The air was filled with the warm aromas of baking pastry and, thank goodness, coffee.

Her eyes roved over the tables, looking for an empty place for her to sit, and found that Adam had already arrived, catching sight of his dark curls as he leaned over the table before him. He had papers strewn across the surface and was sipping what looked like tea. Nora momentarily watched his lips caress the edge of his large earthenware mug before shaking herself and picking her way across the room. Something odd had come over her recently. As she approached, he had to take off his glasses to wipe the fog that had formed on them from the steam of his beverage.

When Nora's shadow fell over his papers, he looked up and beamed, revealing a striking set of dimples.

"You came!" he said, jumping to his feet to shake Nora's hand before shuffling his papers into a neat stack to make room at the table.

As Nora slid into her seat, she watched Adam perch himself on the low bistro-style chair once more, being forced to fold up his long legs in a way that brought to mind vague images of a baby giraffe.

"What were you working on?" Nora asked, inclining her head towards the stack of papers that Adam was now pushing into a beat-up leather bag.

"These? Oh, just grading some papers," Adam said as he snapped his bag shut. "One of the less fun parts of being a professor."

"At Northwestern, right? My sister went there, graduated five years ago. Majored in broadcasting."

"Ah, I wouldn't have had her in my classes then," responded Adam with a shake of his head. "I only started teaching there a few years ago."

"That's probably for the best. She is a superbly disruptive student."

"It's ok," Adam chuckled, the sound musical. "I'm used to disruptive students in my class. I've been told I'm rather...*long-winded* in my discussions of the classic works. My students don't always appreciate it. I doubt a broadcasting major would be very interested in my class anyway. Is she a reporter?"

Nora's chest swelled with pride, as it always did when she got to brag about her sister's career. "Yeah, on weekends, on one of the local channels. She just got the job last year and she's still excited about it. People tried to tell her she wouldn't be able to make it on TV because she has prosthetic legs, but I'm pretty sure that just made her want to do it more."

"She sounds charming."

Nora snorted. "She's a handful. I have vivid memories of Irina chasing her around the house, telling stories of Russian witches that would come out and eat her in the night if she didn't hold still."

Adam chuckled. "And Irina is?"

"Our foster mother."

Adam's face took on an expression that Nora had become familiar with throughout her life, and she automatically moved to wave it away.

"Oh no, don't give me that sorry look. We lived with Irina for almost as long as I can remember, and she spent the entire time stuffing me full of borscht and driving me to marching band practice."

"So, do you speak any Russian?"

Nora shrugged. "I understand it better than I speak it."

At that moment, a cheerful looking plump lady approached the table and greeted Adam in what sounded like French. Adam chatted with her animatedly for a moment, gesturing to Nora a few times, before turning back to her and asking, "Would you like anything to drink?"

"Espresso, please."

Adam exchanged a few more foreign words with the lady before she bustled off, presumably to fetch her coffee.

"So, you speak French?" Nora asked, tearing her mind away from the way Adam's mouth shaped itself around rolling French syllables. Her thoughts seemed to derail so easily around him it was disconcerting.

Adam shrugged one shoulder and Nora spotted a slight blush coloring his bronze skin.

"Yeah, I like to learn languages. I started so I could read books in the language they were written in, and then it sort of became an area of expertise."

"That's part of why I wanted to meet with you today," Nora pushed on, determined to steer their conversation into professional territory. "I'm looking for an expert in languages who can help me translate an engraving on a weapon."

Adam leaned forward in his seat and his eyes sparkled behind his glasses. "What kind of weapon?"

Nora blinked at his enthusiasm.

"Well, there were a bunch of weapons and fragments discovered in a dig outside of Athens, but the specific piece I need assistance with is a short sword. It was found right next to a spear, and both are in near perfect condition. They most likely belonged to the same person, the spear being the primary weapon of the Greek hoplite and the sword being carried as a backup. The sword is the weapon with the engravings on it, but it's in a language that nobody in the field can recognize..."

Nora looked up to find Adam gripping the edge of the table with white knuckles as he listened. His fingers were very long.

"Are you all right?" she asked.

"Oh...yes," Adam seemed to remember himself and leaned back in his chair as he smoothed down his tie with one hand. "I've always loved history. I was so intrigued when I read about the Greek weapons in the newspaper and the prospect of getting to help with them is thrilling. I do happen to know some ancient Greek dialects."

Nora rifled around in her bag to pull out the leather notebook in which she had attempted to copy the inscription on the sword and leafed through it until she found the appropriate page.

"Does this look like something you might recognize?" she asked, turning the paper around to show him.

His eyes widened. "That looks like an ancient language I've been studying in my spare time, but it's hard to learn with so little of it left." He squinted at the page and leaned in further. "I might be able to translate it, but some of the symbols copied here are a little different than what I'm familiar with."

Nora chewed her lip. "I did my best to copy the inscription, but it was hard to replicate an alphabet I'm not familiar with. Do you think that you could translate it better if you looked at the original?"

"You would let me look at the sword?" Adam asked.

Nora knew she shouldn't be inviting someone who was basically a stranger into the lab to look at ancient artifacts, but this was the best lead she had. She wasn't going to let it slip through her fingers. Besides, if she brought him in right now, nobody would even have to know. Nobody else ever went into the office on weekends.

"Sure. Maybe we could take the bus over from here?"

Adam nodded emphatically. "I'm ready when you are."

"Okay," Nora said as she spotted the cheery waitress weaving her way back through the tables with a steaming cup. "We'll leave after I finish my coffee."

PUSHING THROUGH THE SIDE DOORS, NORA LED ADAM DOWN THE hallway to the offices and peered around. She had never encountered any of her coworkers here on a Saturday, but it would be just her luck to have somebody putting in extra hours when she brought in an unauthorized visitor. Finding the hallway empty, she unlocked the office and held the door open.

As they made their way back to her workbench, she told him, "Just don't touch anything, it's all very old and fragile."

Adam made a dramatic show of tucking his hands into the pockets of his tweed blazer, and Nora smiled despite herself.

She made her way to the crate where the sword was being kept and put on the clean gloves she retrieved from a drawer in her workstation. Now appropriately attired, she lifted the bundle from the crate and began unwrapping the sword. As she worked, the warmth from Adam's body behind her seeped through her clothes as he stepped closer. It seemed backwards that warmth would make her shiver, but a pleasant tingle crept up her spine.

As the last of the protective wrappings fell away, Adam inhaled sharply and she spared him a glance. His eyes were wide and shining as he beheld the blade.

She stepped to the side so he could slide up next to her and take a closer look. Putting some distance between them reduced the spine tingling, as well, and Nora decided that was a good thing. Adam leaned in before asking, his tone bordering on reverent, "Where was this found again?"

"On a dig just outside of Athens." Nora watched as his eyes ran up and down the blade, taking in every lethal inch of it. "It was found on a deeper level than most of the other artifacts from its period, although we have dated it to about 400 BC. It was right next to the spear that was found too."

His voice was so soft when he responded that it almost felt as if he wasn't talking to her. "It's in such perfect condition; it looks just like it did when it was left there so long ago."

Nora raised her eyebrows at the odd phrasing of his comment, but then she remembered why she had brought him there in the first place.

"Do you see these markings here on the blade?" she asked, gesturing to the delicate engravings down the top half of the fuller. "Are these the same markings as that language you were studying?"

Adam squinted at the engraving before answering. "They do look similar. I think I could make out what they say if I could get a clearer look at them."

Nora pulled out her toolkit, locating her magnifier in the bundle of tweezers and scalpels. He took it from her without taking his eyes off the blade and held it up.

"Fascinating," he whispered, using the magnifier to look up and down the length of the blade several times. Nora resisted the urge to tap her foot, giving him time to inspect.

"As far as I can translate, the inscription on this blade says, *Through the darkest night.*" Adam straightened and handed her the magnifier.

Nora pursed her lips and repeated the phrase. "Through the darkest night. That's not any sort of army motto we've seen before. It may have been some sort of personal inscription. I wonder what it meant."

Adam's eyes were filled with a far-off look as he responded. "It probably was something important to the person who owned the sword." Nora pondered in the brief silence that followed before he asked, "Does the spear have any markings on it?"

"Not that we've observed. But do you want to take a look at it anyways? It's quite spectacular."

Adam nodded, making his glasses slide down his nose. He pushed them back up as Nora turned to lift the spear onto the table. It went much better this time as she was prepared for its weight. She worked quickly to unwrap it, feeling Adam's gaze heavy on her, although it was likely due to his excitement to see the artifact.

They stood in silence for a moment, staring at the fantastic weapon on the table before them before Nora sighed again. "I think this one is my favorite."

"I can see why," Adam murmured. His voice came from so close to her ear that Nora jumped, not realizing he had leaned in to get a better look. His breath stirred the hairs that had escaped from the messy bun at the top of her head, and she stole a glance at his chiseled profile.

That was when the screaming started.

3

Adam jumped back from Nora as if he had been burned by the proximity. Nora turned to look at him, momentarily dazed from the sudden change, and found Adam's head already whipping back and forth, looking for the source of the danger. There was not just one voice screaming, but many. They sounded panicked, and the pounding of feet accompanied them. Nora thought the noise was coming from near the museum entrance.

Nora's mind flew to the emergency preparedness drill they'd had a few weeks prior and the talk of multiple mass shootings across the country. She started towards the door, but Adam snaked his hand out and grabbed her by the back of the collar so suddenly that her head snapped back.

"Where in blazes do you think you're going?"

Nora gestured towards the noises, confused as to why he was stopping her.

"There's some sort of emergency here. It could be an active shooter or something," Nora explained, working herself free of his grasp.

Adam gawked. "So your first response is to rush *towards* the screaming? That's how people get killed, Nora." He pulled her behind him and then started towards the door himself, keeping her body behind his. "We have to get out of here. We can use the back door by the loading bay."

Nora opened her mouth, but before she could ask Adam how he knew where the back door was, there was a flashing of lights and a deafening, blaring noise as the fire alarms started going off. The office door swung shut of its own accord as the emergency systems went into effect. Right before the door slammed closed, she caught the briefest whiff of the hot and acrid smoke.

Nora yelled over the wild chiming. "The fire must be close, I could smell it."

Adam continued to pull her towards the door as if she hadn't spoken. She yanked on his arm to stop him, not about to let him charge towards a fire after he had just scolded her for running towards what she thought was an active shooter.

"If the fire is in the hallway, we can't go out that way," she shouted.

Adam shook his head, and when he looked at Nora, his eyes had gone as round as dinner plates.

"We have to get out of here," he insisted.

"That's a fire door." Nora jerked her chin towards the now closed entrance to the hallway. "It would take hours to burn through it. We'll be safe in here until they put it out." She cast around, knowing there had to be a fire extinguisher in the office as well.

Adam didn't seem comforted at all. In fact, the color had drained from his face, giving a ghostly cast to his golden bronze skin, and a slight sheen of sweat glistened on his forehead.

"Hey, it's going to be all right," she reassured him, shocked by his fearful reaction. "I'll find the fire extinguisher just in case, okay?"

She made to turn away from him to begin her search, but with surprising strength, he grasped her wrist and pulled her back, making her bang into the workbench.

"Stay away from the door." Adam's voice was harsh.

Nora had already opened her mouth to snap that he needed to calm down when she saw it. At the bottom of the door, a thin line of black smoke was oozing its way through, despite the fire-resistant sealant. It twisted and writhed in a way that Nora found strange. Smoke didn't usually behave like that. The cloud grew larger and denser until it was as tall as she was, then began to gather into a shape. Nora blinked as she realized the smoke was taking on the form of a human, but it wasn't really all that human. It had two arms and two legs, but that was where the similarities ended. All the angles and proportions were wrong, and the thick smoke the thing was composed of continued to writhe and swirl in a way that made Nora sick to look at. As she was frozen on the spot, more smoke crept under the door and formed into dozens of the horrific creatures.

As Nora wondered what on earth had been in the coffee at that café, Adam stepped in front of her and put an arm across her as if to shield her. The first creature then began to roll forward on its warped legs, stretching out too-long arms towards the pair as if to envelope them in a hug. Nora opened her mouth to scream, but at that moment, Adam's arm tightened. She realized he had not put it across her to shield her but was instead reaching for something—the sword. In an instant, his long fingers closed around the hilt and he swung the blade out in front of him in a long arc, slicing the being in a diagonal slash across its torso. The dark creature let out an unearthly shriek before fracturing into hundreds of fragments of shadow that wriggled away like Stygian maggots before dissolving into thin air.

Nora didn't even have a second to process what had just happened before the rest of the creatures began advancing on them and Adam lunged forward into the midst of a swirling vortex of shadows. The creatures descended on him, shrieking in horrible voices that made Nora want to claw at her eardrums. Adam stood at the center of the mass and brandished the sword, slicing several more shadows that dispersed in much the same way as the first. Nora opened her mouth to warn him of more creatures creeping up behind him, but Adam had already whirled around and dispatched them before she could draw a breath. She watched, transfixed as he whirled and bobbed in the mass of creatures, swinging the sword faster than her eyes could follow. Shadow after shadow fell before the blade, but still more oozed under the door.

It had become unbearably hot in the room as the fire alarms continued to sound, and a layer of sweat formed on her skin and dampened her hair. Her back was still pressed against the workbench, her hands on the edge with a white-knuckled grip. Her brain refused to process what was happening in front of her. At any moment, she expected to jerk awake from a very strange nightmare. Or perhaps there was a fire and she was suffering from hallucinatory smoke poisoning. Another small voice in the back of her head, that still clung to sanity, tried to scream at her that Adam shouldn't be touching an artifact with his bare hands, let alone using it like this, but she decided that, in this moment, sanity was vastly overrated.

For a heartbeat, she lost sight of Adam as the shadows around him became denser, and it was the impetus she needed to regain the power to move. She scrabbled on the workbench behind her and grabbed the first thing her hand touched: a long pair of pointed tweezers from her open supply kit.

When she turned back, Adam was grappling with a shadow creature who had managed to grab his tie and was attempting to use it to drag him down into the swirling pit of darkness around his feet. Nora gripped the tweezers in her left hand and, for a fleeting moment, she desperately tried to remember everything Drew had taught her about playing darts. Then she lobbed the tweezers at the shadow creature as hard as she could.

The creature let out a shriek that cut through the already deafening alarms as the tweezers sunk into where an eye would be if it had any sort of conventional features. It immediately released Adam's tie as its arms flew to its face, and he took the opportunity to stab the sword through its chest, looking much less like a lanky college professor and much more like a heroic warrior. As the creature dissolved, Adam glanced over to where Nora was standing, a look of something Nora didn't recognize crossing his otherwise focused face. The moment was gone as quickly as it came as Adam was forced to make a quick turn to dodge under a whip-like arm of blackness. The motion caused his glasses to slip off his face and they were crushed under his heel, but he continued slashing and parrying as if he hadn't noticed.

Nora's use of tweezers as projectiles seemed to have drawn the attention of the other shadow creatures, and she spotted one slithering across the floor toward where she stood. She reached behind her for something else she could throw, hoping for a scalpel of some sort this time, but the creature was too fast for her. Pain seared her ankle and then she was falling. She heard the back of her head hit the edge of her workbench with a sickening crack before she felt it, and the world swam before her eyes in a dizzying swirl of shadows and light.

When her eyes refocused, the monster had a whip-like arm wrapped around her ankle, its grip burning into her flesh. The creature began pulling on her leg, reeling her towards its darkness like a fish on the end of its line. Nora reached behind her to grab the bottom of the work bench, trying to keep herself from being drawn across the floor. As she stopped her own forward progress, the creature shrieked in frustration and began clawing its way up her calf to her body, where she lay on the floor. A scream bubbled up in her throat, but she was unable to get it out around the intense heat clawing its way down into her lungs. Red coals burned where the creature's eyes should be, and the shadows parted in a sick parody of a smile.

Adam screamed her name as she clawed at the table behind

her, trying to find something—anything—to defend herself with as the creature reached her upper thigh. In that moment, her hand closed around heavy metal, and before she could process what was happening, she had swung the spear down in a long arc and jabbed it forward, sending the blade straight through the place where the creature's face should have been. With one last shriek, it exploded into its shadow fragments and the weight on her leg was gone, although the pain was still there.

The spear rested heavily across her lap as she panted in fear and relief. When she raised her eyes, Adam was still fighting the shadows, but only a few remained and the smoke had stopped coming in from under the door. As he dealt with the lingering creatures, Nora's eyes slid closed and she leaned her head against her table, the throbbing from where her skull had collided with the edge forcing itself back to the forefront of her consciousness.

After what felt like a few moments but was probably several minutes, there was a clatter and a warm presence at her side. Nora forced her eyes open to see that Adam had dropped the sword and kneeled on the floor beside her. His hands flew to her face and smoothed over her forehead, trying to meet her unfocused eyes with his. The warmth of his fingers felt nice in her hair, despite how sweaty she was.

"Nora? Nora," he repeated, his tone bordering on pleading.

Her eyes slid over him, distantly noting he had a few small holes charred in his tweed blazer, and the long end of his tie had been singed right off where the creature had grabbed it. He looked otherwise unscathed.

"Nora, are you okay?" His face was frantic, not at all like the grim determination she had seen on it when he was grappling with the shadow creatures.

"Yeah, I'm fine," she said as she reached up and grabbed his hand, which was still smoothing over her sweat-soaked hair. She put her other hand on the floor to push herself up to stand but didn't make it six inches off the ground before she slid back down the table, finding herself quite dizzy and weak. "I think I hit my head a little too hard."

"That's not all." Adam's face was ashen as he looked down. Nora followed his gaze to find that his knees were soaked in a spreading puddle of blood that flowed from a gash in her upper thigh, right where the creature had grabbed her before she killed it. *I killed it,* she thought, her mind unable or unwilling to focus on the blood streaming out of her. She had never killed anything before.

"By St. Boogar and all the saints at the backside door of purgatory!"

Adam swore so colorfully that Nora was drawn back to reality enough to gape at him even in her current delirious state.

"One advantage of being an English professor—you're exposed to a lot of wonderfully creative expletives," Adam commented in a voice so falsely calm that his intent to distract Nora from her injuries was immediately transparent. As he spoke, Adam pulled off the remnants of his tie. As soon as he had jerked the strip of plaid fabric from his neck, he began fastening it around her upper thigh above the gash. After knotting it securely, he reached up into a drawer of her table and retrieved a pen. He forced the pen into the loop he had made around her leg and twisted it until the binding pulled tight, causing Nora to grunt and jerk away in pain. He paid her distress no heed and used the free end of the fabric to fasten the pen in place, leaving the loop taut around her thigh.

A tourniquet, she mused as she grappled with her receding consciousness. Her eyes began drifting closed, but she forced them open again as Adam murmured, "We have to get you to a hospital."

She forced herself to form words even though her tongue felt as if it had turned into a large rubber ball in her mouth.

"Dr. Drew Coleman. The emergency room at Northwestern Memorial." Her voice sounded far away, even to her. "Ask for Drew."

The world spun dizzily around her and, for a moment, she thought she had finally passed out, until she jerked once again and she realized that Adam had scooped her off the ground and began to run. She tried to move her head, but whether it was to protest or to bury her face in Adam's chest, she couldn't say. The last thought she had as she lost her grasp on reality was one of disbelief as she registered that he was reciting a Russian fairytale as he ran with her cradled in his arms.

4

THE FIRST THING NORA HEARD WAS SLOW MECHANICAL BEEPING AND the whispering of voices too low to make out. Finding herself unable to open her eyes, she contented herself with taking inventory of what she could feel. She immediately regretted her decision as her next level of consciousness returned and she became acutely aware of a searing pain in both her leg and her head. She grasped for other sensations to distract herself from the discomfort and found that there was a tight band around her left upper arm, and somebody had their fingers interlaced with hers. She tried to wiggle those fingers and the hand around hers tightened.

"Nora, *zolotse*, are you there? Can you hear me?"

Nora succeeded in fluttering her eyelids and tried to tell Odelle that she could hear but only managed a slight groan. Odelle didn't let go of her hand but called, "Drew, she's awake!"

There were footsteps and a large hand rested on her cheek. She fluttered her eyelids again and then managed to keep them open, a familiar pair of concerned brown eyes coming into focus.

"Oh thank God," Drew rumbled. Her eyes drifted to his blue scrubs and white lab coat. "How are you feeling? Can you talk?"

Nora opened her mouth to respond and all that came out was a whispered, "Ow."

Drew grimaced. "I can do something about that." He looked away for a second. "Odelle, would you go find her nurse?"

The hand squeezed one more time before it was gone, and Drew's attention returned to her, his eyes assessing.

"What...what happened?" Nora croaked.

"You were in a car accident," Drew responded, straightening the blankets around her. "You hit your head badly, probably gave yourself a concussion. I have to say, you're lucky you didn't develop any sort of cranial bleed. And you've got a pretty nasty wound in your leg too."

Nora tried to turn her head to look around but that type of movement was still beyond her.

"How..." she trailed off, unable to complete her sentence.

Drew seemed to fill in what she wanted to know.

"Your...colleague, Adam, carried you in here." Nora's eyes finally focused enough that she saw a muscle in his jaw tighten. "He was kind of crazed, covered in your blood. He kept shouting that he needed Dr. Drew Coleman. He wouldn't let go of you until I arrived. I had to do some fast talking to prevent security from being called."

Images slowly wormed their way into Nora's consciousness. Adam tying his tie around her leg, him reciting familiar Russian fairytales.

"I told him to ask for you."

Drew's smile looked strained. "I'm glad you did. Although I must admit, when I said I wanted to see you again, this was not what I had in mind."

Nora offered him her weak attempt at a smile. "Odelle's been teaching me how to make an entrance."

Drew let out a half chuckle. "Glad to see you survived with your wit intact."

At that moment, Odelle ducked back around the curtain into the room, a nurse at her heels. Drew stepped away, and there was a flurry of activity that Nora couldn't quite follow. The nurse was saying something to Drew about her blood pressure and another unit of blood. An almost empty bag of scarlet fluid hung from an IV pole. She also registered tubing across her face, delivering what she assumed was oxygen. The prongs in her nose were uncomfortable, but she was too dazed to care.

The nurse pushed something into her IV and, immediately, the throbbing in her head and leg lessened, though the medication made her vision swim. She stopped trying to follow what was happening and just rested her head against the pillows again, grateful for the relief. The nurse and Drew were poking and prodding her a bit, pulling back her blankets to look at her leg and using a stethoscope to listen to her chest, but she didn't have the energy to be bothered by it.

She felt Drew's hand on her upper arm, and she peeled her eyes open.

"I'll be back later. I've just got to go check on some other patients, okay? You rest and tell Odelle or your nurse if you need anything."

Nora blinked in response, and Drew gave her another tight smile before withdrawing. His face was replaced by Odelle's, and her sister's fingers wove back between her own.

"Hey, *zolotse*. It's good to see you with your eyes open."

Nora attempted to smile but was pretty sure it came off as more of a grimace. Then another thought floated to the surface of her foggy mind.

"Adam…"

"He hasn't left. He's on a couch in the lounge, taking a nap. We sent him out there to rest. His pacing was making us nervous. I told him we had it under control here and you could call him when you were up to it, but he refused to go. Something about feeling responsible. Odd, but gallant."

Nora grunted her agreement, and Odelle chattered on.

"I didn't know you encountered such attractive men in your line

of work. Sexy professor isn't my type, but do you happen to know if
he has a brother?"

While Nora couldn't exactly dispute the sexy professor
comment, she still mustered up the most withering glare she could
in her current state. While she was sure the oxygen tubing in her
nose detracted from her ferocity, Odelle backed off.

"All right, I'll save the questions for when you're feeling better.
Do you want to talk to him?"

Nora flopped her head side to side as best she could. "No.
Sleep."

Odelle chuckled. "It's okay. Get some rest. I'm not going
anywhere." Odelle settled back into a chair at her bedside and
squeezed her hand again as Nora drifted back into unconsciousness.

THE NEXT TIME NORA WOKE, SHE OPENED HER EYES TO FIND ADAM
seated at her bedside, his nose in a book. He hadn't noticed her
eyes opening yet, and she took the moment to observe that he was
still wearing his charred blazer, albeit extremely rumpled, but
somebody must have dug a pair of scrub pants up for him so he
could change out of his bloodstained ones. They were too small for
him and clung to his thighs. Nora tried not to stare.

"Nora," he whispered, spotting her watching him. He set book
to the side and put his hand on her arm, causing her to wince as he
jostled her IV. Everything still hurt, but it had settled into a dull
ache instead of the agony of the first time she woke.

"Adam," she whispered, her voice like sandpaper in her dry
throat. "I'm sorry about your tie."

He let out an incredulous laugh.

"Of course. You almost die and the first thing you think of is
how my tie must have been ruined."

Nora furrowed her brow.

"I almost died?" she asked, still fuzzy on the details of what had happened. She remembered Drew saying something about a car crash and a concussion, but not much else.

Adam cocked his head to the side. "Maybe that was a slight exaggeration, but you weren't exactly thriving. You had gone into shock from blood loss by the time I carried you here. They had to take you straight to the OR to sew it up, and you received several blood transfusions. You are lucky that the cut wasn't just an inch to the side or it would have hit a major artery. The good news is that you're going to have a rather impressive scar."

"I've always wanted a cool scar," she murmured, the blanks in her memory filling back in. They had been at the museum when she got hurt, and he had taken her to the hospital. "Wait, you *carried* me here?" Her mind performed some sluggish calculations. "That has to be like two miles! Do you have something against ambulances?"

Adam looked down and rubbed the back of his neck. "I was worried about you; I kind of forgot. And I have to be honest with you. I didn't cradle you the whole way. I switched you to a fireman carry after you lost consciousness. Much easier on the arms."

Nora gaped. "You forgot about calling 911?" Her brain managed to put together a few more pieces of what was going on, but she was still missing essential parts of the puzzle. "Wait—Drew said I was in a car accident, but we weren't in a car. We were at the museum."

Adam's face contorted in discomfort and Nora's stomach plunged. She attempted to sit upright but found that she couldn't and settled for an agitated jerk instead.

"Oh my gosh!" Nora gasped. "You touched an artifact with your bare hands, and...and swung it around like a crazy person! That didn't really happen. I hit my head too hard and got confused, right?" Nora practically pleaded with Adam, but he only offered her an apologetic grimace.

"I must say, I'm surprised the first thing you're asking me about in that whole scene was whether or not I touched an artifact without proper precautions," Adam commented, shifting uncomfortably in the plastic chair.

"We left them on the floor!" Nora raged. "Forget about my promotion, this will lose me my entire job."

Adam held up his palms placatingly.

"I went back to the museum while you were out and cleaned everything up. I don't think the weapons are what you need to be worrying about right now."

"You're an English professor," Nora snapped. "You can't possibly know the proper methods for cleaning weaponry."

Adam raised a brow. "You know, they don't teach you how to fight with weapons without teaching you to take care of them too."

"That's another thing! How did you know how to fight like that? And what were those— oh..." Nora trailed off as she remembered the Shadow creatures in the museum, and Adam's comment that she had bigger things to be worrying about made more sense. While her heart still raced at the idea of an improperly cleaned sword, the thought faded in the face of memories of all-consuming darkness. The image of a creature clawing its way up her leg forced itself into her memory and Nora shuddered in revulsion.

"Hey, it's okay. They're gone, and they are not going to hurt you," Adam soothed. He reached his hand out as if to stroke her arm in reassurance, but Nora jerked away.

"It's okay? How in Hell is it okay? What were those things? And how are you some sort of master swordsman?" Nora demanded.

Adam shot Nora a pained look. "Nora I want to explain everything, I do. But not right now. Not while you're in the hospital."

"I almost died and you aren't going to tell me what the things that nearly killed me were?" Nora fumed.

"Well I said that you almost dying was a slight exaggeration—"

"I don't care if I got a splinter; I deserve to know what happened! Not to mention those *things* obviously had something to do with you. I was doing just fine until you appeared and then I start getting attacked at my own job. How do I know you didn't bring those things down on me?" If Nora hadn't been as weak as a newborn kitten, she would be grabbing Adam by the shoulders and shaking him.

"Listen," Adam pleaded, "if I wanted you hurt, I wouldn't have carried you two miles to the hospital. I swear on my life I will tell you what happened. I'll tell you as soon as you're out of the hospital. You still have a concussion and you need to focus on healing. Plus, it's going to be a long conversation that would be better held in private."

The sincerity in Adam's eyes placated her despite her anger. She already felt her energy draining out of her like the air from a balloon after her brief outburst.

"Fine." She leaned back into her pillows to sulk. "But the instant I'm discharged, I demand explanations." She was disgusted by how easily she caved, but she felt worse than she cared to admit.

"I promise, and I'm sure you'll be ship-shape in no time," Adam reassured. "Dr. Coleman has been taking impeccable care of you."

"Drew's still here?"

"His shift ended a few hours ago, but he refuses to leave. Wants to keep an eye on you." Adam paused. "Are the two of you...together?"

Nora's eyes narrowed at his inquiry but found his expression politely curious. It was a question of the type she shouldn't be encouraging from a professional partner, but they had already gotten this far.

"We were, but we broke up a few months ago."

Adam tilted his head and, for a moment, Nora worried he was going to question her further about their relationship, wishing he would instead just let the subject drop. She was saved by a young woman in misty blue scrubs appearing around the curtain.

"Look who's awake!" she chimed. "I'm Sheila and I've been your nurse today. It's good to see you up. Let's see how your blood pressure is doing." She bustled into the room and pressed a button on the monitor, making the cuff on Nora's upper arm tighten. Adam took the moment to duck out of the room, motioning that he would be right back.

"How are you feeling?" Sheila asked.

"Cold," Nora responded, indeed beginning to shiver.

"Hmm, I'll make sure to get you some more blankets after I finish getting your vitals." She grabbed a thermometer off the wall and held it up to Nora, who obediently opened her mouth and put it under her tongue. When it beeped, Sheila looked at the reading with a furrowed brow.

"One hundred and two. Do you mind if I take a peek at your leg?"

Nora shook her head, and the nurse moved the blankets aside before unwrapping the bandage around her thigh. As Nora's wound came into view, she hissed. The long gash had been closed with a line of neat stitches, but an ashy blackness was radiating out from the line of angry red. There was a white, puss-like substance oozing from the wound.

"Oh dear," Sheila muttered. "Dr. Coleman will want to see this right away."

She stepped to the side and pulled a small phone out of her pocket while Nora continued gaping at the gruesome looking gash on her thigh, which still throbbed angrily.

It was only a minute before Drew ducked around the corner of the room.

"Look at you, sitting up and everything!" He gave her a broad smile before his eyes drifted to her leg.

"Okay," he muttered, rubbing his thick beard. Turning to Sheila, he said, "Let's get a culture on that and start her on some IV vancomycin. Increase her fluid rate too."

They moved around her room, carrying a rapid discussion about her blood pressure and something about her labs. Nora became irritated, as if she were being ignored in all of this, but she had begun shivering more forcefully now and was too uncomfortable to worry about inserting herself into the discussion. At that moment, Adam pushed past the curtain, carrying a Styrofoam cup of something steaming, adding to the small crowd of people milling around her already hectic bedside. As he moved to the head of her bed to say something to her, he caught sight of her infected wound. "Oh, that doesn't look good."

"Just an infection," responded Drew as he rebandaged her leg. "We're on it."

Drew's clipped tone was jarring in comparison to his usual unshakeable calm, but he appeared focused on his task, so Nora didn't mention it. Adam's brows pulled together and he was opening his mouth to say something, but Nora decided it was best if they left Drew alone.

"Where's Odelle?" Nora interjected to change the subject.

Adam turned his attention back to her face.

"She had to go to work, but she'll be back as soon as she's done. She left some beef stroganoff in the mini fridge in case you want it."

Nora grimaced and shook her head. While stroganoff was her go-to comfort food, her stomach twisted uncomfortably, and she realized she was slightly nauseous.

"Maybe later; I'm not feeling up to eating right now."

Drew had finished wrapping her thigh in a fresh bandage, and the nurse had exited the room to fetch something or another. He straightened and cleared his throat pointedly before saying, "We are going to start you on some antibiotics for this infection and monitor your fever. You let us know if you are feeling any changes at all, okay?"

Nora nodded, and Drew shot a hard look over his shoulder before pushing past the curtain and out of the room. The two of them were now alone and Adam settled himself into the chair at the head of the bed.

"This is the pits. I hope this doesn't keep me away from work too long," Nora huffed and attempted to cross her arms but was impeded by her IVs.

"I wouldn't worry too much. Dr. Coleman has been...vigilant."

Nora nodded in agreement. There was a pause before Adam continued.

"I don't think he likes me very much."

Nora was about to ask him where he got that idea when another round of violent shivers wracked her body. Adam leaned in and tucked the blankets around her as tightly as he could, commenting, "It must be from the fever."

Nora made to nod, but moving her head seemed to make her unbearably dizzy.

"Adam, something's wrong." She tasted metal in her mouth and her shivering had transformed into more of a constant tremor. Even her vision was distorted.

Adam put his hand on her cheek and tried to meet her eyes but she couldn't bring his face into focus.

"No, no," he whispered. "This isn't an infection. Infection doesn't progress this fast. This is poison." His voice sounded like he was trying to speak to her from underwater.

She opened her mouth to ask him how she could have been poisoned but she couldn't breathe as her whole body went rigid.

"Nora!" Adam cried, but she couldn't respond. Her world had turned a blazing white and she didn't have any control over her limbs as they shook, but she could still hear Adam. Fingers scrabbled at her IVs, ripping them out, droplets of warm blood running down her arm.

The whole time, Adam muttered, "Thad. Thad will know what to do."

Then there were more voices, Drew's deep voice like thunder, barking orders and demanding Adam step away from her. There was more yelling, something about poison and more about whomever Thad was.

Nora tried to scream but made a horrible choking sound instead. She couldn't breathe. She needed them to stop arguing. She needed quiet. She needed the shaking to stop.

Adam's determined voice cut through the haze. "You can follow me, but you can't stop me from taking her."

Her world lurched again as arms tightened around her. Her limbs thrashed against them, but Adam got her over his shoulder and held her tightly.

Drew's voice reached her. "I'm not letting her out of my sight."

Then the world spun away, and Nora was falling but didn't remember ever hitting the bottom.

5

NORA DREAMED THAT SHE WAS IN MILLENIUM PARK, UNDER THE
Bean. She was staring into its mirrored surfaces and recognized
Adam and Drew. Drawing closer to her image, she stared into her
own fevered green eyes. She was so close that her nose touched
the cold metal surface, but it wasn't like metal at all. It felt like
water, and then there were ripples moving out from where she
touched the surface. The ripples warped the reflections around
her, and she lost sight of Adam's and Drew's faces. She opened her
mouth to scream but then she pitched forward and began to fall
again.

Now Apollo the sun god himself stood above her as she lay on a
cloud. His arms were raised, the orb of the sun shining impossibly
close behind him. He was draped in vibrant green fabric,
contrasting with his dark skin, which shone in the light. His voice
was deep as he called her name.

"Nora, you have to wake up."

She tried to tell him that she was awake, but then he was
pouring molten sunshine into her open mouth and she coughed
and spluttered around it. He kept pouring it down her throat until
she was drowning, and her vision went white. She could think of

nothing but the brightness of the sun and the heat coursing through her veins.

Nora's mind slipped gently back into her body. When she opened her eyes, it was to a clear blue sky and the sun above her. As she stared up into it, she wondered why the sky was such an odd texture until she realized that she was not really outside but looking up at a very realistic fresco painting.

Lowering her gaze, she registered that she was lying on a gigantic four-poster bed, cocooned in a fluffy white comforter. Nora was glad to see she was so thoroughly swaddled because her next realization was that she was naked against the silky sheets. While Nora was all for sleeping in the buff, she wasn't sure she felt comfortable being completely exposed when she was... Where was she?

As if in answer to her silent question, the man from her dreams approached from outside her field of vision. He smiled at her and said, "Welcome to the Sanctuary, Nora Zvezda."

"Apollo," she whispered in awe.

His head tipped back and he laughed deeply before continuing in an accent she couldn't quite place. "No, not even I am quite that good looking. My name is Thaddeus, but you may call me Thad. I'm the reason you are still alive."

"Thad," she echoed, remembering the name being shouted during her white-hot haze of confusion. "Adam brought me here." Wherever here was. "Why am I not in the hospital?"

Thad chuckled once again. "The hospital wasn't going to be able to help you, no matter how talented your physician was. Only a Healer here at the Sanctuary can treat the poison you were suffering from."

Nora remembered Adam saying something about poison, but none of this made any sense. She shook her head as if that could somehow straighten out the jumble of thoughts in her mind. Also, why was Thad wearing a green toga?

Thad's expression was sympathetic.

"Adam will explain everything to you. He's waiting outside." He motioned to one side of the room, and sure enough, when Nora looked around the cavernous space, she spied an open archway on one wall, real sunlight shining through.

Thad continued as she looked around. "I put some clothes over there for you to try on. If you then head out into the courtyard, Adam will tell you everything." He took another glance at her confused face before adding, "It's good to see you, Nora." Then he drew back and made his way out of a heavy wooden door.

With Thad's departure, Nora pulled herself into an upright position, keeping the comforter clutched to her chest. She counted it as a small victory that her head didn't spin, and she was able to move with much more strength than she had in the hospital. Sitting up, she was able to take in her surroundings more thoroughly than she had before. The large bed occupied one end of a room that had to be the size of her entire city apartment. While the ceiling was painted to mirror the sky, the walls and the floor were made of polished white stone. A lack of furniture other than a few barren bookshelves made the room appear even more cavernous and foreign.

As overwhelming as her predicament was, Nora concluded that everything would be easier to face when she was no longer naked.

She swung her feet around to put them on the floor and stood, pulling the comforter with her, and was surprised to find that the process had been painless. She padded over to the screen and stepped behind it, finding a low stool with a pile of red fabric folded on it.

Letting the comforter drop now that she was behind the privacy of the screen, she glanced down and drew in a sharp breath. The gash in her leg was now nothing more than a thin pink scar. She ran the pads of her fingers over it in wonder for a few moments before remembering that she was supposed to be getting dressed. She picked up the fabric from the stool, only to be dismayed to find that it was not, in fact, clothes, but instead a large rectangle of fabric with no discernable arm or leg holes. Remembering how Thad had been draped in fabric like the figures of ancient Greek statues, she grimaced. Sure enough, under the pile of fabric, she found a set of small golden clasps and a thin gold cord that could serve as a belt.

Thanking her lucky stars that she was a historian and knew how classical Greek clothing worked, she draped the scarlet fabric around herself, albeit awkwardly, and used the clasps to fasten it at the shoulders, before tying the cord around her waist, gathering in the voluminous fabric. She searched in vain for any undergarments before deciding that going commando under a toga was hardly worthy of her concern at the moment. Nora did succeed in locating a pair of leather sandals next to the stool and tried her best to lace them up her calves with unpracticed fingers. Her hair fell loose around her face and, even without a mirror, she could tell her brown curls had become a mass of frizz, but the hair elastic she normally kept around her wrist was missing, so she had no choice but to leave it. A hysterical giggle bubbled up in Nora's throat as she glanced down at her outfit. Maybe she was still hallucinating.

An image came to her mind then of a swirl of dark creatures and Adam at the center of it, slicing and hacking with a bronze sword. Her smile slid from her face as she remembered how terribly real that had been, and suddenly, it seemed more plausible that this might be real too. Part of her longed to run for the shelter of her cozy apartment and bury her head under the covers and pretend this had never happened, but who knew if she would be able to find her way home from wherever this was. Listening to Adam's explanations was her best option. She stepped from behind the screen and made her way over to the arch that Thad had indicated.

As she stepped out into the dazzling light, Nora was forced to blink rapidly. Once her eyes adjusted, she found she was in a court-yard made of the same white stone as the room and surrounded by towering, Ionic style Greek columns. The gentle murmur of running water greeted her, and as she looked around, she located the source—a fountain at one end of the courtyard. The outside was covered in small turquoise tiles, and at the center of the pool stood a grand statue of a man. The figure had his face turned up, and held aloft in his hand was a spear, the blade pointed straight up at the sky. Water shot out of the tip of the spear, cascading around him before falling into the pool at his feet, the tinkling of the water reverberating around the almost deserted courtyard.

Perched on the edge of the fountain, Adam looked up at the man. The dark jeans and argyle sweater he wore made him look out of place in the sun-soaked courtyard, and Nora felt even more self-conscious in her odd ensemble. When Adam heard her foot-steps echoing off the polished stone, he turned to look.

When he caught sight of her, he froze for a second with his lips parted and eyes wide, probably in shock at her ridiculous outfit. Her cheeks warmed, but the look was gone as quickly as it came, and he jumped to his feet.

"Nora, you're up!" He looked her over and his voice contained an edge of laughter as he continued. "I see Thad gave you a peplos to sort out for yourself. I'll see if I can't find you some real clothes after we are finished talking."

Nora managed a tight smile as he motioned towards the edge of the fountain, and they both sat down, Nora angling her body to face him. She wanted to inspect his face as he spoke. A silence fell between them, and Nora realized she had so many questions that she did not even know where to begin. She opened her mouth to say something, but Adam got there first.

"I thought you would have attacked me with questions by now."

Nora tilted her head in thought before responding. "I'm actually debating whether or not to shove you into this fountain for drag-ging me from a weekend business meeting into a life-endangering fiasco that has me thinking I might be more than half insane, not to mention putting my entire career at risk."

Adam grimaced. "And what's the verdict?"

"I think I'll let you explain yourself and then decide if you deserve to go for a swim."

"Fair enough," Adam conceded. "What do you want to know?"

Nora opened and closed her mouth a few times before admitting, "I don't know what I want to ask first." She paused again and then settled for, "Who are you?"

Adam sighed and ran his hand through his hair. "That's a complicated question."

"Then talk," responded Nora, leaning back on her hands and crossing her legs. Adam quickly looked away from where a large expanse of Nora's bare thigh peaked through the red fabric. Nora tried not to think about the fact that she wasn't wearing any underwear.

Adam took another deep breath as if to steady himself before diving in.

"I am one of the Eteria, an ancient order dedicated to defending the Light. The Light is an endless source of wisdom and beauty, but it is also the source of our power. It allows us to do things like heal the wound in your leg, but it can also be concentrated and used in battle to take out dozens of enemies at a time."

"You're...what? Sorcerers?" Nora knew she should have been dizzy with disbelief, but her mind was strangely logical as she weighed his explanation.

The corner of Adam's mouth twitched. "I suppose you could say that, although that calls to mind all sorts of images of garish hand waving and strange incantations. Our use of the Light is far more... cerebral than that. Not to mention we don't spend all our time haphazardly throwing around balls of Light. We also celebrate the gifts of wisdom and beauty the Light brings us by studying philosophy, art, and literature."

"That explains the whole English professor thing I suppose,"

Nora mused, tapping her chin. "Can anybody learn to use the Light, or are you some special breed of human or something?"

Adam shook his head. "We are human, just born with a unique ability. It's like...being able to roll your tongue or wiggle your ears. Not everybody can do it, and it seems to be hereditary. We haven't exactly used genetic testing, but nobody with the ability has been born outside the Eteria in thousands of years."

"But if you Eteria people can do so much with your Light, then why hasn't anybody noticed you guys?" Nora asked with a furrowed brow.

"Because we can't actually do much with the Light. Not anymore, at least, so we keep to ourselves. When I said we were an ancient order, I was not exaggerating. With the Light, there is also Shadow, a power of darkness that feeds on doubt and insecurity."

Nora couldn't help but snort, and Adam raised a brow at her. "Sorry, it's just that this is starting to sound a whole lot like a sci-fi movie—the whole light and dark sides thing."

"Storytellers often come closer to the truth of the world than people like to think."

Nora had to suppress her disbelief that she was discussing science fiction movies with a sorcerer and dragged her attention back to the issue at hand. "You were saying about the Shadow?"

"Right, about three thousand years ago, the Shadow started gaining power. The Eteria did our best to stop it, but for every bit of power we gained, the Shadow gained even more. It was insidious, worming its way into the dark recesses of people's minds, causing fighting within the Order and turning us against ourselves. Both the Shadow and the Light reached the height of their power in about 400 BC. At the time, the headquarters of the Eteria was located near Athens, which was a center of Light, with art and philosophy being developed there at the time.

"There came a point when the Shadow was threatening the existence of Light itself, and we knew we had to act. The full force of the Eteria marched out to meet the forces of Shadow on the plains outside the city, and we clashed in the largest battle our order has ever seen. At the end of the battle, when the dust had settled, the Eteria learned that we had won, but at a terrible price. While it appeared the Shadow had been vanquished, only a few dozen of us had survived. Nearly all our leadership had been wiped out. Even worse, a barrier had formed between us and the Light, making it difficult to use without exhausting oneself to the point of near death. The survivors used what little magic we had left to take our headquarters, the Sanctuary, and put it in a pocket dimension with points of access all over the world for those who know how to find them.

"What remains of the Eteria have lived here in this Sanctuary ever since, thinking for a time that we had paid a steep price, but it was worth it to rid the world of the Shadow. We stayed out of worldly affairs for the most part, assuming we had done our job and could now hide in our pocket dimension to lick our wounds. We were wrong, though; the Shadow has begun to creep back into the world. With our limited access to the Light and our decimated numbers, we have done what we can to slow its spread, but it's not enough to make a big impact."

Nora was breathless from Adam's story, but her brain was already whirring, reconciling everything that had happened to her with what she had just learned. Unable to hold still any longer, she stood and began pacing back and forth in front of the fountain. Adam followed her movements with unreadable eyes.

"So, the Shadow is back, and for some reason, it decided to attack us at the museum? And you knew how to fight it because you are a warrior sorcerer from an ancient order?"

Adam nodded.

Nora blew out a breath through her lips and stopped her pacing. "You know what? I don't have time for this. I already only get five hours of sleep a night without having to worry about an ancient war. Thank you for saving my life and all, but I'd like to go home now."

Adam's mouth twisted as if he was chewing on his next words in distaste. "I'm not sure that's an option anymore."

Nora froze. "What do you mean, *not an option?*"

"When the Shadow left a cut on your leg, some of its essence was left in your bloodstream, which acted as a poison against you. Thad managed to draw it out of you, but the Shadow does not like being denied a victim." Adam shifted uncomfortably on the edge of the fountain. "There is a chance it might be...drawn to you, now that it has been in your blood. It tends to act as a kind of homing beacon for disasters."

Nora blinked once. Then again. "You mean I can't leave this place without those...things attacking me again?"

"No, we can keep you safe," Adam assured, shaking his head emphatically, "but you have to work with us. You'll need a guard for now, and we can teach you to defend yourself going forward."

Nora sat down hard and dropped her head between her knees. The cool stone was reassuring against her bare legs, but she still felt as if a pair of giant hands had picked up the entire courtyard and thrown it on its side.

"Why did they have to attack me in the first place?" she mumbled towards to floor, but Adam still seemed to hear her.

He sighed from his perch on the fountain before embarking on another explanation. "I'm afraid the attack may have happened even if I wasn't there. The sword and the spear are both very powerful artifacts that the Shadow would be drawn to."

Nora raised her head and squinted up at Adam through the hair that had fallen across her face, doing some very quick mental math. "Powerful artifacts? And you said that the Eteria took their final stand against the Shadow around 400 BC. The battle took place near Athens." It all made sense to her now. "The sword and the spear were left from the battle with the Shadow."

Adam nodded. "They are both Eteria weapons, forged by our Smiths. That's why they haven't deteriorated throughout the centuries; they were created using the Light."

"Explains why you wanted to see them so badly," Nora observed, piecing together the puzzle formed by Adam's explanations. Nora had a sudden thought about the lengths Adam might have gone to see the sword, but she kept that thought to herself for now, putting it away to examine later.

"Well yes." Adam looked down and rubbed the back of his neck as he spoke. "I will admit that I was rather desperate to see the sword once I saw it in the paper. I was particularly interested in it, because, well...it's mine."

"You mean 'mine' as in it belongs to the Eteria?" Nora clarified.

"No," Adam would not meet her eyes as he spoke, choosing his words as if she were a wounded animal who might bolt if he said the wrong thing. "That sword belonged to me personally. It was made for me, and I used it in combat."

Nora pinched her eyebrows together. "But Adam, that can't be your sword. That weapon was left behind over two millennia ago. You can't be..."

Adam grimaced.

Nora's ears rang.

"No, no. If that sword was yours, then you'd have to be—"

"I'm 2600 years old, give or take." He cut her off, glancing up through his lashes.

Nora stared in silence, waiting for him to burst out laughing and tell her that it was all a joke. When she looked into his eyes, though, she found no amusement. She shook her head. She had been trying to take his explanations in stride up until this point, but this tipped her over the edge.

"Our connection with the Light prevents us from aging," Adam began to explain. "Just as the weapons in the museum show no signs of the centuries of wear and tear, we too are protected from accumulating damage and signs of decay. We are immune to most sickness, and we won't die unless we are killed. Even though using the Light is nearly impossible these days, the connection sustains us."

The gears in Nora's brain that had come to a standstill earlier began to move again, attempting to integrate this new bit of information. The theory had made sense when he had been explaining why the weapons did not age, but it still somehow seemed rather farfetched to apply the same principle to human beings.

Something caught at the back of Nora's throat, and for one horrifying moment, she thought she was going to burst into tears. Instead, a small giggle bubbled up, growing into hysterical laughter until she was rocking back and forth on the ground, shaking uncontrollably.

Adam's mouth hung open and his eyes were round as he watched her antics. Nora was not sure what kind of reaction he had expected, but she was sure this wasn't it. To his credit, he did not reprimand her or tell her to calm down as her hysteria echoed around the smooth stone of the courtyard for long minutes as she let the ridiculousness of her situation wash over her.

Eventually, her laughter subsided, leaving Nora gasping for breath and dashing tears from her eyes.

Adam commented mildly. "You took that better than Drew did."

Nora's face fell, her mirth fading. "Drew. Where is he?"

"He's fine. Totally fine," Adam reassured, his palms held out towards her placatingly. "He came with us to the Sanctuary. He refused to let you out of his sight, and he stayed with you while Thad drew the Shadows out of your blood. Kept yelling about breaking sterile procedure while Thad was healing you. Still, after that, he was in a better position to believe our explanation."

Nora's anxiety ebbed a little, a plan starting to form in its place. "But you said I took it better than he did?"

"Well, yes." The corners of Adam's mouth twitched up. "When Thad told him how old he was, Drew fainted."

Nora's hand flew to her open mouth. "Is he okay? Can I see him?"

"Yes, yes, he's fine. Thad saw to it that he was well taken care of and he's probably anxious to see you. If you're feeling up to it, of course."

Nora nodded as she pushed to her feet. "I'd like to see him right away. I need a little space to process all of this."

"Of course, take as long as you need. I'm sure a familiar face will help," Adam said as he also stood, offering her a small smile.

"Thanks. Oh, and Adam?"

"Yes?"

Nora took a quick step forward and braced both of her hands on Adam's chest before giving him the most forceful shove she could manage. He stumbled back a step or two, arms windmilling wildly to regain his balance before his knees hit the edge of the fountain and he toppled backwards into the water with an almighty splash.

When he surfaced, he was spluttering and shaking his soaked hair out of his eyes like an oversized dog. The wet strands were plastered to his high cheekbones as he gaped at her.

"That's for almost getting me killed," she snapped before spinning on her heel and marching out of the courtyard. If she didn't know better, she would have thought she saw the beginnings of a smile on his face before she turned away.

6

XANDER BLINKED RAPIDLY, TRYING TO GET HIS EYES TO FOCUS ON THE scroll in front of him. He realized he had been staring at the same sentence for several minutes without absorbing any of it. He straightened up from the table he was bent over and tilted his face up to the sky, trying to relieve the aching in his stiff neck. The sunshine warmed his features as he let out a huff of frustration. He was attempting to study the eleven attributes of a successful ward, but his progress through the monotonous manuscript had stalled. Wading his way through the first five attributes had gone efficiently enough, but when he'd gotten to the sixth one, his distraction had arrived, and he hadn't made much progress since.

Xander spared a glance down the long table stretching the length of the open-air courtyard to where his distraction sat. She was perched on a stool about four down from his on the opposite side of the table, a heavy leather book open in front of her. She seemed engrossed in the tome, oblivious to the other people milling about the courtyard's long tables, some studying as he was, others chatting and laughing amongst themselves. Given her current focus, Xander reasoned that he could get away with staring a little longer.

Her left elbow was propped up on the table, and in that hand, she held a delicate bronze dagger. Xander was enraptured as he watched it twirl between her deft fingers crisscrossed with scars from her numerous hours of combat training. What fascinated Xander the most, though, were the three balls of light that trailed from the tip of the dagger as she twirled it around and around. The balls were no bigger than a candied date, yet their brightness was as intense as that of the sun overhead.

Xander couldn't help but be impressed by her control of the Light. While he was certainly no slob when it came to casting defenses, and his knowledge of theory and philosophy was unmatched in their class, he could barely do what she was doing now while focusing completely, let alone while he was reading a book. He wondered what she could be reading that had captured her attention so fully.

While Xander had been enraptured by the Lights twirling around the woman's fingers, he had failed to notice a large form walking up behind her.

"Go away, Cyril. I'm busy," she said, neither looking up from her book nor ceasing her twirling of the dagger around her fingers.

The hulking man folded his arms, making the red fabric stretch across his broad pectorals.

"Oh, come on, Aediene," Cyril said. "Don't be such a bore. Come have some fun with me."

Aediene still didn't look up at the man. "I am having fun. In fact, I would be having more fun if you left me alone now."

Xander's lips twitched but he remained silent. He had watched the woman long enough in their years of training together to know where this was going to end.

Cyril scowled, making it clear that this interaction was not going how he had planned. He reached out a meaty hand and placed it on Aediene's shoulder, jerking her away from her book.

"How can you be having more fun with that book than—"

He did not get to finish his sentence because Aediene whirled to her feet faster than Xander could follow. She managed to grab the wrist of the hand that Cyril had placed on her shoulder and now had her nails digging between the tendons of the sensitive inner side in a way that looked most excruciating. Her other hand still held the dagger, which was now pointed with the tip less than a centimeter from the slight bulge at the meeting of Cyril's legs, the balls of light still hovering around expectantly near the tip. Her voice remained calm as she said, "Because at least this book is somewhat intellectually stimulating, something I'm afraid you could never hope to offer."

Xander bit down on his hand to keep from laughing at the outraged look on the big man's face. Cyril was turning an unflattering shade of purple and a vein throbbed in his temple. Still, he managed to splutter, "You're much too pretty to worry about me being intellectually stimulating when I could be stimulating in other, far more fun ways."

Xander's eyes widened, but Aediene only looked amused. Just then, Cyril violently wrenched his wrist, trying to free it from the woman's grasp. Before he could twist free, the three balls of Light flew up from where they had been hovering around the knife. They stopped in front of his face, just inches from his eyes, and burst with an audible pop, getting even brighter than they had been before.

Cyril stumbled backwards, rubbing at his eyes and cursing loudly. "She blinded me! The wretched woman blinded me!"

At this point, the noise of the orbs of Light exploding combined with the large man's yelling had drawn the attention of everybody in the courtyard.

Aediene acted like she hadn't noticed. "Oh, calm down, you big baby," she hissed. "It's temporary. You'll be able to see just fine in a couple of hours." She turned back to the table, looking as if she fully intended to return to her book, but froze when a commanding voice echoed across the courtyard.

"What seems to be going on here?"

Everybody in the courtyard rushed to get out of the way of the woman striding between the tables. She was dressed in swirling fabric from head to toe, her clothing so white it hurt to look at. As she drew nearer to the center of the commotion, where Aediene and Cyril stood, Xander shot to his feet and stepped around the table in order to get closer to the action.

"What is the meaning of this?" the woman demanded. Her tone made everybody in the courtyard stand up straighter.

Cyril spoke first. "Commander, she blinded me! I was just trying to talk to her and she blinded me!" He threw a thick arm out in the general direction of Aediene, the other hand still covering his eyes.

Aediene held her chin high, opening her mouth to protest. "Commander, I—"

"It was me," Xander interjected.

The Commander's eagle-eyed gaze shot to him. "You did this, Xander?" For once, she seemed caught off guard.

"You did?" Aediene echoed, a crease forming between her brows.

"Yes," Xander continued. "I was practicing my control by juggling some balls of Light and I lost focus when I heard Aediene and Cyril arguing, and well...you know my control isn't the best." He looked down at his sandals and rubbed the back of his neck sheepishly.

The Commander's eyes narrowed for a moment as she appraised him. "I thought at least you were intelligent enough to have better judgement, Xander. I do not want to hear of anything like this again."

Xander nodded emphatically, causing his hair to fall into his eyes. "Of course, Commander."

The Commander turned and led Cyril away toward the infirmary. As they went, Cyril looked back and threw a snarl over his shoulder in Xander's general direction.

Xander grimaced at the thought of making a new enemy, especially an enemy who had arms three times as thick as his own lanky limbs. He turned away to find Aediene staring at him with her arms crossed and an eyebrow raised.

"You know I can fight my own battles."

Xander hopped back over to his side of the table to settle onto his stool. "Oh, don't worry, you made that abundantly clear." He chuckled. "However, I get in less trouble than you do, so I could better afford the slip up. Besides, I am a Defender, not a Warrior, so the Commander can't do much to me anyway."

Aediene looked at him curiously as she gathered her book up from the table. "Still, you didn't have to take the fall for me."

"Nonsense. I have far too much fun watching you taking on those meatheads for you to have to stop."

"So, you watch me do that regularly?"

Xander looked down and rubbed the back of his neck again. This time, his sheepishness was not feigned. "Well, that's not... You do tend to make quite a scene."

Aediene giggled at his awkwardness, and Xander couldn't help but hope that he could make her laugh like that more often.

She gestured to the stool across from his. "Do you mind if I join you?"

"Of course not." Xander shuffled a few of his stacks of paper out of the way to make room for her book as she sat down.

Aediene settled into the seat and reopened her book, resuming the twirling of her knife between her fingers.

Xander had a smile on his face as he looked back down at the parchment in front of him. He still couldn't focus on the sixth element of an effective ward, but he found that he didn't care.

7

Nora scurried through the hallways of the Sanctuary, peering into every doorway she passed, hoping to spot Drew. She realized belatedly that she should have asked Adam where Drew was before shoving him in the fountain, but she didn't want to ruin her moment of triumph by going back and asking for directions. She also hadn't expected how distracted she would be by the way Adam's wet hair clung to his throat. It turned out that the Sanctuary was a labyrinth of identical hallways, and at this point, she was unsure if she could find her way back to Adam if she tried.

Nora peeked into another room and huffed in annoyance when she found it, too, was deserted. She moved on to the next, feeling a pang of disappointment that she could not slow down and explore the beautiful building. There was no time to linger if the plan that had begun to take form in her mind was going to work. Still, her eyes snagged on a few of the remarkable paintings adorning the walls before she poked her head around the corner to check the next room.

It was another white stone monstrosity, this one filled with low couches and plush rugs layered over one another in a rich tapestry.

Nora spotted Drew, looking as out of place as possible, seated on one of the low couches, still wearing his scrubs and lab coat.

As soon as he noticed her, he jumped up from his seat, crossed the room in three long strides, and caught her up in a giant bear hug. Nora closed her eyes and let her head rest on his broad torso for just a moment. The hair of his chest tickled her cheek where it poked out of the slight V in his scrubs, and she took in the familiar scent of citrus laundry soap and the faint tinge of antiseptic that always clung to Drew after a shift at the hospital. With all the chaos that had erupted in her life, this was a piece of solid ground.

Remembering the turmoil that had brought her here, she stepped backwards out of his embrace. Drew left his hands on her shoulders and leaned in to examine her from head to toe.

"How are you feeling?" he questioned, continuing his scrutiny of her. "Any dizziness? Pain? Headache?"

Nora cocked her head.

"I feel...great actually," she answered truthfully. "Which is good, because we need to get out of here."

Drew's thick brows snapped together in concern. "Why? Did something happen?"

"*Did something happen*? What happened is that I've been given the same explanation you have, and it's certifiably insane!"

"You mean you don't believe them?" Drew asked with a tilt of his head.

Nora released a heavy sigh from between pursed lips. "After all that I've seen, I don't think I have a choice to believe them about the Shadows and the Light. But it seems like the type of thing I shouldn't be getting wrapped up in. A group of immortal sorcerers who stays secluded in a pocket dimension for thousands of years now wants me to train in self-defense and keep a guard on me at all times? It sounds like they are trying to trick me into joining a cult or something. Not to mention I'm ninety-nine percent sure that Adam is the same man who broke into the museum last week to see the weapons. He's put my work in jeopardy twice now, and I can't risk anymore." Nora threw her hands up in frustration.

Drew tugged at his sleeves before asking, "And your solution is to run away?"

"Of course," Nora huffed. For somebody so intelligent, he was being oddly dense about the situation. "You seem disturbingly calm about all of this yourself."

"Nora, I'm an emergency medicine doctor. Aggressively calm is what I do. It's my way of coping."

"Go ahead and keep up the level-headed act. I'm going to need your help getting out of here since I was unconscious when we came in." Nora grabbed his hand and started towing him towards the door. "We'll need to act fast. They'll come looking for me."

Drew hesitated, causing Nora to glance back over her shoulder at him in irritation.

"I know trying to get in your way might be akin to trying to stop a freight train with my bare hands, but I think you should stay."

Nora turned to face him. "Look Drew, I don't have time for this sort of craziness in my life. Adam shows up and a week later, I almost die. I'm so close to achieving my goals at work. I can't get caught up in something like this. I need to get away while I still can. Do *you* want to stay or something?"

"No, I'm only here because of you, but you might not have a choice in the matter here," Drew pointed out in a painfully reasonable tone. "Like you said, you almost died, and you need these people's help if you don't want it happening again."

It took all the self-control Nora could muster to not stamp her foot like a stubborn child, and Drew knew her well enough to sense her struggle.

"Listen, how about we at least get some food in your stomach so you can make a decision with a clear head," Drew placated. "That man Thad said something about lunch earlier, but I was too nervous to eat at the time. Get your blood sugar up, hear these people out, and if you still feel like leaving, I'll help you."

"How will we keep them from stopping us from leaving?" Nora asked petulantly, even though she was losing ground.

Drew raised a mischievous eyebrow. "I think we could use some sort of distracting wardrobe malfunction. It doesn't seem like it would be difficult with you in... What is that you are wearing exactly?"

Nora looked down at herself and almost giggled, having forgotten how ridiculous she must look. "I'm not entirely sure. It's some sort of traditional Greek garment. Thad left it for me to put on—with no instructions, I might add." Reminded of her lack of underwear, as well, Nora briefly wondered how distracted Adam would be if her makeshift garment were to "accidentally" fall prey to a stiff breeze. Nora shook the intruding thought away, scolding herself for constantly letting her attention drift from the issues at hand.

"All right, it's a deal," Nora agreed, "but I think you should have the wardrobe malfunction if we need to get away. This is your idea, after all."

Nora found herself in a courtyard similar to the one she had met Adam in earlier, but instead of a fountain, there were several long tables. Each table was surrounded by short, backless stools, enough to seat a few dozen. However, the courtyard's only occupants were Adam, Thad, and three other people Nora didn't recognize sitting at the far end—and a bright blue peacock picking its way between the tables.

Drew led the way over to where the people were sitting. Noticing their approach, Adam looked up and motioned towards the unoccupied seat next to him. He was now wearing a dry black T-shirt, and Nora thought about how he must have had to change out of his wet clothes after his swim in the fountain. His dark curls were still damp and clung to his forehead in a way that made Nora's mouth suddenly dry.

As she took her seat, Adam said, "Everybody, this is Nora." The way he said it gave Nora visions of standing up in front of the class at a new school as the teacher introduced her and warned the other children to play nice.

"Nora, this is Ezra." Adam motioned to a square jawed man in red who looked her over before giving a grunt of affirmation.

"This is Antony." The man in purple looked up from his food to give her a dreamy smile.

"And this is Seraphina." Nora glanced to the last person at the table, but the woman didn't even look up and Nora was forced to give her polite smile to the elaborate tangle of pale blonde braids on top of the woman's head. Nora didn't have much of a chance to be offended, however, because her attention was quickly monopolized by the food on the table as her stomach growled.

Thad, sitting across from her, gave her a knowing look and grabbed a plate.

"You should be starved after the massive healing you went through," he commented as he shoveled stuffed dates, cheese, and olives onto the plate.

"Are you sure you didn't replace my stomach with a bottomless pit?" Nora asked as she watched Thad add a pancake-like piece of bread drizzled in olive oil to the pile and her mouth watered. As Thad put the plate down in front of her, she looked around for silverware. Not seeing any, she shrugged and began tearing into the food with her hands.

The blonde woman at the end looked up and sniffed distastefully while delicately nibbling on an olive.

"Speaking of healing, I think we would all prefer it if Thad didn't have to heal Nora like that more than once," Drew started in diplomatically. "Maybe we should talk about how we are going to keep her safe before she eats you out of house and home."

Nora narrowed her eyes at Drew but kept herself quiet by filling her mouth with a bite of cheese.

"Unfortunately, Nora is now going to be some sort of homing beacon for disaster. She will need to have protection around her to be able to continue going about her normal life," Adam explained.

"So, what do you want me to do? Walk around with a fully armed bodyguard? *That* won't raise any questions or get in the way of my life at all," Nora argued, remembering why it had seemed like such a good idea to run away just a few minutes ago.

She almost jumped when the man in purple, Antony, chimed in from the far end of the table.

"I would enjoy being your bodyguard. Chicago sounds lovely." His smile was excited enough that Nora almost felt bad for being frustrated at the suggestion.

"That's not the point! I don't want my entire routine upset by this!"

"I agree with her," the blonde at the end of the table spoke up. "I don't think we should be putting ourselves in harm's way just because she was dense enough to mess with things she shouldn't have."

Nora opened and shut her mouth, uncomfortable with the feeling of being lost for words, which hadn't happened to her in quite a while.

Adam stepped in before she could formulate her response.

"Seraphina," he warned, to which the woman just shrugged and returned her attention to her plate. Adam turned back to Nora and continued. "The guard could be temporary. If we get you trained in at least basic combat, you could learn to defend yourself if there was any trouble."

"I'm resourceful enough. After all, didn't I save you by skewering a Shadow in the eye with a pair of tweezers?" Nora jabbed Adam in the chest with her finger and was thrown off guard by how solid it was.

Thad grimaced. "Yes, but as much as I'd love to see how many

Shadows you can fight with everyday objects, I'm sure Ezra could teach you to fight in a way that won't involve you throwing your tools."

Ezra himself grumbled from the end of the table. "I'm not training anybody."

"Oh, so you're saying you can't train her?" Thad asked.

"Don't be ridiculous; I could train a goat to fight if I wanted to," Ezra responded, his gray eyes narrowed. "But she's too old to start training now. It would be too hard for her to learn, and she would get hurt."

Nora pounded her fist on the table, making the plates rattle as everybody jumped.

"Could everyone stop arguing about what to do with me as if I don't have any say in the matter?" she ground out through gritted teeth.

Adam opened his mouth but remained silent when Nora narrowed her eyes at him.

"I've worked hard for the life I have, and I'm not going to let one weekend of craziness ruin it for me," Nora continued. "Drew, you've been quiet for all of this. You're on my side, aren't you?"

She looked pleadingly at one of her oldest friends, but he wouldn't quite meet her eyes, instead rubbing his beard and looking down at the table.

"I don't know, Nora. I don't want to see you coming through the emergency room doors covered in blood again," Drew said. "Maybe staying safe wouldn't be such a bad idea."

The silence that followed was so thick that it felt as if nobody was breathing. Nora's mouth hung open, and Drew peeked up apologetically through his lashes.

Nora pushed to her feet, making the stool beneath her topple over, causing a harsh clatter in the silence that had fallen in the courtyard. Then she turned and stomped back into the Sanctuary. Another stool scraped as if somebody stood, but Drew's voice cut in.

"Let her go. Just give her a minute."

She didn't look back to see who had tried to follow her.

IT WASN'T LONG BEFORE NORA WAS HOPELESSLY LOST IN THE labyrinthian hallways of the Sanctuary. In her retreat from the courtyard, her only focus had been on putting distance between herself and the people there, and she hadn't thought to look for landmarks or paid attention to where she was going. Now she continued to wander, although at a much more reasonable pace. Her initial anger had faded, but she still wasn't ready to face the group again. Instead, she distracted herself with wondering where all these hallways could lead.

Seeing a door ajar ahead, she peeked in to find an empty bedroom. It looked like the one she had woken up in, except without the elaborate painting on the ceiling. She continued to peer into every open room she passed as she walked, finding the same sight behind every door.

Just as Nora was calm enough to consider turning around and trying to retrace her steps, she came upon a pair of carved double doors, much grander than any she had passed so far. Nora only paused for a moment before her curiosity got the best of her and she pushed it open to step inside.

The room was filled with rows upon rows of weapons, all made of bronze and shimmering softly in the faint light of the hallway. She drifted into the room and had to tuck her hands behind her back to not run her fingers over the racks of swords and spears as she passed. The collection was three times the size of the entire inventory at the Field Museum, and her head spun as she glanced around, hoping to find other types of weapons, or perhaps even a shield.

As she searched, her eyes caught on something else. In one corner, there was a tall case, just like the one at the museum that contained the replica armor of a Greek hoplite. It only took Nora one glance to tell that the armor in the case in front of her now was no replica. She strode across the room to stand in front of it, stepping as close to it as she could manage. Her nose was inches from the glass, so close that her breathe made a thin coat of fog. It was magnificent.

Her eyes ran along the intricate whorls on the breastplate that seemed to dance in the dim light, and she considered the type of mold that would have to be used to craft such a piece. A dent had once caved in one side of the helmet, but somebody had done their best to return it to its original form. This was not just ceremonial; this outfit had seen real combat. Whomever this armor had been made for, they couldn't have been much taller than her.

Nora had become so enraptured by the armor that she didn't hear the footsteps coming up behind her.

"See something you like?"

Nora started so hard that she jumped backwards and landed directly on Adam's foot. She spun around to face him, ready to chastise him for sneaking up on her, but as she turned, she lost her balance and his hands shot out to grab her waist, steadying her. Nora involuntarily stepped into his space at the feeling of strong, warm fingers on her hips before her brain caught up with her. Even if she found Adam charming, Nora didn't know enough about his life as an immortal sorcerer to be having those kind of thoughts. She backed out of his grasp before any more distracting images of his hands on her waist got the better of her.

"I didn't mean to startle you. I assumed you had heard me come in," he apologized, shoving his outstretched hands into his pockets.

"Yes, well. I was distracted by the armor."

Adam glanced over her shoulder at the display case. "I suppose it is worth being distracted by. This set belongs to one of our greatest commanders."

Curious, Nora pressed him. "Really? Who is he? Does he live here in the Sanctuary?"

Adam took a moment to swallow before responding. "They died, a long time ago. In the battle against the Shadow."

Adam's face was obscured, with the light coming from the door behind him, but Nora didn't need to be able to see his face to know the pain she would find there. The tightness in his voice was enough.

"I'm very sorry," Nora looked down at her toes in her sandals.

"It's okay, they would have been happy that you were admiring their armor." Some of the tightness had left Adam's tone, and his usual musical lilt was edging its way back into his voice.

"I was admiring all of it." Nora gestured to the room in general. Then she added sheepishly, "I had an itch to go exploring. I hope that was all right."

Adam chuckled. "I figured you would. I wouldn't have left you alone if I wasn't okay with you poking around a little bit."

"Good, because I wasn't going to be that sorry anyways. I hope that doesn't get you in trouble with your leaders or anything."

Adam shrugged. "There are too few of us to have any sort of organized governance anymore. We all just try to do what we think is best and hope by this age we've managed to develop good judgement."

Nora nodded, and silence fell between them once more. She looked down at her toes and wiggled them in her sandals, knowing they couldn't avoid the inevitable discussion forever, though she didn't want to be the one to start it.

"Are you okay?" Adam asked.

Nora's eyes snapped up, not expecting that to be Adam's opening line.

She thought for a second before shrugging. "I wouldn't say 'okay', but considering the circumstances, I think I'm faring admirably."

Adam nodded, as if considering her answer. "I want you to know that I didn't seek you out with the intention of upsetting your life. If... If there were a way to keep you safe without drawing you into our war, I would do it. If you don't want to train, I'll respect your decision, but it would go against our mission, and my own conscious, to send you out there alone again."

Nora sighed and turned around to face the case, putting her back to Adam as she considered.

"There is no winning, is there? Either I let myself most likely get killed by the incarnation of evil, or I take precious time away from life and work to learn how to defend myself."

"You're too smart to see things in such all-or-nothing terms."

"You sound very sure of that."

"I am."

Nora glanced up at his profile, strikingly defined in the back-lighting, and considered what he'd said. Her eyes caught on the glimmer of bronze behind him and her mind whirred.

"So, if I were to choose to train, do you think Ezra could be convinced to train me to fight with a spear?" Nora asked slowly.

Adam glanced down at her with a smile starting to form on his lips, appearing to try and play it cool.

"He could be."

"And I could be given insight into ancient fighting techniques? Say...even techniques that a well-studied weapons expert may not have known about?"

"Absolutely."

Nora hummed in thought. "And I could maybe even write an academic paper and present my findings about these techniques to my peers at an upcoming conference?"

"Of course." Adam was no longer trying to hide his smile. "But you would need to come up with a way to cite your sources that would be believable. Perhaps you could cite some texts that have been newly translated by a local professor of ancient languages."

"That could work."

"So, do we have a deal?" Adam held out his hand for Nora to shake on it, but she hesitated.

"I have just a few more requirements."

Adam tilted his head, indicating that she should state her terms.

"My temporary guard while I'm learning would have to keep their distance, not interfere unless I was in immediate danger. And they can't follow me around Chicago wearing a toga."

"They aren't togas; they're called peplos. And deal. You won't even know they're there unless the Shadow tries to attack."

Reassured, Nora took his hand and shook on the arrangement, and Adam offered her a grin that made him look almost boyish. As she smiled back, she realized something about him looked off. She squinted as she scrutinized his face, trying to figure out what was different.

"Your glasses! I forgot they were crushed at the museum. Can you see all right?"

Adam shoved his hands in his pockets. "Oh yeah, I'm fine. I don't need glasses."

"Then why do you wear them?"

"I guess I view them as kind of a disguise. Nobody in Chicago is going to recognize me as a member of the Eteria, but still. They make me feel kind of like a superhero with a secret identity."

Nora blinked, incredulous.

"I've had a lot of free time through the years, and I've filled some of it by consuming excessive amounts of pop culture." Adam's tone was defensive.

Nora snorted. "I kind of get why you do it. The glasses suit you. They add to the whole hot professor vibe."

Adam raised his brows. "Hot professor vibe?"

It was Nora's turn to get defensive as she snapped. "I said what I said. Don't let it go to your head." To his credit, Adam didn't press the issue.

"Come on," he said, turning to lead her from the room. "You still need to finish your lunch."

8

A TRICKLE OF SWEAT ROLLED DOWN XANDER'S BACK AS HE SCREWED HIS eyes shut. Trying to keep a ward around this large a group by himself took more concentration than he was accustomed to. He breathed in and let it out slowly as he opened his eyes, settling into the feeling of the Light pouring through his veins and out the tip of his short sword. Seeing the air in front of him glimmer with the slight iridescence of a soap bubble, he smiled in victory and anchored the ward in place.

Xander was used to helping with the renewal of the permanent ward around the Sanctuary, but that was done with the power of dozens of people and they were strengthening something that already existed. Creating a ward out of the Light by himself was completely new. It was a skill he wouldn't have been expected to master for many more years, but these were dark times, and everybody was being pushed past their limits.

With the ward stable around him, Xander returned his attention to the field where the young Defenders and Warriors were locked in a mock battle. By his assessment, the fighters on the East side of the field would soon be victorious.

A grim smile tugged at his features as his team's "injured" fighters panted inside the ward he had created. His eyes swept over the field outside the transparent barrier, seeking out a familiar figure. As usual, he found Aediene at the center of the melee, spear twirling about her in untraceable arcs of bronze. Nobody seemed to be able to come within several feet of her without being forced back by a shot of light from the end of her weapon or marked with the red chalk on the edge of her blunted blade, which designated them as "injured". A few chestnut curls had escaped from her braid and clung to her sweat-coated face. Somebody had managed to tear one side of her crimson tunic, but she didn't seem to notice.

As he watched her, Xander's grim smile turned genuine. There were few times that Aediene looked as glorious as she did in the heat of battle. As she incapacitated the last few challengers from the other team, she shot a glance over her shoulder, her eyes bright from the exertion, back to where Xander stood with a triumphant smile. As she glanced at him, she turned away from the battle and failed to notice the last Warrior from the opposing team sneaking up behind her. Not having time to yell, Xander threw up his hand and a wall of Light sprang up in front of the Warrior for a split second. It only served to slow him down, but it caught Aediene's attention and gave her enough time to whirl around and hit him in the stomach with the blunt end of her spear, knocking him into the churned mud at her feet.

Leaving the other Warrior to catch his breath, Aediene trudged her way over to where Xander was standing, and he let the ward that surrounded him and the other members of their team drop so she could step closer. She was still panting as she commented. "Don't you think casting an entire ward by yourself was showing off just a little bit?"

"Oh, and what you were doing out there wasn't?" he retorted.

She playfully punched him in the shoulder, making him stagger back a step. He was quite a bit taller than her but still rather lanky, and sometimes, after hours of combat training, she forgot that she didn't need to push everybody quite so hard.

Noticing that she'd knocked him back, Aediene grimaced. "Sorry."

Before Xander could respond, they were interrupted by the approach of Ezra, the training master.

"Okay, knock it off, lovebirds," he rumbled.

Xander looked down to study the trampled grass. While everybody teased him and Aediene about their obvious affection, there wasn't much to it besides a close friendship and a pile of borrowed books. After watching Aediene reject every Warrior who approached her, sometimes repeatedly, he knew better than to test his luck.

Ezra's voice made him look up from where he was digging his sandals into the mud. "We're going to have to split the two of you up next time."

"What? Why?" Xander spluttered.

A weary voice piped up from somewhere in the background. "Because always having them on the same side gives them an unfair advantage?"

"Yeah, I'm tired of eating dirt," another voice chimed in.

Ezra held up a large hand for silence. "No." His voice was stern, but his scowl had softened a fraction. "Because the two of you have come to depend on each other too much. You cover for all of each other's mistakes, not allowing yourselves to learn."

He was right. Xander and Aediene had fallen into an automatic pattern in battle. She defended him while he created wards, and he helped her cover holes in her defenses. It was useful, but Xander knew they wouldn't always be near each other in a real battle.

Still, as Xander and Aediene trekked back up the hill to the Sanctuary to clean their weapons, he said to her, "You know I'll still cover your back, even if you're on the other team."

"I know," she said. She glanced over at him as her tone turned teasing. "You can't help but defend somebody who looks as beautiful as Athena with her spear."

Xander almost tumbled headfirst into the ground but struggled to regain his footing and righted himself at the last second.

"I don't know what you are talking about."

Aediene snorted. "I know you're the one who has been leaving notes in my books. Only you have handwriting that painfully neat."

Xander turned as red as her tunic, but she continued.

"Don't be embarrassed," she said. "I like your notes. I think they're sweet."

Xander's stomach clenched. He had been aiming for something more *along the lines of dashing or romantic. Notes from your Grandmother were sweet.*

"I can stop sending them if you'd rather," he offered. "I know you already have plenty of admirers." They had reached the columns of the Sanctuary, and he paused in the shade, almost scared to look at Aediene's face but unable to resist sneaking a glance.

Aediene stopped, too, turning to face him with an inscrutable expression on her face. Xander was tempted to apologize again for the notes when Aediene grabbed him by the front of his tunic and pressed her lips to his. It was a short, chaste kiss, but Xander could have lived his entire life in that moment. Her body pressed against his, and he could feel the warmth of their earlier exertion radiating off her. If Aediene hadn't had a firm grasp on the front of his tunic, he might have melted into a puddle where he stood.

When she pulled away, she met his eyes expectantly, but Xander was mute. She sighed as she turned away and she muttered under her breath. "Well, it was worth a shot."

Xander was generally a man who believed in the beauty of spoken language, but for once in his life, he decided to let his actions speak for him. Before Aediene could make it two steps up the hill, he grasped her by the wrist and pulled her back to kiss her once more.

9

THREE DAYS AFTER NORA HAD LEFT FOR A SIMPLE COFFEE MEETING with Adam, she collapsed back onto her own bed with a sigh. She stretched out, glad for the sense of comfort and normalcy that washed over her. Although she knew there was a guard from the Eteria nearby, Adam had kept his promise and she'd seen neither hide nor hair of them on her trip home.

She took a few moments of comfort in the sound of the traffic outside and the gurgle of her coffeemaker running in the kitchen before her phone buzzed against her thigh.

Sitting up, she pulled it out to see Odelle's name on the screen and grimaced before answering. "Hello?"

Her sister didn't even acknowledge her with a greeting before launching into a tirade.

"Where the hell have you been? I've called you twenty times and you only pick up now?"

Nora winced, pulling the phone away from her ear so that her sister's yelling didn't blow out her eardrum. Apparently, the Eteria had not yet figured out how to get cell phone service in pocket dimensions.

"You were at the hospital after almost bleeding to death, then I go back to see you and you aren't there anymore. You and Drew just vanished without telling anybody where you were going. I would have filed a missing person report already if Drew hadn't called me this morning and told me you were safe." Under the rage in Odelle's voice, Nora could sense a slight edge of hysteria.

"Well he was right. I'm safe. I just got back to my apartment." Nora did her best to sound reassuring, but the effort was wasted on Odelle.

"You were safe the whole time, and you didn't even think to call me and let me know? I've been out of my mind over here. I spilled a cup of coffee on myself on live TV during the news because I was so distracted, worrying about what happened to you."

Nora's heart sank, and she covered her face with the hand that wasn't holding the phone.

"I'm sorry, *zaika*. I didn't have cell service where I was, and I was really out of it."

"Of course you were out of it. You ran out while being treated for blood loss and concussion. And where were you that you didn't have service?" Nora could envision Odelle with her hands on her hips, tossing her hair in exasperation.

"I was...with Adam." Nora gave the only answer she could think of. She supposed she hadn't promised anybody that she wouldn't tell her sister about the Eteria, but somehow, she couldn't bring herself to burden Odelle with everything that had just happened.

Odelle was far from satisfied with her answer.

"You ran out of the hospital with the professional acquaintance who got you into a car accident? I know I said he was attractive, but I didn't mean for you to disappear with him right then! How hard did you hit your head?"

"Drew came with us," Nora offered lamely.

"Of course he did!" Odelle was beyond incensed. "He didn't want you to die when you decided it was a good idea to slip out of the hospital with a man you barely know!"

"I didn't decide to leave. It was more complicated than that."

Nora stood and started pacing back and forth from the window to her closet.

"Then explain it to me. Contrary to common opinion, I'm not stupid," Odelle fired back.

There was a long silence on the line before Nora answered. She opened her mouth, ready to spill the truth to her sister, whom she'd shared everything with for as long as she could remember. The words stuck in her throat. How did one begin when everything they'd believed to be true about the world had just been upended?

Nora thought about how her whole life, everything she had worked so hard for, was in jeopardy. Then she thought of the same thing happening to Odelle's life, all the obstacles she had overcome to get where she was being for nothing. She knew Odelle wouldn't be able to stay out of this conflict if she knew about it, just the way she'd run towards every playground fight when they were kids. Odelle was always jumping in to protect Nora and getting herself in trouble, and Nora would be damned if she didn't try to protect Odelle from this fight.

"I can't tell you," Nora finally whispered.

"That's not true," Odelle answered in her typical obstinate fashion. "You always tell me everything."

"Not this."

There was another long silence and a lump rose in Nora's throat. Finally, her sister's voice came through the line.

"Then I guess we aren't the sisters I thought we were. If you change your mind and need somebody to talk to, you know where to find me." Odelle's voice was followed by a faint click, then she was gone.

Nora slid to the floor where she had been standing, not bothering to make her way back to her bed, and covered her head with her arms. It was as if a wall was sliding into place where there had never been a barrier before—not even through all the struggles they had faced together as foster children. Now Nora had placed something damaging between them, and she wasn't sure if she'd be able to break back through.

As Nora sat on the floor under the window, hot tears squeezed out of the corners of her eyes. They ran down her cheeks, dripping off her chin to form wet pools on her collarbone. For the first time during the ordeal of the last few days, she let herself cry.

THE NEXT MORNING, AS NORA WALKED UP THE STEPS TO WORK, SHE felt as if somebody had dug out her brain with a spoon and replaced it with a pile of soggy cotton balls. It took all her focus to keep her feet moving up the steps after the sleeplessness of the night before.

As she pushed through the doors of the museum, however, her exhaustion faded and was replaced by puzzlement. After hearing that the museum had been closed the day before in the aftermath of the fire, she expected extensive damage. Instead of charred floors and smoke-stained ceilings, though, the museum entrance looked the same as it always had. There were even a few early visitors checking in and milling around the base of the giant T-Rex skeleton in the entrance hall.

Confused, she turned and made her way down the stairs to her office, seeing no signs of damage there either. Adam had assured her that he had returned while she was unconscious and put the weapons back in their places, but she had no idea how the rest of the museum had gotten cleaned up so quickly.

As she pushed open the doors to the basement workroom, she only caught a brief glimpse of the room before a small form barreled into her, almost knocking her backwards.

"Oh my goodness! I'm so glad you are okay!" exclaimed a worried voice, and Nora looked down on a head of sleek black hair.

Nora extricated herself from Mandy with a chuckle. "Yeah, I'm okay. Fit as a fiddle."

Mandy still looked concerned. "Drew texted me from your phone and told me you were in the hospital after a car accident, so you wouldn't be at work. I didn't know what to think! Leo tried not to look too pleased that you were gone, and I just hoped you'd be back before he managed to take over all your projects."

"As if he could handle all my work," Nora snorted as she waved her hand. "Drew was being dramatic. I was just a little banged up. Nothing major," she lied smoothly. She was disturbed by how believable the lie sounded, even to her own ears. "It seems like you guys were having a much more exciting time here with the fire and all. I expected there to be more damage."

"We all expected that too. According to the eye-witness accounts of all the museum guests, the fire was gigantic. But you know people, always exaggerating things to make a good story and get on the news."

Nora hummed in assent, still looking around the office in masked disbelief.

Mandy continued. "They kept the museum closed for a few days while they were investigating the cause of the fire, but they didn't find anything. Guess it must have been a freak accident of some sort. In terms of damage, there were just a few charred walls and some smoke stains at the end of the hall. They got that all cleaned up rather quickly."

"And what about our office? Any damage in here?" Nora attempted to sound as nonchalant as possible.

"Nope. The fire doors closed and kept all the smoke out."

Nora had to work to suppress a shudder as she thought about how the fire door had failed at keeping the smoke out. Meanwhile, Mandy pressed on.

"All our artifacts should be fine, but we haven't taken out the pieces from the new shipment to see if any changes in the climate control may have affected them. That should probably be our project for the day."

Nora nodded. "Good thinking. I'll take the sword and the spear since they're already by my bench." She didn't add that she was anxious to assess them for damage caused by something other than an increase in humidity.

A few minutes later, Nora stood in front of her workbench, where Adam had kneeled in a pool of her blood just a few days earlier. The floor was spotless, and she surmised that Adam must have cleaned up the mess when he came to put the sword and spear away.

It was quick work to inspect the weapons, finding them to still be in immaculate condition. She supposed she shouldn't be surprised that Adam had done a good job cleaning them after all his insistence. He did seem serious about doing his part to keep her life as normal as possible.

Thankful her work hadn't been jeopardized, Nora turned to making plans to integrate the new artifacts into the existing displays upstairs in the museum. She chewed on her pen as she paused in drawing out her idea to put the sword and the spear in a prominent new case. It seemed odd to display the pieces when she now knew the person who had fought with them, but Adam hadn't actually asked her to give him the sword back, so she decided to press on with her plans.

Nora was still considering things when she headed down the steps at the end of the day. She slowed when she noticed more than a few people staring at the bottom of the stairs and giggling. Nora followed the direction of their stares, and her gaze landed on Thad, jauntily perched on one of the railings as if he owned the place.

When Nora saw what he was wearing, she could understand why people were staring. She strolled up to him with raised eyebrows.

"Nice threads, Thad," she commented as she took in his lavender suit. As she got closer, it looked to be made of velvet.

"Thank you," he said, straightening his silver ascot, the movement making his matching drop earrings twinkle in the sunlight. "I've been told the color compliments my complexion."

"You were told the truth," Nora said as he hopped down off the railing. Nora had to look down a few inches to meet his eyes.

"What are you doing here anyways? I got the impression you didn't leave the Sanctuary much."

"I don't," Thad began walking and motioned for her to follow him. "I'm here to pick you up and bring you to the Sanctuary to train with Ezra."

Nora fell into step beside him. "We're starting that today?"

"Adam convinced him to train you, and as long as he is going to do it, he is going to take his job seriously. You'll be coming every day after work."

"I guess he really plans on whipping me into shape then."

"Oh Nora, you have no idea what you're in for." Thad shot her a pitying look.

"Then why don't you fill me in while we walk? I still have a lot to learn about the Eteria."

Thad glanced at her out of the corner of his eye. "What do you want to know?"

Nora wasn't sure where to start, but she settled for asking, "Why does nobody but Adam leave the Sanctuary very often?"

Thad looked pensive for a moment before he spoke.

"It was hard watching the world around us go by as if nothing had happened after the Defeat. The Eteria as we knew it had come crumbling down. Our leadership was dead or disheartened, and with the Shadow vanquished, we had no real purpose. It was easier to stay in the Sanctuary and grieve all we had lost. After that..." Thad shrugged. "It exhausts you to your very soul to watch everybody you ever met grow old and die."

Nora walked in silence for a moment, considering how horrible the defeat must have been to send the entire Eteria into hiding.

"Then why does Adam stay out in the rest of the world?" Nora eventually asked. Adam was a mystery she couldn't resist trying to solve.

"Adam is in a...unique situation. He always has been curious about where the world is going. It's been good for the rest of us, too, to have him bringing pieces of the world back with him. Keeps us young, as it were."

"What kinds of things does he bring back with him?"

"Have you ever tried chili cheese fries? Life altering."

Nora laughed. They had reached Millenium Park and Thad led her towards the spectacle that was The Bean. He pulled her under the curved edge of the perfectly polished, kidney bean shaped structure. They stood beneath its wide arch, facing towards one of the mirrored sides.

Nora shook her head in disbelief as she commented. "I still can't believe this is the entrance to the Sanctuary, just out in plain sight like this."

"You should see the Paris entrance. It's straight through one of the walls in the Hall of Mirrors at Versailles."

Nora's mouth fell open. "But how do you keep people from just falling through the wall into the Sanctuary? Or are you constantly besieged by extremely confused tourists? And don't people notice you popping in and out of walls?"

"You'd be surprised what people miss when they aren't looking for it. Besides, that's the thing about these portals that's so brilliant —you can only get through them if you know where you're trying to go." He took her hand and drew her a step closer to the mirrored surface. "You could do this on your own, I'm just here for insurance this first time. After this, you should be able to come and go as you please."

Nora raised a brow and glanced down at him. "Are you sure you want that? You know you will never see the end of me if I can get in here and explore all I want."

Thad's smile was crooked as he responded. "Oh, I'm sure. we could use a little variety around here after two thousand years. You're just the change we need."

Nora hit the dirt with an ungraceful thud for what had to be the twelfth time in the last hour and rubbed her backside as she clambered back to her feet. She didn't bother to dust off her clothes, surrendering to the fact that the red tunic Thad had supplied for her was now hopelessly crusted with dirt from the ground of the training ring.

"Take your stance again, and this time, keep your weight on your back foot." Ezra's voice reminded her to focus on what she was doing, not on how silly she must look. She moved into the position he had taught her, and he crossed his arms as he appraised her, looking like a human mountain as he scowled. Nora couldn't say whether he was scowling because of her form, though, because she hadn't seen another expression from him the entire time she had been here, and she had begun to think that was just the way his face looked.

Nora brought her attention back to her own feet and focused on keeping her body angled to the right, with her weight on her right foot and the ball of her left just resting on the packed dirt. She lifted her hands with her left arm forward and fingers slightly open, ready to grab or strike as the occasion arose.

Ezra sighed and uncrossed his arms, making the black band tattooed around his left bicep ripple. "You must round your back more and lean forward. If you stand up straight like a board, you will not be behind the defense of your hands."

Nora attempted to get into the position he described and felt supremely silly. It was hard to believe that just two hours ago, she had been excited to learn the Greek hand-to-hand fighting style of pankration, hoping to discover more about the techniques than anybody else ever had from examining the depictions of famous fights on pottery. Now, though, she was mainly regretting never going to Pilates with Odelle, thinking maybe more exercise would have given her a better sense of coordination. As it was, Nora was a shaking ball of bruises and sweat. History lessons had rarely been so hands-on.

"Enough," Ezra grumbled, running his fingers through his sandy hair, and she gratefully stood up out of the fighting stance. "You are too tired to make any more progress today. You are only going to practice bad habits. Especially harmful for beginners."

Nora hobbled over to the edge of the fountain where there was a towel for her to wipe the sweat away from her eyes.

"I haven't been a beginner at anything in years," Nora grumbled as she mopped at her face.

Ezra snorted. "I'm not surprised. You lack the patience that comes with learning new things."

"You can't always get good at things by taking it slow."

"And you can't always improve at things simply by wishing it were so," Ezra continued with a glare. "Now stretch or you'll hurt yourself. I don't want to hear about you being sore when we train again tomorrow."

Nora groaned but flopped down onto the ground and reached for her toes. Ezra was so big as he loomed above her that he blocked out the sun. She couldn't help but ask, "So how do you end up getting stuck with training the newbies?"

"I am a Warrior. It is my job to train all the new Warriors in the Eteria."

Nora squinted up at him as she pulled an arm across her chest to stretch her shoulder.

"But I thought everyone here at the sanctuary was a warrior?"

"We all fight against the Shadow, but not all of us are Warriors. Warriors are one of the four orders of the Eteria, charged with defending the Light in battle and known for our physical prowess. We wear red to symbolize our position in the Eteria."

Nora glanced down at her own red tunic. "Am I a Warrior now?" she teased.

"Most definitely not." Ezra's scowl deepened a fraction. "Most of the training tunics we have lying around are red, since the Warriors do the most combat exercises."

Nora contemplated, envisioning Adam's skill with a sword in the museum, and asked, "Is Adam a Warrior too?"

"No," Ezra scoffed. "Adam is a Defender. He has the basic combat training that all members of the Eteria receive. He's more a librarian than a fighter."

Nora blanched, imagining what the Warrior's skills must be like if what Adam had done was "basic". She also thoroughly appreciated the image of Adam as a librarian but jumped to distract herself before she fell into a hole of library-based fantasies. Nora grasped for something else to ask.

"Thad was wearing green yesterday. What order is that?"

"Healers wear green, and before you ask, the last order is Smiths, and they wear purple." Ezra pointed accusingly at where Nora was now sitting cross-legged at the ground squinting up at him. "Now are you done stretching, or are you just going to sit there and interrogate me?"

Nora pried herself off the ground with a barely stifled moan. Despite her minimal attempts at stretching, she knew her muscles would feel the day's exercises when she woke up in the morning.

"I'll ask you more later," she said, and Ezra glared. "I have to get home and answer some emails anyways."

"I'll see you back here at the same time tomorrow. You have a lot of work to do. And by Zeus, eat some meat tonight. You are going to have to put on a lot more muscle if you are going to stand a chance against the Shadows."

10

THE NEXT DAYS FELL INTO THE SAME PATTERN OF WORK AND TRAINING.
Today, as usual, Nora burst through the doors and scanned the
broad steps in search of Thad, able to pick him out easily in an
oversized fur stole with his face obscured by the largest sunglasses
she had ever seen.

"A fashion icon, as always," she commented as they fell into
step, enjoying the easy comradery that had sprung up between
them. However, a tiny piece of her heart always sank when Thad
met her on the museum steps. She tried to squash the quiet voice
in her head telling her it was because she hoped one day Adam
would be the one to escort her to the Sanctuary. She supposed she
didn't even need an escort anymore, and Thad was only walking
with her to be nice anyways. To placate herself, Nora asked Thad if
he had any stories of himself and Adam when they were younger.

Thad launched into a tale about the time he and Adam had
drunkenly decided to attempt to make all the books in the library
fly on wings made of their own folded pages, and she found herself
chuckling at his antics. Nora had the fleeting thought that she
would have given almost anything to know Adam when he was
younger and more carefree.

As usual, Thad left her in the training yard with Ezra, who offered her barely a greeting before barking at her to fall into her stance. She moved into place more naturally than she ever had before, and she patted herself on the back for practicing the position in front of her narrow bedroom mirror the night before.

Nora began to move through the increasingly familiar forms, resuming her habit of counting how many times she managed to sprawl across the training ring floor. When she finished her exercises, she had fallen a record low of two times, and she even saw Ezra nodding approvingly out of the corner of her eye when he thought she wasn't looking, but that might have been her imagination.

Still, when she flopped down on the ground to do her stretches, she thought she had earned the opportunity to ask him a few more questions about the culture of the Eteria.

"What's the meaning of the tattoo?" she added, nodding towards the band around his bicep.

Ezra sighed and seated himself on the edge of the fountain, resigning himself to her curiosity.

"It is a symbol of our commitment to the Eteria, and each person chooses their unique pattern as a reflection of their individuality and skill set."

Nora snorted the word, "creative" under her breath as she glanced at Ezra's plain black line. While the furrow between his brows deepened at her jibe, she thought she detected a faint spark of amusement in his gray eyes.

Taking that as a sign she could ask another question, she chewed at her chapped lip as she considered what to ask.

"Why weren't there any shields or crossbows in the armory? They were pretty popular weapons around the time of the fall of the Eteria."

"We don't need them," Ezra answered as Nora pulled a leg up to stretch her hamstring. "Our Warriors use weapons as a conduit for the Light more than anything else. That is why they are made

completely of bronze, because it is better conductor of Light than wood or steel." Noticing that she had opened her mouth to ask another question, he cut her off, saying, "Don't ask me why. It's all very complicated, and only the Smiths know the answer to that question."

Nora snapped her mouth shut as Ezra continued. "We don't use shields because we form our own much more durable defenses using the Light. And crossbows are just impractical. It seems silly to go to all the trouble of imbuing a bolt with magic only to shoot it far away, when you could just use the Light to incapacitate your enemy from a distance anyways."

"So why use weapons at all then?"

"Because," Ezra groped for the proper words. "Having a weapon makes it easier to...focus the energy. The Light is always there, nebulous and undefined until you shape it for a purpose. It is easier to shape it around a physical object, to ground the power. It's why Defenders almost always use swords for creating wards, even though they rarely enter direct combat."

Nora sat up and examined the array of bruises on her forearms. "Then why all the combat training if you are just going to use the Light anyways?"

"It builds character," Ezra stated matter-of-factly. "Sometimes a soldier is unable to channel the Light, but they can still do some major damage at close range, like Adam did with his sword at the museum. He fought back the Shadow without using the Light at all, relying on his weapon."

"Hmm, what about cavalry? I only saw armor for ground soldiers."

"We don't ride horses into combat," Ezra answered as though it should be obvious. "The magic scares the horses."

"Oh," Nora was taken aback. "I thought you would have some sway to train the horses to not be afraid. You know, be the Warrior heroes with your trusty steeds charging bravely into battle."

Ezra frowned. "You read too many fantasy novels. This is the real world."

11

THE TEXT ON THE SCREEN OF NORA'S LAPTOP BLURRED AS SHE TRIED to work, drafting a manuscript about the discoveries she had made from the sword and spear, frustrated that her findings didn't sound as impressive as she had anticipated. Granted, she couldn't exactly share the details she had learned with the general public, but she had agreed to train because she could get something out of it. So far, though, she hadn't gotten any research done that she could apply to her work. All she had to show for her time was a tapestry of bruises, and her chest burned when she thought about how she had let the Eteria distract her from work so much. It was time to fix that, and she thought she knew just where to start.

A short while later, Nora marched up the path to the front doors of the Sanctuary, anxious to begin her search for the great library that Thad had mentioned once in passing. She wandered the vast halls for a few minutes, wondering if she should start looking near the training courts, or if she should attempt to find her way back over to the area where she had located the armory.

A commotion around the corner from where she had been walking distracted her from her thoughts. Curious, she followed the sounds and peeked around a pillar towards the source.

In the hallway gathered a small crowd of people, mostly dressed in green but with a flash of blue and purple here and there. She started in surprise at the sight, realizing that she hadn't seen anybody else in the Sanctuary before. She had known that other people must live here, but she had only ever seen Thad and Ezra, as well as Adam, Antony, and Seraphina on that first day.

At the center of the group, she caught a glimpse of two men carrying a stretcher between them. There was a person on the stretcher wearing navy blue, and the men quickly carried it through an arch into what she assumed was one of the numerous bedrooms. As she watched, Nora recognized Thad following behind the stretcher.

Once the door was closed, Nora examined the other people in the dispersing group and recognized Seraphina. She was in a green peplos, as before, and despite the apparent gravity of the current situation, Nora couldn't help but take a moment to admire the way the fabric effortlessly dripped off the woman, and she could just make out the tattoo encircling her left bicep in the image of a peacock feather. Seraphina had even braided a silver cord into her golden hair. She'd been rude to Nora when they'd first met, but Nora had to admit that the woman had style.

Nora stepped out from behind the pillar and waved to get Seraphina's attention.

Seraphina sneered. "Oh, it's you." Although she stood a head shorter than Nora, she still somehow managed to look down her nose at her.

Ignoring the hostility in her voice, Nora asked, "What's going on?"

Seraphina's perfectly arched brows rose. "What's going on? We are at war."

"Oh," Nora stammered, taken aback. She knew the Eteria fought the Shadow, but nobody had put it quite that bluntly.

"Another one of our Defenders was just injured trying to protect *your* city." Seraphina made the statement sound accusatory, as if Nora was personally responsible for everything that happened in Chicago.

"Why so many Shadows in Chicago?" Nora asked. While she certainly admitted that she lived in a world-class city, it seemed odd to Nora that the Shadow would be so prevalent there. There must be other cities for the Shadow to terrorize.

"It seems that an agent of the Shadow has taken up residence there. Why, we don't know."

Nora made a mental note to look up what Seraphina meant by 'agent of Shadow' when she got to the library. "Is there anything I can do to help?"

Seraphina had turned to leave, but now whirled back to face Nora, her chin raised like a commanding queen. "You can help by staying out of the way." The words hit Nora like a punch to the gut, but Seraphina continued ruthlessly. "People like you, prancing around thinking they know everything and acting like they can save the world, are what get people like us killed. If you want to help, just go home and leave the world saving to the experts."

Before Nora could gather her thoughts to respond, Seraphina had turned back around in an elegant swirl of green cloth and marched off down the hallway. The way she held her head as she strode away made it clear why she had chosen a peacock feather as her tattoo.

Nora was frozen in place for a few moments as she watched Seraphina turn down a side corridor. A slow heat started to pulse in her gut. It made her hands tremble and her heart pound in her ears until she couldn't hear anything else.

How dare that woman imply that this was somehow Nora's fault? Nora had been thrown into this after almost dying in an attack by the Shadows herself. And to suggest that Nora couldn't help with all her expertise, when it was her city that was endangered... While Nora may not have thousands of years' worth of experience, she was no cowering damsel, and she knew how to grit her teeth and get things done. Nora stomped off with renewed determination, looking for the library.

Turning another corner, Nora found herself staring at a surrealist painting she didn't recognize. This was an area of the Sanctuary she hadn't come across before. She made her way down the quiet hall and glanced through open doors she passed. As she peered through the last door in the hallway, she found a wall covered in bookshelves and sighed in relief.

Nora slid inside and was greeted by the scent of ginger and something warm that brought to her a fleeting image of her favorite cozy reading nook for late night research. As she took a few deep breathes, she glanced around and was struck by the realization that she was not, in fact, in a library, but in a rather eclectically decorated bedroom.

It had been easy to mistake it for a library, with two of the walls being completely covered in bookshelves, but the far wall was dominated by a gigantic four-poster bed with navy blue silk curtains. Nora squinted in curiosity as she spotted a cozy art-deco-style armchair, upholstered in brown leather situated next to the bed, as well as a white bearskin rug draped over the polished floor.

Nora told herself she shouldn't be poking around in somebody else's room, but the place just felt so full of personality that she drifted inside a few steps more. She made her way over to the bookshelves, interested in what a person who decorated their room like this might like to read. She found that while the shelves contained many books, they also housed a wide variety of knickknacks. She spotted a dagger on a small cushion, no longer than her hand and simple in its design. On another shelf, she spied a locket, it's oval face covered in swirling engravings with the letter "C" at the center.

"May I help you?"

Nora jumped and spun around. Adam stood propped against the doorframe, hands shoved into the pockets of his jeans, his eyebrows raised. He had gotten his glasses replaced in the past week, and they sat crookedly on his face in a way that made her itch to straighten them out.

Nora shifted her weight from foot to foot. He had just caught her snooping in the Sanctuary for the second time in a week.

"I was just looking for the library," she explained, although she was sure he could tell she was quite aware that this was not the library.

"And your search for the library led you to my bedroom?" Nora was relieved that his tone was teasing instead of angry, but then the content of what he'd said struck her.

"This is *your* bedroom?"

"Well, it was when I was younger." Adam pushed off the door-frame and took a few steps towards her. "And I still come and stay here occasionally, although I mostly live in an apartment in Lincoln Park now."

A fresh surge of embarrassment took Nora as she processed that it was Adam's things she had been poking through. She cursed her inner historian, who encouraged her to sort through people's things to put together what their life must look like.

Avoiding looking into Adam's twinkling eyes, she gestured to the room at large. "You have rather interesting taste."

"I suppose I do. Mostly this is just a collection of things that I haven't been able to part with from my various lives."

"Various lives?" Nora probed.

"I've done a lot of different things throughout my centuries on this earth." Adam stepped up next to her, and Nora unconsciously shuffled closer. "Every thirty years or so, when people start to realize I'm not aging, I pick up and move to a different place, changing my name and starting over again. Although I end up being a teacher or librarian more often than not."

"So, Adam isn't your real name?"

"Well it currently is my legal name, but no, that's not the name I was given when I was born."

When Nora asked what his first name had been, he hesitated

for a long moment before murmuring, "Xander. My name is Xander, although nobody has called me that since… Nobody has called me that in a long time."

"Xander," Nora repeated. The name suited him. "Is it weird not to have people call you by your real name?"

"It doesn't bother me." Adam raised one shoulder in a lopsided shrug. "It's who I am right now. Adam Scott, English professor, wearer of argyle sweaters, lover of chai tea and the color green."

"Wait, let me get this straight. You are an immortal member of a secret magical society and actually teach English at Northwestern? That isn't just a cover story you used to get to see the weapons?"

"Of course I am," Adam said, sounding wounded. "I don't lie about everything. And I like having a job. For one, my apartment doesn't just pay for itself, and second, it makes eternity feel like it has a bit more purpose."

Nora stayed silent, trying to put herself in Adam's shoes and finding it incredibly lonely.

Adam continued softly, as if he could read her mind. "It hasn't been all that bad. I've met a lot of great people and had a lot of great experiences. I even had a drink with J.R.R. Tolkien once."

Nora's attention had been fixated on Adam's knuckles momentarily brushing hers, but that snapped her back to reality. "Really? What was he like?"

"We didn't talk that much. I just ran into him at a bar once when he was a professor. I had no idea the legend he was going to become at the time. I thought he was just a guy with a really weird fixation on elves." Adam chuckled wryly. "Actually, that is how a lot of it has been. I didn't realize when important things were happening until long after they passed."

"But you must know so much about history," Nora argued. "You are a walking primary source! You could solve so many disputes, unravel so many mysteries."

Adam shook his head. "I don't really think I could. I lived through the birth of Jesus Christ, and I missed the whole thing because I was screwing around trying to teach myself how to sail on the Mediterranean Sea. Unsuccessfully, I might add."

Maybe that was the way of the world. Life threw important things at you when you were least expecting them.

"It doesn't bother me, though," Adam continued thoughtfully. "The best part of living forever is all the great people you get to meet, and most of those people don't end up in history books."

It was a more positive outlook than Nora would have predicted from somebody who had watched everybody they had ever cared for grow old and die. It made her wonder how close he had become to the people he had met, if he'd ever fallen in love with any of them.

Turning from that train of thought, Nora asked, "Why didn't you just stay here at the Sanctuary like the rest of the Eteria?"

"The people who have remained throughout the centuries tend to get callous. I never wanted to be like that." There was a long pause where Adam seemed to debate whether he should continue. "I suppose I was also searching for something...someone. I didn't want to spend all my time on this earth alone."

Nora met his eyes and found that it was an oddly relatable sentiment from somebody who had seen more of life than she could imagine.

Realizing she had been staring for far too long, Nora broke the silence with a frustrated huff.

"I get what you mean when you say that people get callous. All the time away from humanity hasn't done anything to soften Seraphina's temperament."

Adam brushed his hand through his already tousled mop of curls. "Oh don't let her get to you. She hasn't always been so...high-strung."

"Really?" Nora snorted in disbelief. "Because she seems to have some sort of vendetta against me."

Adam became very interested in inspecting his loafers as he responded. "Seraphina has experienced a lot of loss in her life, and she's had a long time to sit with her grief. It's made her unusually bitter."

Knowing it was probably rude to ask but also unable to curb her natural curiosity, Nora asked, "What happened to her?"

Adam scuffed a toe against the polished floor as he responded. "She lost her husband in the Defeat. She was pregnant at the time and lost the baby soon after. The loss of the connection to the Light made it impossible for any children to be born into the Eteria."

Nora found herself also looking at the floor. A soft "oh" was all she could manage in response as she contemplated Seraphina's tragedy. She might not have had many maternal instincts herself, but her heart still clenched in sympathy.

"Would you like a cup of tea?"

Adam's non-sequitur caught Nora off guard.

"I don't suppose you have any coffee?"

Adam mimed himself retching enthusiastically. "I would never keep something so vile in my own room. But I have any type of tea you could want."

"Then I'll take English breakfast."

Adam motioned her towards the leather armchair she had noticed earlier. As she sat down, he busied himself with the tea. Nora took the opportunity when his back was turned to breathe in her fill of the intoxicating scent of chai tea and books that clung to the chair. Adam picked up an electric kettle from its place on a cart near the fireplace and carried it into an adjoining bathroom to fill it up.

"I'm surprised to see you have electricity and indoor plumbing here. Wasn't this place built before that sort of thing?" Nora commented, her tone teasing but her question legitimate.

He gave her his signature boyish grin as he returned. "It was, but I convinced everybody to put it in a while back. I consider it my personal responsibility to keep these old fogey's up with the times."

Once their tea was made, Adam took a seat at the foot of the massive bed, and Nora settled back into the armchair, the teacup nestled between her hands, the warm steam caressing her face.

They sat in amicable silence for a while before Nora asked, "You must know all of the Greek myths really well if you were around when they were first being told."

When Adam nodded in confirmation, Nora asked, "Could you tell me some of them? The way they were told when you were young?"

Adam gave her a soft smile before he obliged and launched into the tale of Hades and Persephone. Adam's voice drew her in, soft and melodious. Nora experienced the familiar myths in a way she never had before. She blinked back tears when Adam told the tale of Eros and Psyche and found herself holding her breath during the tense moments in the adventures of Jason and the Argonauts. Adam was a master storyteller, pausing at all the right places, letting his voice rise and fall gently like the tides, sending tingles up Nora's spine.

Later, Nora was roused by Adam's knuckles brushing her face. For a moment, Adam continued stroking her cheek, and Nora allowed herself to imagine that he was enjoying touching her before her consciousness returned fully. She pulled herself upright and thanked her lucky stars that she had not started drooling when she dozed off.

"It's late," he murmured. "I can take you back to the city if you want, or you can sleep in the room you were in when you came here the first time. It's just across the hall."

Feeling particularly cozy at the moment, Nora was not enthused by the idea of a cold bus ride across the city.

"I'll stay the night, if that's ok."

Nora pushed herself up from the chair and padded her way over to the door. Before she entered the hallway. though, she looked over her shoulder.

"Thank you for the tea, and goodnight."

"Goodnight to you. too, Nora. Dream good dreams."

12

NORA STRETCHED LUXURIOUSLY, UNABLE TO REMEMBER THE LAST TIME she had been woken by the sun instead of her blaring alarm. After rubbing the sleep from her eyes, she made her way down the hall to thank Adam for letting her stay the night. She found the door to his bedroom ajar, but when she pushed it open, the room was empty. The bed was made, and there was no trace of the man who'd slept there, other than the now familiar scent of chai and books.

She wondered where he could have been up and off to so early on a Sunday and suppressed the little bubble of hurt she felt that he hadn't stayed to say good morning. Nora told herself his leaving had nothing to do with her presence.

Remembering what had brought her to the Sanctuary in the first place, she mentally kicked herself for not asking Adam where the library was. Now she was going to be back to square one with her search.

She started in the direction she had come from the night before, hoping she would at least be able to retrace her steps back to the entrance. As soon as she rounded the corner, though, she ran into something very warm and solid.

"Oh, there you are Ad—" The words died in Nora's mouth as

she looked up to find that she had not in fact run into Adam, for the figure was much too broad across the shoulders. Instead, she saw a curling beard and dark brown eyes, wide with surprise.

"Drew? What are you doing here?"

"Oh—well, umm…" Drew's gaze darted around the hallway. "I was looking for…"

"Wait, were you looking for me?" Nora realized she had not told anybody where she was going when she'd left the day before. "Sorry if you called me. I don't get cell service here. I should have let somebody know I was staying the night."

"Oh no, that's— What were you doing here overnight?"

"I came looking for the library to do some research. I guess I lost track of the time. Adam told me I could sleep in the room I'd stayed in before if I didn't feel up to the journey home."

The furrow between Drew's brows smoothed. "I'm glad you didn't have to go home by yourself at night."

"Did Odelle ask you to check up on me? Sorry if she put you up to this. I haven't told her about everything," she gestured around the Sanctuary at large, "and she is too smart to not figure out when I'm hiding something from her. It's made her get all worried about me."

"No, Odelle hasn't texted me. I didn't know you would be here." Drew rubbed the back of his neck.

"Oh," Nora internally sighed in relief that her younger sister hadn't resorted to involving her ex-boyfriend. She cocked her head. "So, wait—what are you doing here then?"

"Well…" Drew cleared his throat. "I asked Thad if he could explain to me some of the, ah, techniques he used while he was healing you. Being an ER doc, I was really interested in the science behind it. He agreed to teach me a few tricks that he has learned over the years. I've been coming here occasionally to see him."

"That's great!" Nora said, and she meant it. "I've been working in some weapons research with my combat training, too, so I'm glad we've both found a way to use this experience to our benefit."

"I'm sorry if everybody ganged up on you to get you to train in self-defense." Drew shifted from foot to foot as he spoke. "I'm just glad you're going to be safer now."

Nora waved him off. "Don't worry about it. I needed some time to...reframe the situation."

"Right. Did you say you were trying to find the library? Thad showed me where it was. I could take you to it if you'd like."

"That'd be great," Nora conceded. "I've wasted enough time trying to find it on my own."

A few minutes later, Drew led Nora into a vast circular room that took her breath away. The library overflowed with golden light, streaming in from above. The distant ceiling was composed of a mosaic of glass panels held in place by a latticework of gold. Turning her attention back to the main room, Nora couldn't help but find the bookshelves themselves to be one of the most impressive parts. Instead of being made of wood, the shelves were carved into the white stone walls themselves. They were packed haphazardly with books of every size and color, running in both directions, stacked on top of each other, and even shelved two-deep in some places.

Nora wove her way through a collection of stools and study tables to the center of the circle, which was clear of furniture. A bronze symbol emblazoned the pale floor. It was the shape of a sun, crossed by a sword and spear. The way the light danced through the glass above caught on the metal and made it shimmer, making it look more like the sun hanging in the sky than just a symbol on the floor.

Nora had been so enchanted by her surroundings that she had forgotten Drew was with her until he chuckled. "You look like you've died and gone to Heaven, although I can't say I'm surprised. This suits you perfectly."

"I have always loved books," Nora breathed, still staring around in awe.

"True, but it's not just that," Drew continued, a wistful note in his deep voice. "This whole place, you just...fit here. You've always seemed like you belonged in a place like this, so full of art and history and knowledge."

Nora cocked her head up at him, finding herself unsure how to respond to a comment that profound. She settled on a whispered, "Thank you." A few moments passed before she asked, "Shouldn't you be going to find Thad? If he's expecting you, I wouldn't want to be the reason you're keeping him waiting."

"What? Oh—Thad. Of course." Drew reached out and gave her shoulder a squeeze before turning to go. "Have fun with your explorations. I'll see you around."

As Drew's footsteps faded down the hallway, Nora turned back to the books in front of her, puzzling out where she should start. She stepped up to the nearest shelf and began to peruse, unable to stop herself from running her fingers along the spines of the books, seeing titles on dozens of topics from every age all mixed together in no particular order.

She paused when her finger brushed a particularly ancient looking tome titled *The Birth of Shadows*, Seraphina's haughty voice playing in her mind, saying something about an agent of Shadow. Nora pulled the tome out and tucked it under her free arm before continuing to browse. There was no harm in doing some research on her potential enemy.

By the time Nora reached the end of the shelf, she carried two more tomes , both very old with titles hinting at information on weaponry. She considered setting herself up at one of the study tables, but then thought of how she couldn't receive work emails while she was in the Sanctuary, and how she wished she could have a cup of coffee while she read. So, she tucked the books more firmly under her arm, thinking that it was better to ask for forgiveness instead of permission when it came to removing the books from the library.

As soon as she stepped through the portal and into the cool city air, her phone vibrated insistently with the tone she reserved for her work email. Fishing it from her jacket pocket, she crossed her fingers that she didn't have to go into the office when she had just come across such great reading material.

When she read the subject of the email, she whooped so loudly that a flock of nearby pigeons took flight. She was going on a trip.

Nothing could dampen Nora's mood that weekend, and she was still practically skipping as she made her way into the training ring on Monday afternoon.

"You seem...bouncy today," Ezra commented as she approached.

"And you'll be bouncy, too, when you hear my news. You're going to get a few days off from me next week."

Ezra furrowed his brow. "Why would it make me bouncy to hear that my student will be slacking off and forgetting most of what she's learned?"

"It's not slacking," Nora snapped. "I have to go on a trip for work. I'm presenting on my research at the Carnegie Museum in Pittsburgh, and I'm sure it's just a precursor to my promotion!"

To Nora's disappointment, this only seemed to further concern Ezra.

"Where is Pittsburgh again?"

"Not far. The plane ride should be less than two hours," Nora answered, still bouncing on her toes in excitement.

"Plane ride? I'm not sure you can do that."

Nora froze. "What do you mean I can't *do* that?"

Ezra pinched the bridge of his nose with his thumb and forefinger as if having to explain this to Nora was already giving him a headache.

"Because your guard would have to come with you, and it's been hard enough to keep up with you during your crazy skipping around the city. Seriously, do you have to go an extra mile every day to get your coffee when there is a coffee shop right across the street?"

"Yes, their espresso is distinctly better," Nora insisted. "Also, how do you know that? Are you my guard as well as my trainer?"

Ezra shrugged one thick shoulder. "We all take turns. There aren't that many of us after all. And none of us can come on a plane with you. It's not as if I have a valid photo ID, and that makes it hard enough to get around one city."

Nora planted a hand on her hip in frustration. "The only reason I agreed to any of this was because it could advance my research. If you think I'm going to give up this opportunity because you don't have enough brains in your head to figure out how to keep me safe while I travel, then you have another thing coming."

Ezra held out his hands placatingly. "Calm yourself, young firecracker. There is one of us who might be able to come with you."

Nora looked up from her laptop, which she had propped on top of her suitcase, when a pair of loafers stopped just inside her field of vision. Adam juggled two paper cups while trying to keep his beaten leather bag on his shoulder.

Nora jumped to her feet, relieving him of the cups so he could settle himself into the uncomfortable airport chair beside hers. When she moved to give him back his beverages, he took one but inclined his head towards the other cup in her hand.

"That one's for you. One black Americano." He reached into his bag as he spoke. "And I got you something else that you will love." Nora took the crumpled brown bag from his outstretched hand as he proudly proclaimed, "One chocolate croissant."

She tried not to wrinkle her nose as she passed the bag back to him. "No thank you. I'm not really one for sweets."

Adam blinked. "You're not? I could have sworn..."

"It's not a problem." Nora shrugged. "It's not like you've ever seen me eat dessert."

"I suppose I haven't," Adam said, still dumbly clutching the bakery bag as if the idea that Nora could refuse a croissant had turned his entire world upside down.

"Hey, don't worry about it," Nora reassured, taking a sip of her coffee, which was much more to her liking. "I forgive you, since you don't know me very well."

Adam settled back in his chair and considered her. "We do have thirty minutes until our flight boards. Why don't I get to know you a little better?"

"I have to go over my presentation one last time," Nora lamented, even as the corner of her mouth pulled up.

"You've gone over that presentation three times since we got here. And I took a day and a half off from work to fly with you to a conference where you will be presenting details about weaponry that I am already familiar with. Humor me."

Nora snapped her laptop closed and turned to face him. She crossed her legs and asked, "What do you want to know?"

Adam took a sip of his tea as he debated where to start.

"Pet peeve?" he asked.

"Slow pedestrians who don't stay to the right side of the sidewalk."

He nodded as if adding this to a mental catalogue.

"Favorite food?"

"Hot sauce."

"That's not a—"

"Just go with it," Nora warned.

To his credit, Adam let the issue drop and moved on to his next question.

"Best friend?"

"Easy. My sister."

Adam tilted his head. "That doesn't count. She's family."

"It counts to me," Nora argued. "I spend more of my free time with her than with anybody else."

"You have to have other friends, though," Adam insisted.

Nora shrugged. "Some, but I've never really done the inseparable group of besties thing. I would almost always rather be alone than be around stupid people."

"You think most people are stupid?" Adam asked with one corner of his mouth twisting up. Nora could tell he was baiting her, but she refused to give him satisfaction.

"Well, less interesting than Odelle, at least," she shot back.

Adam took a long sip of his drink as he hummed. "Then it's a good thing I'm well studied, or this might be a very long trip for you."

Nora rolled her eyes and searched around in her bag until she found what she was looking for as she said, "Now if you are done with the twenty questions act, I'm going to try to get some reading done."

When she pulled the thick tome onto her lap, Adam's breath hitched, and she peered at him out of the corner of her eye.

"Should I not have taken this out of the library?" she asked.

"No, it's not that," he hedged. "That's just...very heavy reading for a plane ride."

"I figured I might as well learn about the creatures that are going to try to kill me."

Adam shook his head and ran his long fingers through his hair.

"That book is about more than just the creatures. It describes the nature of the Shadow itself and it can get quite...graphic. I would not recommend it. I had to read it in my training to become a Defender and I still have nightmares."

Nora chewed her lip thoughtfully. "What do you mean by 'nature of the Shadow'?" Adam hesitated and Nora pressed him. "If you don't tell me, then I'm just going to read the book myself."

"Ok, I'll do my best to explain," Adam said, folding his hands under his chin and propping his elbows on his knees. He didn't look at her as he began speaking.

"The creatures at the museum are actually just fragments of the enemy, broken off from the greater whole to wreak havoc. The real enemy is much more insidious. It creeps into people's minds to hide, masquerading as a piece of their own self-doubt. It feeds upon every negative thought in the person's head until they can think of nothing else. It's evasive, though, weaving itself so thoroughly into a person's insecurities that they can't tell where they end and the Shadow begins. Once the Shadow fully overtakes a person, they are no more than a puppet for the Shadow to use as they will—not even human anymore. At that point, we call them an agent of Shadow."

Nora tried to take a sip of her coffee as she listened, but the liquid was suddenly too bitter for her to stomach, and her hands shook. She put the cup down and pressed her palms into the armrests of her seat to steady herself.

"What about things like the fire at the museum then? Where do they fit in?" Nora managed to ask.

"The agent has the power to call down natural disasters of all sorts, even plague, in a hope to bring death and terror. The Shadow can then use the pain sowed in the survivors to create more agents, creating an endless cycle." Adam inclined his head towards the book in Nora's lap. "That book details the worst disasters the Shadow has ever brought down, and how it used them to shroud the world in its darkness."

Nora glanced down at the heavy leather tome that lay open in her lap before slamming it closed and shoving it into her bag.

She swallowed a few times before responding. "I think you're right. I really don't want to read that on an airplane. I'm a nervous enough flyer as it is."

"Probably wise," Adam agreed.

Nora resolved to keep the book safely shut in the bottom of her bag for the remainder of the trip.

ADAM AND NORA MANAGED TO FIND THEIR SEATS NEAR THE REAR OF
the aircraft, but not without a fair amount of grumbling from Nora
about how people really needed to learn how to pack their carry-on
baggage more effectively and not waste everybody's time trying to
shove too-large bags in the overhead bins. Adam, for his part,
appeared to find her tirade very amusing and had no trouble slipping his practical luggage into the bin above their seats.

Determined to cheer herself up, Nora put in her earbuds and
closed her eyes as the plane taxied toward the runway. The pilot
made some announcement about high winds and turbulence in
their flight path, but Nora couldn't quite hear it over her music. She
had just drifted off to sleep by the time the plane lifted off, but she
was jerked awake by Adam violently shaking her shoulder shortly
after.

"What is your—" she began to scold him but cut off when she
saw the wild look in his eyes.

"We have a problem," he said, gesturing past their already
sleeping row-mate to the window.

Nora could just make out the wing of the plane through the
clouds as she squinted. She stared for a moment, confused, before
her eyes suddenly widened in realization. Clinging onto the end of
the wing was the swirling, gray, but still unmistakable form of a
Shadow creature.

13

Nora choked before whispering, "I'm now glad that Ezra convinced me to bring you along as a guard."

Her heart was pounding so hard that it might have been fighting to get out of her ribcage, and her skin crawled as she watched the creature claw its way up the wing of the plane, getting closer to the main body by the second.

Adam glanced around frantically.

"By the Titans' tentacled testacles!" He swore loudly enough to wake up their row mate, an elderly lady whose eyes went wide with shock as she glared at him.

"Sorry, just realized I forgot something," he offered by way of explanation. That satisfied her as she closed her eyes again and Adam turned back to Nora.

"I don't have a weapon with me," he whispered into her ear, making Nora draw back in shock, doing nothing to help her still accelerating heartrate.

"You're supposed to be my guard and you didn't bring anything to fight with?"

Adam shushed Nora, her rising hysteria having made her careless with her volume.

"I can't exactly get a sword through airport security. Not to mention the Shadow hasn't attacked you while you've had a guard before. We figured just having one of us here would be the equivalent of a nuclear deterrent for them."

"Did you just compare yourself to a nuclear weapon when you didn't even have the sense to bring anything to use to protect yourself?" Nora hissed.

Adam chanced a glance out the window toward where the Shadow was halfway up the wing. "Now is not the time for scolding, Nora. We need solutions."

Nora furrowed her brow as she observed the creature's progress. "It won't be able to get inside the plane anyways, will it? The fuselage is designed to be airtight."

"I wouldn't be so sure. That is a Shadow born of wind and storm, and they don't have a particularly high regard for the laws of physics. What I need is something to fight it with."

Nora wracked her brains.

"Coffee pot? You could smash it and use one of the shards as a dagger?" she suggested.

Adam nodded. "Maybe we should have let you continue to use household objects as weapons. I'll go to the galley in the back to grab it, but I need you to create a distraction so the flight attendant who's back there doesn't stop me."

Before Nora could ask what he had in mind for a distraction, he was out of his seat and striding to the back of the cabin. The creature was mere feet away from the body of the plane, and she unbuckled her seatbelt as quickly as she could, improvising as she went. The sudden spike in adrenaline made her fingers as useful as raw sausages, but she freed herself and launched into the aisle.

She hesitated a moment before doing the first thing she thought of that would get everybody's attention and not end with her in handcuffs. She gave a dramatic gasp before crumpling to the floor as loudly as possible in her best impression of a faint. The hand pressed to her forehead might have been a little much, but she was fully committed to the role of damsel in distress.

The reaction in the cabin was instantaneous and feet pounded down the aisle towards her from both directions even as she kept her eyes closed. It was only a few moments before cool hands grasped her shoulders and there was an announcement over the communication system.

"Could any licensed medical professional on board please report immediately to the back of the aircraft?"

The hands on her shoulders rolled her over, but she let her head loll limply to the side, still feigning unconsciousness. She needed to keep all eyes on her for a few moments longer. It was difficult to stay limp when every muscle in her body strained for any indication that the Shadow had boarded the aircraft.

Just as fingers searched her neck for a pulse, a violent bout of turbulence shook the cabin so forcefully that Nora slid into the base of the seat next to her, hard enough to knock the wind from her lungs. The fingers flew from her throat from the motion and a crash came from the back of the cabin. Nora prayed that it was Adam smashing the coffee pot even as she wheezed to catch the breath that had been knocked from her.

As soon as she heard voices screaming, Nora sat bolt upright and whipped her head around. Swirling down the center aisle from the back of the plane was the Shadow, this one the dirty grey of the tornados Nora saw on TV. It looked like a nightmare of storm clouds and dust, but with the same glowing eyes and demented shape of its fiery counterparts. Catching sight of her where she was sprawled on the floor, it advanced down the aisle, and Nora scrabbled away from it as best she could in sort of a demented crab walk. The skin of her hands burned as they dragged against the carpet.

Just as the Shadow was within arms-reach of her, so close that Nora could practically taste the death and dust that made up its flesh, there was a wild cry from the back of the cabin. Adam barreled down the aisle, a long shard of glass clutched in his raised fist. The sound was enough to draw the Shadow's attention, and it whipped away from Nora, the motion causing hot wind to lash across her face so hard that she almost fell backwards again.

Adam's battle cry had given the Shadow just enough warning of his position. It flung a long arm out and caught Adam by the throat even as he attempted to charge forward. He was lifted clean off the ground, the toes of his loafers scrabbling for purchase on the rough carpet of the aisle. He made a terrible gargling noise and swung the glass shard wildly with one hand, the other trying to dislodge the creature's grip on his neck. The Shadow just held Adam away from its body, its arm long enough to keep Adam at a distance where none of his attacks could connect.

Nora sprang to her feet, ready to go at the Shadow with her bare hands. The flight attendants yelled behind her, but she didn't spare a moment to look at them. She drew her arm back, but before she could throw a punch that would make Ezra proud, Adam's eyes began to roll back in his head. With his last flail, he managed to fling the glass straight at the creature's chest, where it embedded itself.

The Shadow let out an earsplitting screech, dropping Adam to the ground with an ungraceful thud. Nora lunged towards where he lay crumpled in the aisle, but she never reached him.

The Shadow creature, which had begun writhing in its death throes, coalesced into a swirling ball before shattering apart with a clap like thunder. The force of the detonation threw Nora to the ground and shook the plane even harder than the continuing turbulence.

There was a horrible sucking sound that came from nowhere and everywhere all at once, and Nora clapped her hands to her ears, which exploded in her head. Within seconds, yellow masks dropped from the bulkheads and people hurried to put them on. Nora was already lightheaded, and she scrambled to her feet to snatch the one above her unoccupied seat, clutching it to her face.

Within two deep breaths, Nora's world steadied, even as her

skin grew cold and she could taste blood dribbling from her nose onto her lips. She glanced around, still holding the mask to her face with one hand, but nearly fainted all over again as she caught sight of Adam still sprawled on the floor.

She inched towards him, reaching her hand out as far as she could, but her fingertips could just brush his hair while keeping her mask pressed to her face. She took in Adam's pale face, turned to the side so Nora could just make out his dusty blue lips and the blood trickling from one ear. She took one last bracing breath before letting go of her mask and lunging towards him.

She managed to catch Adam's limp body under his arms and heaved him towards her. He only moved several inches with the first tug, but she kept yanking at him, pulling so hard that she was surprised his arm didn't pop right out of its socket.

Her other hand reached towards the dangling mask, still just out of reach, as black spots began forming in front of her vision, but she willed herself to keep moving. Several other passengers, noticing her struggle, reached out to help her, and Adam's body slid more easily down the aisle. Nora gasped for breath and gave one final heave, moving Adam the final inches. Her fist closed around the mask, and she smashed it to her face, taking deep panting breaths. She snapped the elastic around her head before scooping Adam up into a seated position, silently thanking Ezra for her better developed upper body muscles. As quickly as she could, she grabbed the mask from above Adam's seat and brought it to his face, working the elastic over his head with trembling fingers.

There was a horrible moment of stillness filled with nothing but the shaking of the plane and Nora's own panting breaths raking at her throat. It could have been one second, or it could have been a minute.

Adam's long eyelashes fluttered a few times, and when his eyes opened to meet hers, Nora choked on a sob. She didn't try to speak to him through her mask, just nodded at him in reassurance. He blinked in understanding. She helped him into the seat as the pilot announced an emergency landing, and the plane started to descend.

NORA SLID INTO THE SEAT OF THE RENTAL CAR AND SLAMMED THE door behind her, resting her forehead on the steering wheel in relief. Ever since the airplane had touched down in Cleveland, she'd been holding her breath all over again.

Thankfully, Adam had recovered from his unconsciousness and handled most of the questions from authorities. Nora did her best to play the part of hysterical woman too rattled to remember everything clearly, which was remarkably easy after the harrowing flight. Everybody readily believed that any number of strange hallucinations could be caused by oxygen deprivation and wrote the whole thing off as a freak accident.

As Adam slid into the passenger seat beside her, Nora mumbled into the steering wheel, "You're remarkably good at explaining impossible happenings away to authorities while simultaneously brushing off the paramedics."

He tried for a joke as he buckled his seatbelt. "It's almost like I've done it before."

Nora wasn't in the mood to laugh and just nodded against the steering wheel.

"Are you sure you don't want me to drive?" Adam continued more softly. "You're pretty shaken up, and a nap might do you some good."

Nora hoisted herself upright and put the key in the ignition as she shook her head.

"No. I'd rather drive. I think I just need to feel...in control for a second. Thus, the renting a car and driving back to Chicago."

It was dark by the time Nora pulled up to a sleek apartment building in Lincoln Park to drop Adam off, and she had begun to breathe easily again. After grabbing his luggage out of the trunk, Adam stepped up to Nora's window, and she rolled it down.

They were quiet for a moment longer, and Adam's throat bobbed in the dim light from the streetlamp behind him.

"I'm sorry about your conference. And...thank you."

"Any time," Nora replied, trying to sound casual but failing when her voice cracked.

Adam's hand gripped the edge of the car window, and Nora chose to examine the gold ring he was wearing instead of meeting his eyes.

"Seriously, I owe you my life today," he said.

Nora continued to examine his hand as she responded. "The way I see it, I still owe you one. I think you've saved me more than once."

"I wasn't keeping track."

When Nora lifted her head to meet Adam's eyes, they glittered in the streetlights, full of something so heavy that it was hard to look at. Nora's mind was so preoccupied with the thought that his expression was almost one of longing that she didn't notice him leaning in until his breath tickled her face. His lips just brushed her cheek, but a shiver still ran through Nora's body, colliding with the residual adrenaline and causing frizzling sparks to dance across her skin. Before she could recover, Adam turned away and made his way into his building. She shook herself before rolling up the window and pulling away from the curb.

Nora thanked her lucky stars when she managed to find street parking near her apartment, telling herself she could return the rental car tomorrow. However, as she dragged her suitcase towards her apartment door, she found somebody already sitting on her stoop.

"Nora!" Odelle shot to her feet and crashed into her, clutching her so tightly that Nora's ribs creaked.

"Odelle! What are you doing here?" Nora asked, her voice

muffled by her face in Odelle's hair, which smelled of expensive perfume and roses.

"Oh my gosh, you're all right! I was at work when we covered the story about the flight to Pittsburgh, and I heard from Irina you were going there for the conference this week. I was so worried it was your flight but I couldn't get away while we were on the air, so I came here right after work and—"

"I'm okay, Odelle. I'm here now and I'm just fine," Nora said, trying to sound calm, even as her eyes grew damp.

Odelle took a step back and held Nora at arm's length as if to inspect her. Odelle seemed to be fighting a case of wet eyes, too, although she was doing a much more admirable job of it, managing to look teary without ruining the thick mascara she still had on from an evening of broadcasting.

"I just kept thinking about how, if your plane crashed when we weren't on speaking terms, I could never forgive myself. And then you weren't home and..."

"You don't have to worry about it. The plane depressurized and made an emergency landing, but nobody was hurt," Nora reassured.

There was a tense pause and Odelle's hands stiffened on her shoulders.

"You mean you were on that flight?"

Nora flinched. "Umm..."

"This is the second major disaster you've been a part of this month." Odelle's voice trembled a little, but she still sounded icy as she stepped away and dropped her hands to her sides.

"This one was just a coincidence," Nora tried, taking a step towards her sister, but Odelle was having none of it.

"So, you're saying the other one wasn't a coincidence?" she asked with a raised brow.

Nora buried her face in her hands for a second. "That's not what I... I thought you were regretting not being on speaking terms?"

Odelle sighed and Nora took her face out of her hands to find that Odelle's had softened and now looked resigned.

"I am. And I'm glad you're all right."

"Thanks."

There was a long silence, and Nora was about to invite Odelle upstairs for tea when her sister spoke again.

"I'm not letting this rest, you know." The severity of Odelle's tone was enough to make Irina proud. "But please, call me sometime, okay?"

Nora chewed at her lip. "Okay. Goodnight, Odelle."

Odelle nodded and stepped out into the street to hail a passing cab with a flick of her fingers while Nora trudged up the stairs to her apartment. By the time she flopped down onto her bed and buried her face in her pillows, she was wondering just how much more it would take before her life imploded like the airlock on the plane.

14

THE NEXT MORNING DAWNED, GRAY AND FOGGY, WITH NORA tramping down the sidewalk toward the park before the sun had fully risen. She was sure there were dark circles like bruises under her eyes, and she hadn't even brushed her teeth, but she couldn't bring herself to care. Nobody was hanging around the Bean this early in the morning to see her disheveled state anyways.

She mechanically stepped through the portal and weaved her way through the hallways of the Sanctuary to the training yard. It was odd to enter the space and not find Ezra waiting for her at the other end, eyeing her as he considered the best way in which to put her through her paces.

Nora positioned herself in the middle of the ring and fell into her usual warm up routine of kicks and punches. Her limbs heavy with exhaustion, she pushed every hit as hard as she could. She imagined every blow connecting with the sickly gray Shadow from the plane yesterday until he dispersed into clouds of mist.

With every kick that she performed that didn't meet her standards, she pictured Adam's blue lips as he lay sprawled on the cabin floor. She kicked until the sweat ran into her eyes, burning until she could barely see, but still, her strikes weren't strong enough. She spun around, hands flying to her sweat-matted hair as if to tear it out.

A polite cough echoed from the far end of the courtyard, and she froze. She lifted her eyes to find Antony perched on the edge of the fountain. In the bright sun, his softly curled copper hair shone like a new penny.

"Hello Nora," he greeted her, his voice warm.

"Hey Antony," Nora looked around, wondering how long he had been sitting there. To her surprise, a peacock was hovering around Antony's feet, picking at what looked to be pieces of torn up bread. "I'm sorry to bother you."

"On the contrary, I just came out to feed Pags here, and I'd enjoy some company." He turned his face up to look at the sky. "Although, I'm afraid if you've come out here to find shapes in the clouds, you are out of luck. We don't have any clouds here."

Nora followed his gaze upwards and found that he was right. The sun was shining in a clear azure sky, and there wasn't even the slightest wisp of cloud to be seen.

"It makes me sad that we never have clouds here. I always did have a good time pretending they were dragons or trying to spot Pegasus."

Nora couldn't help the smile that tugged at the corners of her mouth, and she made her way over to the fountain to perch on the lip next to Antony.

"If you miss them that much, feel free to visit us in Chicago. We have more than enough clouds to go around there."

"Maybe I will sometime."

They enjoyed the sunshine in silence for a moment, but even the quiet company and the warmth could not banish the anxiety still gnawing at her gut.

"How do you find it in yourself to watch clouds go by when you are constantly at war with the Shadow?" she asked him eventually.

Antony dropped his eyes and tilted his head. "How do you mean?"

"I just mean that... Well, Adam told me about what the Shadow can do, and then we were attacked on the plane and..." She struggled to articulate her thought but pressed on anyways. "It's all so terrifying. How do I go on with my normal life when I know what's out there, constantly endangering everything I care about?"

"Well I guess that's the point, isn't it," Antony's dreamy eyes grew serious. "If we don't take the time to enjoy our lives then the Shadow has already won. By being afraid, we give it exactly what it wants."

"But you march into battle to fight the Shadow. Isn't fear and hostility part of the whole package when you're in battle?"

"Yes," Antony conceded. "But when your enemy is fear itself, you can't just fight it with more fear. You can't forget that we also express our connection to the Light through poetry and art and music. People don't talk about that as much because it lacks the same drama as hacking Shadows to bits with a spear. Between you and me, though, I think it's the more important part of what we do."

"So, you are saying we can fight the doom of the world with... art?" It sounded a little ridiculous to Nora when she said it out loud, but Antony nodded seriously.

"And love and joy and hope. The best part is that normal people do it every day and they don't even know it. You fight the Shadow by putting so much of yourself into your work at the museum. All that beauty and history—it keeps the Shadows from taking over everybody's minds."

Nora considered. "I suppose that's good but... I could do more to fight back. To help stop the Shadow."

Antony peaked at her out of the corner of his eye. "Then I'm sure you will. But don't forget that it's the little acts of beauty that add up to save the world."

"You guys really take being warrior poets to the next level, don't you?"

The twinkle returned to Adam's eyes as he responded. "Don't

forget dancers. We used to have the best dances here." He turned his dreamy gaze back up to the sky as he talked. "Adam was always a fantastic dancer. It's a shame that it has been so long since he's had a partner."

Nora was glad that Antony was looking at the sky when her cheeks turned hot—not just from the sun.

"It's too bad I don't know of any good dance partners for him then. The best I can do is the chicken dance," Nora deflected.

Antony just hummed knowingly and continued to study the sky.

They remained in the courtyard for a while longer, Antony once again feeding Pags the peacock. Now, though, Nora was not quite as overwhelmed by the threat she knew waited for her beyond the walls of the Sanctuary.

WHEN NORA SHOWED UP FOR HER TRAINING WITH EZRA ON MONDAY, the sight that greeted her made her want to skip over to the big man and give him a giant hug. She contained herself, however, and settled for a brisk walk over to where he was standing with a spear clutched in each meaty hand.

"Today's the day?" she asked by way of greeting, inclining her head toward the weapons in his hands.

Ezra nodded. "Don't get ahead of yourself. Normally, you would train in pankration for a full year before you even got to hold a weapon, but considering the circumstances, I have been persuaded to make an exception. Knowing how to use a weapon sooner rather than later might prove to be...beneficial for you."

Nora reached to snatch the weapon from Ezra's hand, but he yanked it out of her reach.

"Don't think you get out of your warm-up exercises just because of these. Show me your forms before I change my mind about letting you use this."

Nora huffed but settled into her stance without further complaint. She progressed through her punches, moving on to her kicks, which she managed to complete without overbalancing even once. By the time she was done, and Ezra approached her with the practice spear in hand, she was bouncing on the balls of her feet in poorly contained anticipation.

"Calm yourself, young firecracker. It's a weapon, not a piece of candy," Ezra grunted, but Nora could still sense his pleasure at her excitement. It must have been many years since he had gotten the chance to train anybody.

He handed her the weapon, and when the smooth wood touched her palms, she smiled. This felt real. This felt like she could make a difference.

Nora blinked, and her hour of training was over. As Ezra instructed her to begin her cool down exercises, she griped.

"We just covered the basic stances and grips," she argued as she flopped down in the dirt.

"And that is a quick progression for the first day with a spear. You had barely learned the basics, and now you have to adjust to accommodate three meters of wood. If we go much further, you'll hurt yourself," Ezra pointed out.

She began stretching her arms and hissed to find out that he was right. She may have gotten used to exertion, but her muscles seemed permanently knotted from the added weight of the weapon. As she moved to stretch her other arm, she silently thanked Ezra for starting her with a wooden training spear instead of the bronze ones traditionally used in combat.

Still, as she took stock of her aches and pains, she was pleased to find that she had accumulated fewer bruises today than she had in prior weeks. It seemed that training with a spear involved far less of her getting dumped on her backside. She mentally added another tally in favor of the weapon.

Over the next week, Nora continued to train with the spear. Her suspicions that this would go much better than her initial training were confirmed. She found that she was granted a surprising amount of confidence with its length in her hands, almost as if it were an extension of herself that she didn't know she had been missing until now. The stories from her favorite childhood fantasy novels about heroes who slept with their weapons started to make a bit more sense to her. She only trained with her battered practice spear a few hours a day and she had already grown attached to it. It did not seem that farfetched to think that she would never want to be too far from her weapon if she had used it her entire life. With a little more practice, perhaps she could prevent herself from acquiring more injuries that would necessitate a trip to the emergency room. The scar on her thigh did have a roguish appeal, but she had no desire to repeat the experience.

15

XANDER RUBBED HIS ACHING TEMPLES WITH THE PADS OF HIS LONG *fingers. Glancing over at his candle, he found that it was almost burned down, and he would have to fetch another one soon. He debated just letting it sputter out and calling it a night, but he really should finish the research he was doing. With the dwindling ranks of Defenders, his work on fortifying the Sanctuary's wards was becoming critical.*

He glanced up at the glass ceiling of the library to where the silver crescent of the moon hung high in the sky. It must have been well past midnight. He turned back to his work, telling himself he would make sure he was in bed before dawn.

He started, almost knocking over his candle, when a hand slid onto his shoulder. He heard a feminine chuckle, and a voice said very close to his ear, "Leaving me cold and lonely again tonight?"

Xander relaxed. He had forgotten how silent Aediene could be when she wished. He reached up to take the hand resting on his shoulder and pulled her around until she was in front of him. Instead of standing before him, however, she slid onto his lap, placing a hand on each of his shoulders.

"You know how important this is, Aediene," he said, but his fingers somehow made their way to her waist of their own accord. "If I don't

figure out a way to strengthen the wards with all the losses we are taking..." he trailed off.

"Are you really making much progress this late at night? Maybe it's just me, but I don't think you will be much good to the Defenders if you collapse from exhaustion every time you try to stand up."

Xander closed his eyes and let his head fall forward, resting against her muscular shoulder. One of Aediene's hands left his shoulder to card through his hair and he melted into the sensation.

"I just can't sleep," he whispered into her shoulder. "Every time I close my eyes, I keep envisioning what will happen if the wards fail. All I can think about is how I could be doing more to help."

"You can help by getting enough sleep to be a functioning human being," Aediene chided, but he just let out a puff of air against her skin.

She pushed off him and stood up, and Xander kept his hands on her waist, having half a mind to pull her right back down so he could continue hiding his face in her shoulder. Instead, she took his hands in hers and tugged, saying, "Come on, I have an idea."

Xander pushed himself to his feet, and they both giggled as his knees creaked audibly from sitting in the same position for so long. The warm cadence of her laughter reminded him that they were alone in the library, and nobody was there to see them if he were to lay her down on the paper strewn table and take comfort in her body. Before he could act on the thought, she began leading him out of the library, and he trailed in her wake.

They wove their way out of the Sanctuary to a grassy slope, and Aediene flopped down, patting the grass next to her for Xander to do the same. Once they were both seated, Aediene turned her face up to the night sky and said, "Remember how we used to fall asleep out here, looking up at the stars with you telling me stories about the constellations? We haven't done that in a while."

Xander laid back on the grass, pulling Aediene with him so her head was resting against his shoulder.

"I do remember," he said. "They were some of my favorite nights. It seems like there are fewer and fewer stars every time I look up now, though."

"It does seem like things have been getting darker, but there is still plenty of light up there if you look for it."

Xander propped his head up to gaze down at her moonlit profile. "I suppose you're right. I still see plenty of light."

She glanced up at him and smiled, knowing he wasn't talking about the stars.

"Then I'll always stay and be your light, even through the darkest night," Aediene promised him.

Xander, normally quite comfortable expressing himself with words, couldn't come up with a fitting response to her promise. He settled instead for cupping a hand around the back of her neck and bringing her face to his to kiss her soundly. It was a promise of his own, and when Aediene smiled against his mouth, Xander knew she understood what he was trying to say.

They spent the rest of the night in the grass, telling each other stories like they had on nights past. Eventually, they drifted off to sleep, limbs wrapped around one another. This time, when Xander closed his eyes, he didn't worry about anything else he should be doing.

16

THE NEXT DAY AT WORK, NORA FOUND THE CASE FOR THE DISPLAY OF the sword and the spear had arrived, along with a memo on her desk. She didn't even have time to set her bag down before Mandy pranced over with a delighted squeal.

"Oh, did you see? This is going to be so much fun!"

Nora slid into the chair at her desk and picked up the official-looking envelope while responding. "I haven't had a chance to see yet, considering that you ambushed me the moment I walked in the door."

As she skimmed over the memo in her hand, the reason for Mandy's delight became clear. To celebrate the reveal of the new weapons in the arms and armor display, the museum was holding a black-tie celebration, and the entire department was invited.

"After all this time in the basement covered in plaster dust, we get to show off! And you know, an event like this would be a perfect time to announce something like, oh I don't know, a big promotion," Mandy nudged her elbow into Nora's side knowingly.

"Yup, they are letting the nerds out and letting us play dress up for a night, no doubt so we can suck up to some of the major donors," Nora brushed Mandy off, although she bristled with excitement at Mandy's suggestion. A public celebration of her work did seem like the perfect backdrop for a promotion announcement.

"Oh, that's right. I forgot that you hate having fun."

"I don't hate having fun," Nora countered. "I just don't have anything to wear for an event like this. And it's next week! How am I supposed to get an outfit on such short notice?"

It was true. Nora was spending all her time when she wasn't at work either training with Ezra or studying in the library at the Sanctuary. Any other free time she may have had, she spent asleep, her body exhausted from all the sudden additions to her routine.

"Why don't you ask your sister?" Mandy offered. "I'm sure she'd be happy to get an outfit together for you. She's got better taste than both of us put together."

Nora's gut twisted at the mention of Odelle. They hadn't spoken since the night on the street in front of her apartment. Nora had managed to distract herself from the pain of their disagreement by throwing herself into life at the Sanctuary. Mandy's casual mention of Odelle reminded her of their strained relationship and reopened the wound it had caused.

Mandy prattled on, unaware of Nora's inner turmoil.

"We each get a plus one too! Maybe Odelle can set you up with somebody, or do you already have somebody in mind?"

Nora wrenched her thoughts back to the conversation.

"Oh, I'll probably just go alone. Make sure I have plenty of time to make a good impression on the donors," she hedged.

Mandy pursed her lips.

"Just when I thought you were getting the hang of work-life balance by leaving work at a reasonable hour, you refuse to have fun and show off at a party being thrown in honor of your work. There has to be somebody you want to impress!"

Nora envisioned a lanky figure and intelligent eyes framed by glasses.

"Well," Nora debated before continuing, "there is this one guy, but..."

"But what? You're smart, beautiful, young..."

"That's the thing," Nora struggled to explain. "He's quite a bit older."

It was an overly simple way to explain her struggles when it came to her attraction to Adam, because she had found there was no denying she found him charming.

Mandy's eyebrows shot up and she whistled low.

"Girl, you go get it. Nothing like a more mature guy who can actually keep up with an intelligent woman like yourself. Ask him!"

"I'll focus on the outfit first, then worry about the date," Nora responded noncommittally.

Mandy had been right. Having Odelle help her get dressed up for a gala might be a peace offering of sorts. She would just have to do something about the bruises on her skin first, and she thought she knew somebody who might be able to help.

THAT EVENING AFTER TRAINING WITH EZRA, SHE FOUND HERSELF wandering through the halls of the Sanctuary in search of Thad. Ezra had told her he thought he might be in the music room.

Nora turned down the hallway the music room should've been in according to Ezra's instructions. As she made her way across the marble floors, the slight tinkling of a piano assured her that she was headed in the right direction. As she got closer, though, laughter drifted down the hallway, and she furrowed her brow.

"Thad?" Nora gently pushed on the broad wooden door leading to the room where the sounds of the piano came from.

Thad was indeed seated at the piano bench, idly picking out a melody on the keys, much more focused on another figure perched on the corner of the piano, clad in a plaid shirt and laughing.

"Drew?" Nora asked.

At the noise, both men jumped, Drew so hard he nearly fell off the piano, having clearly been so distracted by his conversation he hadn't heard her enter.

"Ah, Nora, how lovely to have you join us," Thad remarked, and Nora detected amusement in the crinkles at the corners of his eyes.

Drew hopped down off the piano, smoothing down the front of his plaid shirt with fidgeting hands.

"Hi Nora," Drew offered, obviously trying to sound casual. "I didn't know you would be here tonight. I was just... I mean, we were... Um, Thad was showing me—"

"I was just teaching Drew how to play the piano," Thad interrupted.

"Of course," Nora teased. "It's a logical extension of discussions of emergency medicine."

"Funny enough, Drew has managed to spend a fair amount of time clutching his pearls over my lack of sterile technique, but he's also quite good company."

Drew attempted to clear his throat and succeeded in falling into a fit of coughing. Thad gave him a hearty clap on the back before returning his focus to Nora.

"So now that we've got you here, is there a reason that you interrupted our piano lesson?"

Nora blinked. "Oh. Ezra mentioned that you might be able to help me fade these bruises." Nora held out her arms, showing the men the scattered marks on her skin. "Not that I'm not proud to have earned these the hard way, it's just that they might raise some eyebrows when I'm forced to wear short sleeves at a work event next weekend."

Thad clicked his tongue thoughtfully. "Not the worst I've seen on somebody who has just started training with a spear. You must be doing Ezra proud. I think I've got something that can help you.

Nora and Drew emerged into the clear Chicago night and stepped out from under the shelter of the Bean into a crisp wind that whipped Nora's curls into her face. Nora carried a miniature Mason jar filled with a yellowish ointment that smelled vaguely of rosemary with a sharper undercurrent that she couldn't place. She had thought the container a bit odd when Thad passed it to her, but he'd just commented that Drew shouldn't have introduced him to Pinterest if he didn't want his concoctions to look rustic-chic.

Drew and Nora walked to the nearest bus stop in a companionable silence, calmed by the familiar sounds of honking cabs and the rumble of the train passing a few streets over. Drew had insisted on accompanying Nora back to the city, saying that he was heading home anyways, but Nora didn't miss the familiar hug Thad gave Drew as he left.

"So you've been hanging out at the Sanctuary with Thad a lot?" Nora asked, breaking the silence.

Drew shoved his hands into the pockets of his coat and shrugged. "I mean, we've become friends. He seems to enjoy having more of a connection to the outside world, and he is…"

"Handsome, charming, funny?" Nora supplied, her tone teasing.

Drew coughed. "I don't want things to be awkward between us, and I know our breakup is still sort of fresh, but I saw you and Adam and I thought… It's not really anything, though. I think Thad flirts with everybody."

They reached the corner of the bus stop, and Nora turned to look up at Drew. "It's not awkward. We said we would be friends, and friends want each other to be happy, even when it seems like they are being intentionally dense about how much a certain Healer might like them."

She was being completely honest. In the past few weeks, the ache deep in her chest had faded. Every day she came to the Sanctuary, the Drew-shaped hole in her life had been slowly filled in with bits of information she was gathering in the library and the confidence she was gaining from Ezra's training. Without her even realizing it, she had started to find a new place for herself among the Eteria. She was feeling the beginnings of a sense of belonging that had been missing since she'd broken up with Drew—and even before, if she thought about it.

"You're just being nice," Drew huffed. "It's so obvious with you and Adam, but Thad... It can be so hard to tell."

Nora blew out a breath that clouded in the night air as she turned to look out at the street. "Do you know something I don't? Adam and I are pretty far from being a thing. I haven't had any contact with him since we almost crashed a plane together."

As much as she tried to sound light, Nora couldn't keep a small amount of disappointment from her tone. She had hoped to see Adam around the Sanctuary this week, but she was hesitant to seek him out herself.

"I think he only reached out to me in the first place to get to see the sword, and now he's kept me around because he feels responsible for what happened."

The assessment seemed to go against Adam's character, even to her own ears, but it was what she had been telling herself to explain why she had seen so little of him.

Drew threw his head back and laughed. When Nora glared up at him in confusion, he said, "You just accused me of being dense when you're acting like this? I forgot how oblivious you can be when somebody is into you. It's like back when you were in grad school, and I was always coming up with any excuse to bother you in that café you used to study in. And it's probably even worse now that you haven't had practice in the dating game for a while."

"Be serious, Drew," she scolded, slapping his arm lightly.

"I am being serious. Anybody who was there when that man charged into the emergency room covered in your blood would bet their first-born child that he cares for you in a way that goes beyond responsibility."

The tips of Nora's ears heated, but she remained obstinate. "If he really felt that way, then he would have sought me out. It's not like he doesn't know where I've been. I've been at the Sanctuary constantly!"

"Exactly." Drew had the smug look of somebody who knew they had argued their opponent into a corner. "He knows you're so busy with all this new stuff that has been thrust on you, he probably thinks you're a little overwhelmed. Plus, considering you were attacked by literal demons the last time you guys spent time together, he may be trying to be a gentleman and let you make the next move."

Nora was growing increasingly sheepish by the second. Adam was trying to be chivalrous, and here Nora was getting all up in arms like a spurned teenager.

Drew continued thoughtfully. "Also, I know the man is from ancient Greece, but he has a phone, right? You could always just shoot him a text and see if he wants to do something that doesn't involve swords or a trip to the hospital. Although, given that it's you, I think pretty much anything will end up involving swords."

THE NEXT DAY AT LUNCH, NORA'S THUMBS HOVERED ABOVE HER phone screen as she chewed on her tuna sandwich. She had taken Drew's advice and decided to ask Adam if he would like to attend the gala with her. After all, they were revealing his own sword in its new position of honor in the display, and he deserved to be there to see it. Adam had responded promptly that he would love to come, and Nora was amused that he did not let the fact that he was over two millennia old deter him from the uninhibited use of emojis.

Now, Nora was in the predicament of finding herself a suitable dress for a black-tie event in a closet dominated by flannel, over-sized sweaters, and a smattering of sharp suits appropriate for professional presentations. She had composed a careful message to Odelle, imploring her to take pity on her and help her pick out a dress, and to her endless relief, Odelle had replied with the name of a boutique and a time this evening.

Nora made her decision and shot off a quick text to Drew, asking him to tell Thad that she would not be coming to the Sanctuary tonight for training, so he could pass the message on to Ezra. The lack of service in the Sanctuary certainly complicated things, although now that she thought about it, she wasn't sure anybody outside of Adam or Thad really used much modern technology at all.

Putting her cell phone down and taking another bite of her sandwich, guilt twisted in Nora's stomach about calling off training tonight. Juggling her work-life balance had started to get to her, although that probably had something to do with the fact that her life outside of work had now stretched to include preparing to fight the physical incarnation of fear.

THE SUN WAS ALREADY ON THE HORIZON BY THE TIME NORA STEPPED off the bus near the store that Odelle named. It was approaching the time of year when it would be dark when Nora left work, and she was forced to pull her scarf up to protect her face from the wind that was cold even for late fall in Chicago.

Nora shouldered her way through the door and spotted Odelle already perusing. She made her way over to the younger woman and stepped up beside her to squeeze her in a one-armed hug. "I'm glad you could make it, *zaika*."

Odelle did not turn away from the rack of gowns in front of her or move to return the hug, but she did incline her head into Nora's embrace so that her cheek rested on Nora's shoulder.

"Yes, well, I wouldn't want to deprive you of my impeccable taste," Odelle responded airily. Considering Odelle's legendary stubbornness when it came to giving people the cold shoulder, Nora considered this greeting a win.

Odelle swept a black dress off the rack that had entirely too many straps for Nora's taste. "This one might look nice on you."

She handed it to a saleswoman while she continued to browse, next selecting a dress in a pomegranate color that Nora thought might be flattering but had a slit up the side that would spark a disagreement about what was appropriate for a work event.

The next dress Odelle pulled off the rack had Nora's eyes widening. Lengths of shimmering gold fabric flowed from a gather at one shoulder to a cinched waistline and a softly draped skirt.

"Let's try on that one first," Nora piped up enthusiastically.

Odelle peered at her out of the corner of her eye, smiling triumphantly as she handed the dress to the dutiful saleswoman to take to the changing room.

"I had hoped I would convince you to go to the gala in a show-stopper."

By the time Nora was stepping out of the dressing room, she was sure Odelle wasn't going to have to do much convincing. Sure, it might be frivolous to drop as much as she would on groceries for two weeks on an outfit she was going to wear once, but it was not every week that a girl had a date with a legendary warrior sorcerer. It wasn't unreasonable to put her best foot forward when trying to impress a man that had lived through every age of ridiculous fashion.

As Nora pushed aside the curtain and stood in front of the mirror, Odelle looked up from her phone and let out a soft, "Damn, girl."

Nora's gaze connected with her sister's in the mirror over her shoulder, and Odelle beamed. Nora made a mental note to thank Thad again for the miracle balm as she looked over herself in the mirror. Explaining so many bruises to Odelle would have been a nightmare.

Odelle circled around Nora so she could view the dress from every angle.

"I know I'm good, but we knocked it out of the park on the first try here. That's a record even for me."

Nora twisted this way and that in the mirror, admiring how the fabric cascaded over her curves in soft folds. The draping was reminiscent of the clothes that a Greek goddess would be painted in, and the significance was not lost on her as she appreciated her reflection.

As Odelle stepped around once more to stand behind Nora, she let out a low whistle.

"Have you been going to the gym more or something?"

"Oh yeah, I've been...taking kickboxing classes," Nora said, attempting to convince herself that this was not technically lying. "I've gotten a lot better."

"It's paid off." Odelle's tone was approving. "Your butt has never looked this good before."

Nora twisted to see her backside in the mirror, and she had to admit that Odelle was right. Her training with Ezra had done her some favors when it came to the view of her posterior. What a lovely bonus that one of the side effects of training to survive an attack by evil monsters was a perkier behind.

"Be careful or I might get jealous. Everybody knows I'm supposed to be the hot one," Odelle teased, stepping up next to Nora in the mirror before softening her tone. "But seriously, you look breathtaking."

"Thanks," Nora said before pausing, taking a moment to fiddle with the waistband of her dress before continuing, "We're good, right?"

The silence was brief before Odelle said, "It's the two of us. We'll always be good."

Nora nodded gratefully. She opened her mouth, considering spilling the truth about everything that had happened in her life right then and there. *A little bit longer.* She could wait until she could confidently tell Odelle that she was able to defend herself from the Shadow so Odelle wouldn't have to worry.

Nora shut her mouth, and Odelle broke the silence.

"And to show you how good we are, I have a little surprise for you," she said, a playful glint in her eyes.

"Oh?"

"I managed to get a press pass to your gala, so I get to cover the event for a special interest piece and play up how wonderfully accomplished my big sister is," Odelle said, lifting her chin proudly. "Plus, I wouldn't want to miss them announcing your promotion."

Nora's jaw dropped and she turned to face her sister. Her mouth worked open and closed a few times before she asked, "Why aren't we finding you something to wear then?"

"Bold of you to assume I haven't already got something in my closet." Odelle waved her question away. "Just be sure you save some interview time for me."

Nora nodded enthusiastically before her mind hit a snag.

"I should warn you, though," she started. "I'm bringing a date to the event, and I don't think you're going to like it."

"Why wouldn't I like the fact that I seem to have finally convinced you to get back in the saddle?" Odelle said with a quizzical tilt of her head.

Nora chewed her bottom lip before admitting, "It's Adam."

"The Adam from the hospital?"

Nora nodded before trying to defend herself. "He helped with the translation of the inscription on the sword, and we've been working closely together, and... Yeah," she finished lamely.

Odelle pursed her lips, but to her credit, she seemed to try to reign in her skepticism. "I won't ruin your night. But I swear, if something goes wrong at this gala, I'm going to find a way to embarrass that guy on national television."

"Are you really going to disapprove of me seeing a perfectly good guy just because he was present when I got in an accident?"

"And an almost plane crash? Until you prove to me that he didn't have something to do with either, then yes. Now come on, take the dress off so we can check out," said Odelle, shooing her back into the dressing room. "We've still got to find you shoes to go with it."

Nora did as she was told, but not before stealing one more glance over her shoulder at herself in the dress and grinning. She had a feeling Adam was going to appreciate the view from behind too.

17

NORA STOOD ON THE FRINGES OF THE PARTY, CLUTCHING A GLASS OF champagne in one hand while using the other to negotiate with the bobby pins stabbing her in the head. After acquiring a dress fit for a literal goddess, she had decided to use a forgotten gift certificate to get her hair done for tonight's gala. While she had to admit the stylist admirably wrestled her hair into a twist at the crown of her head, it came at the cost of feeling as if a pack of vultures were attacking her scalp.

Catching a glimpse of her reflection in the glass of a display case, Nora decided it was worth it. Even Adam would be impressed —if he ever showed up.

Nora berated herself for being impatient. Adam was not the type to go back on his promise to come, and he had seemed excited for the event, even offering to pick her up beforehand. Nora had declined, wanting to get to the museum before the event started, to make sure everything was perfect for the unveiling of the new display. Now, she felt as if she had been waiting for an age, even though the party wasn't in full swing yet.

As if her thoughts had summoned him, a tall figure stepped up beside her and sighed.

"Here I thought I was a gentleman bringing you a drink, and you already have one."

Nora turned to look at Adam and had to suppress the urge to let out an appreciative whistle. The navy tux he wore brought out the deep golden hues in his skin, and the cut perfectly accentuated his statuesque figure.

"Oh, you must be assuming that I am a lady then and wouldn't accept another glass of champagne," Nora responded before throwing back the last of the contents in her flute. She reached for the full replacement in Adam's hand before continuing. "I need more than one drink if I'm going to socialize with the paleontology department. They think they are all that just because their T-Rex is the biggest display in the museum, but I think they're compensating for something."

Adam coughed into the champagne he had just been sipping. Once he had recovered from his spluttering, he asked, "Oh, and you don't think that spear might be compensating for something just a bit?" His eyes held a devious twinkle as he baited her.

"Not at all," Nora defended. "Because you'd actually have to be strong to use it, making you a legitimate badass who's not faking it at all." She refused to let anybody malign the weapons on their special day, and she had to admit that her newfound affinity for her own practice spear had only made her more attached to the bronze masterpiece.

Just then, Nora spotted a familiar figure drifting in through the main entrance. It was hard to miss Odelle on any given day, but tonight, she had made it impossible by donning a scarlet silk jumpsuit with a dramatic overskirt attached in the back that dragged in a short train.

At the sight, Nora passed off her empty champagne glass to a waiter with a quick thanks.

"Before I drink too much champagne, though, I have a few professional obligations to fulfill," she explained, taking Adam by the elbow and leading him across the room to her sister. They weaved through the glittering crowd to where Odelle stood, conversing with a cameraman she had brought in with her.

"Well aren't you dressed to kill?" Nora greeted.

"There are so few opportunities to wear couture. Might as well take advantage. It makes me feel like I'm in a James Bond movie," Odelle said, fluffing her skirt in response.

Nora made Odelle do a little twirl to show off the whole look as she complimented, "You look like a Bond girl."

"Life goal accomplished. Do you want to see if there are any eligible high rollers in the crowd this evening who might want to take us on a ride in their Aston Martin?"

Nora gestured to Adam, who had been standing dutifully beside her. "I have already acquired my James Bond for the evening."

Adam opened his mouth to greet her, but Odelle barely even glanced at him before cutting him off with a dry, "Shame."

Trying to diffuse the bomb this conversation was about to become, Nora changed the subject. "Are you ready to make me look like a boss on the evening news?"

"I was born ready." Odelle stepped up to position Nora appropriately as the cameraman produced a microphone for her to use. Adam still stood at Nora's side, but when Odelle shot him a poisonous glance, he raised his hands and took a few deferential steps away, giving Odelle space to continue arranging Nora to her liking.

"Turn slightly to the side, like this. Pop your hip, and shoulders back," Odelle instructed as she demonstrated. "Perfect."

Odelle then positioned herself opposite Nora and said with a grin, "All right, *zolotse*, time to show off that big brain of yours."

She motioned to her cameraman to roll and began asking Nora a few educated questions about the weapons, which Nora did her best to respond to with terms that wouldn't alienate the casual viewer. It all passed so fast that Nora wasn't even sure if she had spoken in English, but Odelle reassured her with encouraging smiles. They wrapped up quickly, and Odelle gave her sister a wicked grin.

"Wait until that guy Leo gets a load of this. He got passed over for the promotion in favor of you, and now you're on TV."

Nora tried to hug her in thanks, but Odelle brushed her off. "Don't wrinkle my outfit yet, I've still got to get a few more statements. Maybe I'll find Mandy and interview her. She always did seem nice. Then we can break some hearts."

With that, Odelle turned and pranced off through the thickening crowd, cameraman in tow, and Adam returned from where he had been hovering to the side.

"You really do the artifacts credit with your knowledge," he complimented.

"Speaking of, we should go see the pieces of honor." She grabbed Adam's hand and turned to tow him through the milling crowd. When he hesitated, she glanced over her shoulder to find him wearing an expression that clearly indicated he was enjoying the view as much as she thought he might. She raised a brow at him over her shoulder, and he had the decency to blush high on his cheekbones before allowing himself to be led across the room. Still, Nora could feel his eyes on her as she walked and did her best to suppress the heat that built in her body in response.

The cluster of guests around the centerpiece of the exhibit was dense with Nora's coworkers and impeccably dressed people, whom Nora assumed were significant donors to the museum there to appreciate the fruits of their generosity. It was difficult to edge through, but Nora was taller than most of the guests in the heels she had managed to wedge her feet into, and Adam's statuesque frame aided her in clearing a path. Coworkers who recognized Nora stepped back deferentially, recognizing her as a subject of tonight's celebration, and she felt a bolt of pride under the thin layer of self-consciousness caused by the gesture.

Reaching the front of the crowd, Nora looked up at Adam expectantly to see him beaming down at his long-lost sword, encased in protective glass and positioned on a stand to show off its unique inscription down the blade.

"You've really outdone yourself, Nora." He leaned close to speak directly into her ear so she could hear him clearly over the rumble of chatter and laughter now filling the space. His breath stirred an artfully curled tendril of loose hair framing her face as he spoke.

Nora grinned even as she teased. "You know I didn't have to do much to get them looking this good. It's unfair to be getting so much attention when they showed up almost exactly like this."

"Maybe, but this exhibit does make them shine." Adam tilted his head pensively as he continued. "Besides, it's nice to see them shown off for their beauty and craftsmanship instead of as tools of destruction. Antony would be pleased."

Nora's eyebrows pulled together. "Antony?"

"He made both of these," Adam responded, bending down to the case to get a better look at the plaque bearing the "estimated" date of origin and location of recovery. "He always viewed his work more as art than as weaponry anyways. Seeing it treated as such would be right up his alley."

"And what about you? It's not strange to see a personal belonging of yours in a museum?"

"On the contrary, it feels right to have relics from such an important moment in time immortalized like this. And it means more than I can say to see these two next to each other again."

As she watched Adam stare at the weapons with reverence, something she had forgotten to ask Adam about before came to the front of her mind.

"You didn't happen to...break into the museum to try to see these, did you?"

Adam chuckled even as he winced. "I did break in, but it was actually more of a preventative measure. I sensed Shadows in the area, and I figured they knew that the weapons would be coming. I'm sorry for giving you a fright."

"I was wondering if you knew it was me that chased you," she said. "I'm glad that I wasn't just imagining things."

They fell silent in their contemplation of the display once more.

Nora's brow furrowed. "Who did the spear belong to?" Nora questioned, realizing she had no idea how it had ended up on the field so near where Adam's Xiphos had fallen.

Adam kept his eyes on the spear and paused so long that Nora began to think he hadn't heard her question. She was just about to repeat herself when his response came, his voice so low that Nora had to lean in close to hear his response over the chatter around them.

"It was my wife's."

Nora jolted back hard enough to slosh several drops of champagne on her dress. She distractedly brushed them away as she scrabbled to form an adequate response. She settled on, "You're married?" She attempted to feign a casual tone but grimaced when her voice came out an octave higher than usual.

Adam turned his face back to Nora, now wearing a neutral expression of somebody trying hard to seem casual and succeeding a little too much to be convincing as he said, "I was—a long time ago."

Nora knew that it was probably rude to ask, but she supposed that had never stopped her before. "What happened?"

"She died," Adam answered simply. His voice was calm, but a small twitch beneath his left eye betrayed his emotion. Sympathy twisted low in Nora's gut, and she opened her mouth to apologize for bringing up such a painful subject, but Adam continued, as if now that the subject was broached, he was compelled to share. "She was killed in the Defeat, but she was incredibly brave. She fought to the last and died a hero."

Adam's voice had a trace of pain in it that even millennia of healing had been unable to erase, but as he spoke, his face broke into a soft smile, as if talking about her brought him real joy. His expression made Nora inexplicably wistful.

"She sounds incredible," Nora offered, unsure of what the appropriate response was when the man that she had been shamelessly flirting with moments before suddenly divulged the details of the death of his till then unmentioned wife.

"She was," Adam responded.

Nora searched for something she could say about a loss that happened two thousand years ago that Adam wouldn't have heard dozens of times before. Adam, thankfully, saved her from uttering any of her woefully inadequate options.

He plucked the champagne out of her hand as he spoke. "And she would not want us to stand around like melancholy lumps on her account." He passed the flutes to another white-gloved waiter and grabbed her hand. "She would most definitely want us to dance."

Adam's eyes were gleaming with mischief and a little something else as he began to lead her towards the center of the atrium, where there was indeed a dance floor. A string ensemble in the corner had begun to play at some point as well.

"Oh, uh, I really don't know how to dance for an occasion like this," Nora protested, caught off guard from the sudden change in subject. She glanced at the elegantly dressed couples on the floor, moving in graceful steps that she assumed would only be practical to learn if you lived the kind of life where you attended black-tie galas on a regular basis. "In case you haven't noticed, events like this are not a part of my normal repertoire."

"Lucky for you, I am well versed in all sorts of dancing," Adam replied, unperturbed as he continued to usher her forward. "One of the distinct advantages of living though the Regency period is the ability to perform a solid waltz."

They had reached the outskirts of the dance floor, and before Nora could protest again, Adam had twirled her around towards him in a way she thought only worked in movies and put one hand on her waist to pull her close. She would have been inclined to tease him about it if she hadn't just gained a whole new appreciation for the phrase "weak in the knees".

With that, they began to sway gently as Adam guided her around the floor. To Nora's relief, he didn't seem to mind that her only dancing experience involved jumping up and down like a fool to obnoxious pop music on the rare occasion that Odelle had managed to convince her that a few irresponsible decisions really wouldn't kill anybody. If Adam noticed her initial stumbling, he had the decency not to point it out and simply tightened his arm around her waist so he could pull her with him around the dance floor.

As they rounded a curve, Nora caught sight of Odelle's distinctive red jumpsuit and avoided looking at her in favor of watching her footing. She didn't want to think of her sister's disapproval at the moment.

Once Nora was confident that she wasn't going to trip Adam with her incompetence, she looked up from their feet to meet his twinkling eyes. This close to him, she was able to make out a thin white scar across his forehead, as well as faint lines around his eyes, showing that he spent far more time smiling than not. While his gaze was playful now, there was also an intensity behind it that made Nora want to fidget.

Distracting herself from her own awkwardness, she picked up the threads of their former conversation.

"You really can perform a solid waltz."

She wished she could come up with something more engaging to say, but at that moment, she got distracted by Adam navigating her through a pivoting turn around the floor.

"I'd like to think so," Adam responded lightly, as if carrying on a stimulating conversation while making sure neither he nor she collided with any of their fellow dancers was as easy as breathing. "I really do love to dance. Although I don't get the chance to do it very often anymore."

"Antony mentioned that the other day."

Adam's brows raised as he hummed in amusement. "Did he now?"

Nora nodded, continuing to split her focus between the dancing and the conversation while simultaneously trying not to focus on Adam's wiry arm wrapped firmly around her waist. The warmth from the contact was spreading down her body, making Nora very aware that she was still at a work function.

Thankfully, Adam didn't require a verbal response and continued to carry the conversation for her. "He's right. I do wish I had more opportunities to dance. I usually try to avoid saying things like this because it makes me feel like a walking cliché, but people really don't dance like they used to."

Nora chuckled. "I take it the dancing at night clubs isn't digni- fied enough for your mature tastes?"

"On the contrary," Adam scoffed. "I can make a fool of myself with the best of them. But I miss the days when you could ask a beautiful lady to dance with you and then spend the next few minutes getting to know her while impressing her with your coor- dination." He sighed dramatically. "Take that away from me, and I really don't have any good moves."

"What are you talking about? I thought carrying a woman to the hospital for blood loss was your big move," Nora teased.

"Exactly. You understand my plight now."

Nora giggled and Adam took the opportunity to guide her through a small twirl under his arm. She surprised herself by not tripping and thanked Ezra for her newfound sense of balance.

"In all seriousness, though, thank you for inviting me tonight," Adam said as he settled his arm back around her. "The life of an English teacher by day and Defender by night doesn't really lend itself to attending many galas. With everything that's been going on, a little champagne and dancing with a pretty woman is good for me."

Nora tried to keep from preening internally at being called

pretty as she processed the rest of his statement. "Everything that's been going on recently?"

Adam nodded. "With the attacks by the Shadow. We haven't seen a series of hits in such close proximity to each other since, well, since before the Defeat, really. It's all hands on deck at the Sanctuary, and with all the research I've been doing to try and figure this out on top of working, well... I can't remember the last time I had a good night's sleep."

Absorbing his words, Nora felt childish for complaining about Adam's recent absence. He, too, had been fighting with everything she had been battling for the past weeks, working himself to the bone. And yet, when she had asked him to come to a party with her, he had immediately made himself available.

"I'm so sorry. If you want to turn in early tonight and try to catch up on some sleep, I totally understand. I can take a rain check on dancing and champagne when the fate of the city is at stake."

"Nonsense," Adam said with a forceful shake of his head. "This is way better than sleeping. Besides, parties are full of hope and fun." Adam leaned in to whisper conspiratorially in her ear. "Both things the Shadow hates."

Nora's chest heated, but the warmth could not manage to fully diffuse the knot of concern buried below her sternum.

"What kind of research have you been doing?" she asked, hoping to help in some way. If there was one thing she was good at, it was research.

"I've just been trying to come up with anything we could use to get an edge over the Shadow. We know it has to have an agent in the city for the attacks to be so concentrated. And I have a hunch that the Eteria's increased activity here has drawn its attention. So many of us have been coming and going, and the weapons them-selves are great wells of power that the Shadow can sense. Hell, with your blood now being a beacon for the Shadow, its only because we've had a guard keeping an eye on you that you haven't been attacked at work yet."

Nora flinched involuntarily in Adam's arms, and he looked down at her apologetically before continuing. "The problem is that they are so damn slippery. The attacks are so random, and the Shadows and their agent are always gone or retreating by the time we can get there, leaving a disaster for us to clean up. I've been trying to come up with a way to track them, but..." Adam ended his rant with a long-suffering sigh that perfectly encapsulated the struggle of every researcher stuck on a troublesome project.

Nora, however, was still milling over his earlier statements, feeling a pang of guilt that she had brought the weapons here, contributing to all the activity that was drawing the Shadow's eye. She pushed her guilt aside, though, feeling like there was something else she should be seeing here, turning Adam's statements around in her head to look at them from all angles.

"There is a way to know where the Shadow will strike next," she blurted out, stopping in their dance so suddenly that a nearby couple bumped into them.

Adam's eyes were wary as Nora, ignoring the now grumbling couple, pulled Adam to the side so they could stand still as they talked.

"They are going to attack me at work, like you said."

"Nora," his voice was low with concern. "I assure you that we are keeping you safe. We've been extra cautious since the plane fiasco, and Ezra says you are progressing—"

Nora batted at his arm to get him to shut up as she explained herself.

"No, you can get them to attack me on purpose. Send me out without a guard to use me as bait, then set a trap." She continued to brainstorm out loud in her enthusiasm. "It'll be perfect. We can do it at night so there are no civilian casualties. Control the situation."

Looking up, Nora could read on Adam's face that he was not quite as taken with the idea as she was.

"If I'm making you feel like throwing yourself into the worst kind of danger is the solution, then I really have failed," he grumbled.

"Oh, come on, you're just being bitter because you know this is a great idea and you're embarrassed you didn't think of it first," Nora said with exaggerated grandiosity, trying to distract Adam as well as herself from the fact that this was a terrifyingly dangerous plan.

"Who's to say I didn't think of it but was smart enough not to bring it up because I realized it was a harebrained idea?"

"Then you should have known that I would also be smart enough to insist on this plan, because I know that it is just obvious enough to circle right back around to being clever."

"You know I can't possibly like any idea that involves intentionally endangering somebody, right?" Adam said, his expression clearly broadcasting just how much he didn't like the plan.

"You're not intentionally endangering me; I'm doing it myself," Nora insisted. "Besides, by not doing it, everybody else is constantly being endangered, so there."

Adam heaved another sigh and gave her a pleading look. "I suppose there is nothing I can say that might talk you out of wanting to do this?"

Nora raised her chin and shook her head. Seraphina's words echoed in her head.

People like you get us killed.

She would not let herself stand by when there was something she could be doing. She might still be shaken from her last encounter from the Shadows but facing them head-on appealed to her more than living in fear of the next attack.

"I guessed as much," said Adam resignedly. "But if we are going to do this, we should make sure we do it right. Start by running the plan by Thad to get his input."

"Wait—really?" asked Nora. "I've convinced you that easily?"

Adam offered her a wry smile as he grabbed her hand and

started weaving through the crowd towards an unknown destination.

"Through the years, I've learned to pick which hills to die on. Something tells me that trying to be more stubborn than you isn't a fight on which I want to waste my emotional capital."

Nora was unsure if he meant for his comment on her tenacity to be a compliment, but she decided to feel flattered anyways.

"Now come on, let's go run your plan by Thad. See what he has to say."

"We're going to the Sanctuary right now?" Nora asked. "I can't leave, I still need to do some schmoozing. And I hate to break it to you, but I don't think I can make it all the way there in these shoes."

Adam continued to guide her by the hand, but instead of continuing towards the exit, he turned to head up a wide stone staircase.

"Lucky for you, Thad isn't at the Sanctuary. He volunteered to be your guard for the night."

"Oh." Nora paused to pick up the hem of her dress so she wouldn't trip on it while climbing the steps. "I thought you counted as my security detail."

Adam shrugged as he reached the top of the stairs. "I didn't think I would make a very good guest if I was constantly looking over my shoulder for threats. And I certainly would not make an effective guard while drinking champagne."

They rounded a corner at the top of the staircase, and Nora immediately spotted Thad leaning jauntily against a pillar, surveying the party going on in the space below him over a railing. He was, unsurprisingly, sporting an immaculate set of white tuxedo tails as he turned to them.

"And to what do I owe the pleasure of this visit?" he asked, pushing off the pillar he had been leaning on.

Nora ignored his question in favor of asking, "How did you get in here without an invitation?"

Thad waved his hand dismissively. "I've been sneaking into

parties before they invented champagne. I know how to charm a doorman."

"Stop bragging, Thad," cut in Adam. "Nora has an idea I think you should hear."

"You mean the idea where she uses herself as bait so we can catch the agent?" Thad asked with an arched brow. "I was wondering when that was going to come up."

"What?" Nora and Adam said in unison.

"I mean, it's a pretty obvious solution, and Nora is far from stupid. As soon as she got the relevant information, she was going to think of this. You had to know that, Adam."

Adam huffed indignantly, but Nora pressed ahead.

"So, you think it could work?"

"It could," That hedged. "But it would have to be planned carefully, and I think we should really only resort to it if we're desperate."

"I'm pretty desperate to not have to be looking over my shoulder all the time," Nora grumbled.

"If we are going to do it, we should do it at a time when the museum would be mostly empty, so Nora can come in and use the combined pull of herself and the weapon to lure the Shadow without danger to civilians," Thad mused out loud.

Nora chimed in. "The museum closes early on Tuesday to give workers time off after spending so much time prepping for the gala."

"Hera's hairy asscrack," Adam swore under his breath. "That doesn't give us very long to organize if we really want to do this. I'll have to get started right away to pull it off by then, get everybody up to speed on the plan." He rested his hand on Nora's arm. "Will you forgive me if I take a rain check on another dance? If we are even thinking of attempting this without letting you get hurt, I'm going to need to get going on mapping out our strategy right away."

Nora nodded, her head spinning slightly from the rapid sequence of events. "It's fine, do what you need to. I'll probably be spending the rest of the evening chatting up potential benefactors anyways."

Adam paused a moment with his hand still on her arm, looking torn, before nodding briskly.

"I'll see you soon." Then he turned and left, his long legs carrying him swiftly around the corner and out of sight. Nora's arm felt cold where his hand had been.

Once he was gone, Nora let out a deep sigh and let her shoulders slump. She turned back to Thad.

"I suppose you will have to leave too?"

He shook his head, offering her a warm smile. "No, I'm here to keep you safe as long as you are here. You're the guest of honor after all."

Nora propped her hip on the railing beside him, looking down at the sparkling sea of party guests below her and feeling rather distant from the celebration.

"I'm not sure I want to celebrate anymore."

"Don't be silly, you just need a fresh glass of bubbly."

"I'm not sure champagne can fix my problems."

Nora glanced over at Thad to find him looking at her expectantly, giving her time to continue. She took a moment to gather her thoughts, afraid that she sounded like a petulant teenager, but hoping Thad would understand what she was trying to say.

"I just... feel like my life has been split in two. One moment, I'm a girl getting ready for a party, worrying about how my hair looks and what pair of heels makes my ass look the best. The next moment, I'm waging a war against the physical incarnation of fear. It's giving me whiplash, and I don't even know who I am anymore. Am I a nerdy historian who gossips with her sister? Or am I some sort of warrior in training with a responsibility to save the world?"

Thad snorted. "Funny, I never took you to be someone lacking imagination."

Nora shot Thad a quizzical look, and he sat himself on the railing next to her.

"Look, take it from somebody who knows," he continued. "Putting yourself in a box of who you think you're supposed to be gets boring after a while. Let yourself be new things, even if you aren't quite sure how they fit with the old things. No reason you can't have it all, the way I see it."

"You sound like my sister," Nora said, finding Odelle's crimson form winding through the crowd below.

"I'll take that as a compliment. She seems like she has impeccable taste. Do I get to meet her?"

Nora bit her lip and avoided Thad's gaze. "I don't know. I haven't really...told her about all of this."

"Well no wonder your life is being split in two. You're hiding yourself from the people who are supposed to know you best."

"I know you're right," Nora admitted. "I want to tell her. I just..."

"I get it. But she can handle it."

Nora thought on the truth of his words.

"I'll find time this week to sit down and talk to her about it. I won't ruin her fun tonight."

Thad nodded in approval. "Speaking of ruining the party, you should go down there and celebrate with her. Don't waste the evening feeling sorry for yourself with this old hermit. I'll stay up here so I can have a bird's eye view."

Nora did as he suggested, making her way back down the stairs into the frivolity below. She scanned the crowd and managed to spot Gerald Krinkle. *Jackpot.* He was notorious for large private donations to passion projects, and he was standing alone.

Nora made a beeline through the crowd towards the man with the deep pockets, but she was interrupted before she could get there by Leo stepping in front of her. She bit back a groan of frustration and looked up into his face with the emptiest smile she could muster.

"Enjoying the celebration, Leo?" she asked with an extra helping of forced cheeriness.

He pursed his thin lips in response.

"You can quit with the sass, Nora. I came to make peace." He offered her one of the two champagne flutes in his hands.

Nora blinked in surprise.

"Oh, well, that's very big of you."

"I know we both wanted the same promotion, and they are going to announce that it is going to you later tonight, and I have to admit, you've done a very good job." Leo looked like the words were physically paining him, but he pushed on. "I thought it would be nice if we could be on the same side for once."

"I... That might be nice."

Leo raised his glass to her. "To new beginnings."

"To new beginnings," Nora echoed, taking a small sip. She had already had two glasses, and she didn't want to drink any more before she got a chance to talk to all the big wigs.

Leo inclined his head and weaved off through the crowd as Nora looked around for Gerald Krinkle. Before she could take another step forward, though, a hand grabbed her elbow and she was thwarted for the second time in a row. She turned to snap at whoever was stopping her but was cut off by Odelle.

"Don't drink that!"

Nora froze in confusion and looked at the glass in her hand.

"The champagne? Why?"

"I saw Leo put something in it."

"But he just came over to... Oh that little..." Nora's face heated in anger, and she began searching through the crowd for Leo's retreating form, itching to show off some of the punches Ezra had taught her

Odelle caught sight of him first, slipping through the doorway leading to the stairs down to the office.

"I'm going to go confront him about what he tried to give you," Odelle said. "It wouldn't look good for you to lose your cool at your own party. You go find a glass of water and a place to sit down."

Odelle then slipped away, stomping through the crowd with a look on her face that made people jump out of her way. Before

Nora could do as her sister had instructed, though, Thad stepped up beside her.

"Glad Odelle got here first," he commented, plucking the champagne out of Nora's hand and giving it a sniff. "Hmm interesting choice of drug. Wouldn't have hurt you, just would have made you act extremely drunk."

Nora growled. "Probably trying to get me to embarrass myself in front of the board members. If I'm not going to keel over, I'm going to join Odelle in giving him the chewing out of his life."

"That sounds like something I want to watch," Thad said, gesturing for Nora to lead the way through the crowd.

Nora and Thad had just made it to the door when Nora caught the faint whiff of smoke, making her freeze and bringing her back to the day of the fire in this very building. The moment was broken by a shriek. Nora shoved through the door and found Odelle standing at the foot of the stairs over a crumpled form. Leo lay at the bottom of stairs, pale and lying in a pool of dark blood that spread over the white tile. Odelle's skirt spread in a matching puddle on the floor as she fell to her knees and felt for a pulse.

Odelle cursed before overlapping her hands on Leo's chest and beginning to pump. Thad was already halfway down the staircase. Fishing her phone out of her clutch, Nora opened it and had to try three times to dial the right number.

"911. What's your emergency?"

NORA SUNK DOWN ON THE STAIRS IN FRONT OF THE MUSEUM AND pulled Thad's suit jacket more tightly around her shoulders as she watched the ambulance carrying Leo's lifeless body drive away. She couldn't feel her face, but she wasn't sure if it was from the cold or from whatever drug Leo had slipped into her drink. She was only alone for a few seconds before a warm body appeared next to her and an arm was draped around her. Nora let her head fall to Odelle's shoulder and tried to let the smell of roses comfort her.

"I'm sorry they didn't get to announce your promotion," Odelle murmured, smoothing her hand over Nora's hair, which had fallen halfway out of its elegant twist.

"I think that's the least of my worries at this point," Nora sniffed. "They'll probably just email me about it."

Odelle nodded against her head, and silence fell for a few moments as Odelle continued to stroke Nora's hair.

"It's all my fault," Nora whispered.

"It's not your fault that a man had too much to drink and fell down the stairs after trying to drug you," Odelle countered, but Nora knew the truth.

She had smelled the smoke of the Shadows in that stairwell, and she knew they were there for her. Leo had just gotten in their way.

Nora swallowed. "Odelle, can we...talk sometime? Not tonight —but soon?"

"Of course. I'm free on Thursday. Want to come over for dinner? I'll make borscht."

Nora nodded silently into Odelle's shoulder. Thad was right; she could no longer carry this burden alone. Odelle would help her.

18

*T*HE GROUP AROUND THE TABLE HAD BEEN ARGUING IN CIRCLES FOR *hours. Right now, Seraphina was talking again. One hand rested on the gentle swell of her pregnant belly under her green peplos as she said, "Marching out and meeting the Shadow would be playing right into its clutches. We are supposed to be promoting peace, not war!"*

Xander propped his elbows on the table and buried his face in his hands. They had been down this road before and were getting nowhere. Half of the people around the table were arguing for marching against the Shadow, forcing it out into the open, while the other half were trying to convince them to take a more conservative approach. They had been at a stalemate for weeks, and the situation had only become more dire.

As frustrated as he was, it was nothing compared to the agitation of his wife, sitting to his right. Her fists clenched under her folded arms, and a muscle twitched in her jaw. Xander reached out and placed his hand on her arm, rubbing his thumb in small circles. The tips of his fingers just brushed the tattoo encircling her bicep, and he felt like it had been months instead of years since they had received the tattoos that marked them as official members of the Eteria.

As Xander's fingers traced the shape of the spear that circled her arm, Aediene glanced over at him, and her eyes softened as she met his. She uncrossed her arms, and her hand found his knee underneath the table to give it a squeeze.

As the woman finished her familiar speech, Aediene took the opportunity to cut in. "I know you aren't comfortable with open war, Seraphina, but what exactly is your plan? To hide in the Sanctuary while we are slowly picked off, until there are not enough people left to fight even if we wanted to?" Aediene's tone was reasonable, but Xander could sense the effort it took to keep her from shouting given the death grip she had on his knee.

Aedine turned towards the head of the table, where the Commander sat, wearing her usual blindingly white peplos.

"We've been arguing long enough," Aediene implored. "Let's put this to a vote, Commander, and decide whether we are going to fight once and for all."

The Commander steepled her fingers and rested her sharp chin on them as she considered. Her eagle like gaze was fixed firmly on Aediene, and although it was usually enough to make people flinch, his wife didn't even blink.

"Very well," said the Commander brusquely. "This conversation has ceased to be productive. We will vote, starting with you, Aediene. Yea for meeting the Shadow in battle, Nay for continuing with our defensive strategy."

"Yea," answered Aediene. The vote moved around the table, away from Xander. His wife's vote was followed by two "nays". Next to vote was the soft spoken Smith, Antony, who brought the votes to an even two for each side by voting "yea", surprising everybody. Well, everybody except for Aediene, who offered the man a knowing nod across the table. Xander should have guessed that his wife would have calculated exactly how this vote was going to go before suggesting it. The next two votes were Seraphina and her husband, Demetrius, who both unsurprisingly voted "nay." The Commander added her vote of "yea," before turning to the man next to her for his vote.

Xander looked at his best friend, who was sitting to his left, as he made his vote. Thad fiddled with his golden arm bands as he stole a quick glance over at Xander.

"Yea."

Xander let out a huff as he tallied the votes in his head. The votes were tied with four on each side. His gut clenched, knowing that it was his turn to cast the final vote and break the tie. He had been so sure of which way he was going to vote, but as he drew in a breath to give his answer, he paused. The next word he uttered could decide the future of every member of the Eteria. He would have to live with the death and destruction that could result from his answer. He felt as if he held the threads of fate in his hands and somebody had just given him the scissors.

In the pregnant silence, Aediene squeezed his knee, and he looked to his right to meet her eyes. Instead of finding frustration or impatience at his hesitation, he found that they were full of trust. He remembered her words from a night years ago, telling him that she would stand with him through the darkest night. Xander realized in that moment that he would have her undying support, even if he voted against her.

Using the strength he found in his wife's gaze, Xander opened his mouth again and voted, "Yea."

There was another long moment of silence, interrupted by a violent scraping noise. Xander broke eye contact with Aediene in time to see Seraphina push herself up from the table with murder in her expression. She looked as if she were about to curse their ancestors, but instead, she turned away in a swirl of green and stormed off. Demetrius stood up with an apologetic glance to the table before hurrying after his wife.

The seven remaining members of the council finished the meeting quickly. The leaders of the four orders of the Eteria would need to make preparations within the groups before reconvening to organize for battle. The end of the discussion was somber, a sharp contrast to the contentious discussion of earlier.

When they left the meeting room, Aediene's fingers laced between his, the rough calloses on the pads of her fingers familiar against the back of his hand. She gave him a gentle tug and whispered, "Come on, I have something to show you."

He followed her in silence, unable to focus on anything other than the gravity of what had just happened. After a few minutes, he found them back at the room he and Aediene had shared since getting married. Tugging him through the door and shutting it behind her, she directed him to sit on the foot of the bed. He sank down on the soft mattress and gave her a questioning look. Her only response was to say, "Close your eyes and hold out your hands."

He did as she asked and listened to the faint noise of the wardrobe opening and her rummaging around inside. A few moments later, the air stirred as she returned to stand in front of him, and he sensed the warmth of her presence even from a foot away. His hands dipped as something smooth and surprisingly heavy pressed into his palms.

Xander opened his eyes to find a sword sheathed in a simple leather scabbard. He glanced up at Aediene, who looked at him expectantly, not saying a word. He grasped the sword by the hilt and unsheathed it in a single, swift motion, revealing two feet of glittering bronze. Xander's eyes widened as he took in the lethal edges of the leaf-shaped blade. As he twisted and turned the weapon, letting the curved edges scatter the dim candlelight around the room, his eyes caught on an engraving on the flat of the blade. He held it up closer to his face and read the words that were written there with a smile.

Through the darkest night.

"I had Antony make it for you a few weeks ago. You gave me my spear as a wedding present. I thought it was about time that you had a sword to match your skill," Aediene explained.

Xander had never had an issue with using the standard issue sword of the Defenders, and he had never felt uncomfortable casting wards or charging into battle with one. Still, as he gripped the hilt of this new weapon, a sense of surety settled over him that he had never experienced with any other weapon.

"Antony certainly has a gift," he murmured, running his fingers along the words set into the blade.

"No matter what happens on the battlefield, I want you to have a

reminder that I'll be with you," Aediene said, her eyes following the path
of his fingers across the blade.

Xander turned and placed the sword on the midnight blue sheets next
to him before reaching out to his wife, pulling her forward until she came
to sit on his lap. He cupped her serious face in his hands and leaned
forward to press his forehead to hers.

"Whatever lies ahead, loving you is what has given me the strength
to face it without fear."

Aediene brought a hand up to brush his curls away from his face. "No
matter what you chose to do in that meeting, I would have followed you.
I can think of nobody I would rather trust with my fate."

Xander moved his hands from her face to wrap his arms around her
waist and pull her as close to his body as he could manage, taking comfort
in the fact that, for now, she was safe and whole in his arms. He tucked
her head under his chin and murmured into her hair. "Then let's hope, for
all of our sakes, that I prove to be worthy of that trust."

19

W<small>HEN</small> N<small>ORA</small> <small>STEPPED THROUGH THE PORTAL EARLY ON</small> T<small>UESDAY</small> afternoon and out into the sunshine on the Sanctuary lawn, she sighed in relief and unzipped her leather jacket. The pleasant crispness of early fall had given way to actual cold that Nora would be inclined to call "wintry" if she didn't know much worse weather was around the corner.

She was there to go over the final plan for that night's trap at the museum with Adam and Thad. Nora had ducked out of work early, complaining that she wasn't feeling well. She hadn't had to do much to convince her coworkers of her apparent illness; she had been pale and distracted for days. Very little was getting done in the office right now anyways, with everybody still reeling from the shock of losing Leo. He wasn't well liked among most of the workers, but historians weren't accustomed to losing men on the job, and the days seemed to drag on in shocked silence.

Now that the time to execute her own self-sacrificial plot was finally here, she felt something halfway between relief and debilitating stomach cramps.

She made her way to the courtyard with the long tables and entered to find that, not only were Thad and Adam seated there, but they were joined by Ezra, Antony, and Drew. It was still odd to see Adam in a tweed jacket and Drew in a flannel among a group of men wearing brightly colored chitons. Nora wondered how many years it would take her to find such a sight ordinary as she approached the table and slid herself onto an empty stool between Adam and Drew.

Adam offered her a gentle smile as she sat, although she could still sense how nervous he was from the way he fidgeted with a ring he was wearing on his right hand. What little conversation there had been at the table seemed to die as she settled in, and Nora attempted to break the suffocating silence. "I didn't expect to see you here Drew."

He shrugged one broad shoulder, but his eyes betrayed his seriousness.

"Thad filled me in on what you were planning, and I couldn't stand to just wait at home by myself wondering if you were all right. Besides, it's never done any harm to have a real emergency medicine doctor at the ready in a dangerous situation."

"I told you, there's already a doctor at the ready," Thad interjected, but his words were gentle.

"Yes, but this doctor has real suture kits in his bag, not just fancy herbs," Drew countered.

Adam butted in before a lengthy discussion about healthcare practices could break out. "I think the point here is to go over the plan so nobody ends up needing any healing. If we could get to business now..."

With everybody's attention on him, Adam began to outline how they would spring the trap. Nora was shocked to hear that other Eteria members who resided in the Sanctuary would be joining them for the ambush.

Noticing her surprise, Thad leaned around Drew to murmur to her. "Just because some of them are shy of strangers and keep out of your way when you're here doesn't mean they don't want to help."

A wave a gratitude washed over Nora as she returned her attention to what Adam was saying. She began to fidget when Adam started to detail how she wouldn't be able to carry any weapons into the museum to not tip the agent off to their plans. Her sleek black manicure from the weekend before had been halfway picked off by the time it became apparent she was going to be alone and minimally armed with the Shadow for a few minutes as the attack party rushed in.

"Your best bet is to get the agent talking," Thad piped up once Adam got to this part of the plan. "The evil ones are always so mouthy. It's how they spread their lies and fear."

Nora wrinkled her nose at him. "Really? I thought the bad guy speech was just an action movie trope."

"It's a trope for a reason," Adam responded. "Getting them talking is a good strategy for keeping them distracted while we get there."

Adam turned back to Ezra and Antony to start interrogating them on their plans for the attack party, but Nora was too distracted to follow any of the conversation.

While the others were occupied, Drew leaned in to whisper in her ear. "You know you don't have to do this, right?"

"You know I'm going to do it anyways, right?"

She felt his slight huff of breath that passed for an unamused laugh against her hair. "I know how stubborn you can be, so yes, I do know that." He paused for a second before adding, "I'll go with you if you want."

Nora started, having not considered that she might have the option to not be completely alone with the enemy. She tried to envision what it might be like to have company at the museum, but instead, the vision of Leo lying at the bottom of the stairs in a pool of his own blood came to mind.

"I don't want to take the chance that it would give the plan away, or that you would get hurt. Safer to endanger one person instead of two. Besides, it makes me feel better to know you'll be there after to help take care of anybody who is injured."

Drew nodded his understanding. "As long as you're sure."

By this point, Antony and Ezra were discussing weapons between the two of them and Adam seemed to be done with his part. He turned to Nora before standing and inclining his head to indicate she should do the same.

"Come with me and we'll see if we can get you geared up a bit more."

Nora rose from her seat and followed him from the courtyard, trying not to let her hands fuss too much as they strode down the hallway. Normally not at a loss for what to say to each other, they were both quiet, their footsteps echoing harshly in the vast and empty hallways.

They turned through a doorway and Nora found that they had not come to the armory but were instead in Adam's bedroom. Adam ushered her inside and strode over to his kettle in the corner.

"How about some tea to calm our nerves? English breakfast, right?" he asked, pulling out some teacups.

"All right," Nora agreed. "Although I think a weapon in my hands right now would do more to calm my nerves than tea."

Adam snorted. "Don't worry. We're getting there. But I might need a nice cup of tea to keep my sanity right now."

As the water heated, he made his way over to the numerous shelves lining his walls and perused them until he came to the short bronze dagger she had noticed the last time she'd been in his room. He plucked it off its stand and brought it to her, offering it to her hilt first.

She plucked it from his fingers and examined the finely crafted blade.

"It's not a spear, for sure," Adam said as he watched her. "But it's better than nothing, and if you can take on a Shadow with tweezers and a coffee pot, I think you'll make do."

"I thought it was decorative," Nora commented as she touched her finger lightly to the edge and was rewarded with a striking pain in her finger. She hissed and shoved the finger into her mouth to suck off the few drops of blood that had gathered there.

Adam chuckled. "It's pretty, but that doesn't mean you can't stab people with it. Besides, this one's special. It's good luck."

Nora raised her eyebrows at him, index finger still in her mouth, but he didn't elaborate. Instead, he turned to the trunk at the foot of his bed. He rifled through it for a moment before surfacing with a small sheathe that he handed to her.

"Here, that should keep you from disemboweling yourself with that when you tuck it inside your jacket."

Nora took it from him, slipped the dagger into it, and slid it into the inner pocket of her jacket as he'd instructed. As she worked, Adam brought over their finished cups of tea and passed her one, which she lifted to her lips to let the steam wash over her face.

"Nora, I need to warn you of something."

Nora looked up to find Adam watching her, his tea forgotten in his hands.

"Something beyond the fact that I'm being used as live bait for evil incarnate?" Nora winced as her attempt at a joke fell flat.

"This is serious, Nora." Adam's eyes left no room for argument. "I know you are going to have to get the agent talking to keep him distracted, but you can't listen to what he says."

"What?" Nora drew back. "Won't that make it difficult to keep them talking?"

"You may have to listen to them, but you have to promise me you won't believe anything they say. The Shadow grows by instilling fear and doubt in their enemies, which is why they love to talk so much. They use their words to feel out weaknesses and turn allies against each other. You can get them talking, but you can't let them poison you. Don't let your guard down, not even for a second."

Nora gulped. The hairs on her body stood on end as she remembered what Adam had told her about what the Shadows could do to a person's mind. Then Antony's voice came to her, reminding her that love and hope could help keep the Shadow at bay. Glancing around the collections on Adam's shelves, she took in all the beauty that was at stake here at the Sanctuary. She looked back at Adam to find his eyes searching her face with a seriousness that bordered on desperation.

"Ok, I can do that." Nora was pleased by how steady her voice came out.

Adam let out a breath and some of the tension drained from his shoulders at her promise. He was still visibly nervous, though, and Nora's eyes landed on his fingers, fidgeting on the handle of his teacup.

"I do have something else to give you while we're here," Adam continued. "I was planning on giving it to you the other night at the gala, actually, but then... Well, that didn't really turn out to be the type of evening either of us planned on."

Adam picked her teacup out of her hand and turned to the trunk behind him to set them down. Nora wondered where on her person she might be able to hide another weapon with her one pocket already occupied by the dagger, but when Adam turned back around, his hands were empty.

"Where is it?" Nora inquired, but Adam didn't answer, instead stepping towards her until their toes were almost touching. He brought one hand to rest gently on her arm as the other came up to cradle her cheek. As he leaned in, Nora had the split-second thought that this was a very different sort of a gift than a weapon, then his lips pressed against hers.

Nora thought she might be nervous about kissing Adam for the first time, but the experience was not what she'd expected at all. She might have been more prepared for a searing kiss like she had seen in dramatic movies before the leads leapt into a certain-death situation, considering what Nora was about to do. Adam, however, managed to surprise her.

He kissed her gently, savoring her warmth and closeness as if this were all he ever wanted. It felt like warm honey filled Nora's veins as her hands drifted up to grip the lapels of his jacket, and she began to kiss him back in earnest, causing him to sigh into her mouth.

Adam's hands grazed her body, leaving sparks in their wake as they came to weave into her hair. He tipped her head back, opening her up to his mouth for further exploration, and Nora went willingly. The honey in Nora's veins pooled in her belly and she found herself pressing against Adam's body, wanting to feel more, to mold herself to the shape of him.

It was over far before Nora would have liked it to be, but when Adam pulled away, he left his hand cradling her face. She might have been proud of the distinctly dazed expression on his face if she hadn't been sure she looked equally stricken.

"I hope that was all right." Adam's musical voice came out breathier than usual. "I just had you to myself for a second and well...I'm not exactly sure what the protocol for first kisses is anymore."

His earnestness earned a soft chuckle from Nora. "Neither do I." She let go of his lapels and tried to smooth out where her fists had rumpled them. "It's been a while since my last first kiss."

Adam snorted as he finally dropped his hand from her face, his other hand on her arm brushing down to intertwine with her own. "Not as long as it's been since mine."

"Really? How long has it been?" Nora knew it was rude to ask, but after being shocked by the fact he had once been married, she realized she knew very little about his romantic history.

Adam cleared his throat and shifted his weight. "Let's just say it's definitely been longer than you've been alive."

Nora's mouth fell open, but before she could even draw breath to launch into her next line of questioning, Adam jumped in and skillfully changed the subject.

"Isn't there a group of people waiting on us to join them so we can set out to vanquish evil or some such thing?"

Unfortunately, he was right. Nora closed her mouth and tucked away this tidbit of information about him for later examination as she followed him out his bedroom door, their fingers still intertwined.

As Nora let herself into the museum, the rattling of the door sounded deafening in the empty vastness of the space beyond. The one security guard had recognized her from her many nights working late in the past and waved her on with a smile as she told him she had forgotten her phone in the office. She hoped he wouldn't come check on her when the Shadows were present as she stuck a rubber stopper under the door, leaving it cracked open so the attack team could enter after her.

They were currently stationed in Soldier Field about a third of a mile away, hoping it would be far enough for them to not be noticed by the Shadow but close enough to respond quickly when Nora called Adam using the cell phone that was already in her hand.

Nora recalled the image of them gathered there, ready to leap into action at a moment's notice, to calm her nerves and remind herself that she was not really alone. Ezra, Antony, Thad, and Adam were all there, as well as a half dozen other members of the Eteria that she had been briefly introduced to but was too nervous to remember the names of. She had been surprised that so many strangers had agreed to join her harebrained mission, but they had all smiled at her warmly as if they were pleased she was there.

The entire crew had assembled under the tall pillars of the stadium, looking like they felt extremely uncomfortable in the black leather jackets and jeans Thad had acquired for them, instead of being clad in their traditional armor. The effect of their modern clothes was somewhat ruined by the fact they were all armed to the teeth with spears and swords, making the group look more like a biker gang who enjoyed going to Renaissance festivals than an actual fighting force. Drew had also seemed rather amused by the picture they painted but had managed to keep a straight face, given the gravity of the situation.

Drew had wrapped her in a bone-crushing hug when she parted ways with them, offering again to come with her if she had changed her mind, to which she shook her head. She warmed when Antony, Thad, and Adam had all hugged her before she left too, and even Ezra gave her an affectionate pat on the head that sent her off into the night feeling braver than she had before.

Now that she was alone in the museum, though, most of that bravery had dissipated into the thick darkness surrounding her. She used the light of her cell phone, already opened to the call screen with Adam's number typed in, to illuminate her path up the side stairs to the arms exhibit. As a group, they had decided that the Shadow was most likely to respond if she stood close to the powerful artifacts.

Nora wove her way through the darkened exhibit, moving slowly so she wouldn't run into any displays in the blackness. The silence was only broken by her footsteps. It was as if the suits of armor she passed were watching her, haunted by ghosts of dead warriors waiting to watch her plunged into her own battle.

Nora shook the image from her head. Instead, she thought about joyful things that would bolster her when the Shadow tried to poison her with its words, like Adam had warned her it would. She pictured the beautiful sunlit library at the Sanctuary and Drew crushing her to his chest in one of his signature hugs. She pictured Adam's face after he kissed her.

She stepped up to the glass case to look down on the weapons of Adam and his late wife. The light from her cell phone was dim enough to cause her to squint to make out the engravings. She remembered then that she hadn't had the chance to ask him what the phrase meant to him. Nora added it to the long list of things that she would have to ask at some point.

A ripple of heat danced across the back of her neck. She

whipped around, frantically searching the darkness in front of her for the glowing eyes of a Shadow creature or movement that might belong to the agent. Her thumb hovered above the call button on her phone and her other hand shot into the inner pocket of her jacket to grip the hilt of the dagger concealed there. Seeing nothing, Nora attempted to calm her breathing so she wouldn't call Adam too soon and alert the Shadow to their plan.

After several tense moments with no further signs of company, Nora let the hand gripping the dagger hilt slide out of her jacket pocket. As soon as her hand fell back to her side, Nora felt a sharp tug at her ponytail, forceful enough to pull her backwards and cause a shriek of surprise and pain to tear from her throat. Her phone slipped from her grasp as she fell, right before her head cracked against the glass of the display case behind her and she lost all awareness.

20

NORA WAS DISAPPOINTED TO FIND THAT COMING TO AFTER BEING knocked unconscious did not get any less unpleasant the more you did it. In fact, this time was definitely worse than waking up in a hospital bed after her prior encounter with the Shadows. This was mostly because she was facedown on hard, cold concrete. As she stirred, the rough pavement under her scraped against her cheek, and she groaned as her body protested her positioning on such an unforgiving surface.

The awareness of her discomfort was followed swiftly by memories of what had happened prior to her blow to the head. Remembering the trap she was supposed to be setting, she attempted to scrabble into a more dignified position, only to find that she was no longer in the museum at all. Instead, she appeared to be in a concrete tunnel, and she had the distinct impression that she was underground. It was a small space with thick pillars on one side, and she could hear traffic on the other side. She must have somehow gotten to Lower Wacker, she thought in confusion before muttering some creative expletives she had borrowed from Adam under her breath.

"Such a filthy mouth for somebody who serves the Light."

Nora spun around on the ground to locate the source of the voice. Behind her, the outline of a man stood in the gloomy arch leading out of the space.

"Who are you?" The question was out of her mouth before she could think. She grimaced, knowing the man's identity was relatively clear from his comment and the circumstances leading up to her awakening.

"I'm exactly who you expected to fall into your trap, although it was really my trap all along."

"What second rate heist movie did you steal that line from?" Nora snapped, although she had to admit that she was slightly off balance.

"Oh, don't be bitter that I knew you would be stupid enough to try a plan like this. I knew all you would need was a little push in the right direction, and the apparent death of poor unfortunate Leo did the trick." The man's voice was somehow familiar sounding, but it was unnaturally modulated, sounding almost like each word was too well enunciated for somebody who spoke the language on a regular basis. The entire effect served to make Nora even more anxious than she already was.

"If this is your trap, then why am I not restrained?" Nora shot back, only to have to stop herself from slapping her hand to her face. There was apparently no end to her ill-advised questions.

The shadowy silhouette of the man shrugged one shoulder in a soundless motion.

"Because it's impolite to tie up your guests and not very conducive to good conversation."

She got to her feet as she responded, extremely uncomfortable being on the ground as her captor loomed above her, even if he was keeping his distance for now.

"Good conversation?" Nora prompted, trying to buy herself time.

"Of course. That's why I brought you here. So we could chat without being interrupted by a group of idiots with spears."

Nora remembered Adam's words of warning. She tried to surreptitiously pat her jacket to see if the dagger he had given her was still hidden in her inner pocket. Apparently, her movement was not as subtle as she hoped it would be.

"I'm hurt that you would instantly reach for your weapon when I've shown no intention to harm you. I assure you, though, I am no petty thief. I did not take your sentimental keepsake from you."

As the man spoke, he leaned sideways to prop against the wall to his left, leaving a gap on his other side. Nora made the split-second decision that this was her moment, hoping that if the decision was rash enough to surprise her that it would be unexpected enough to catch her captor off guard. As she dashed towards the gap to the man's side, she lowered her front shoulder as Ezra had taught her, hoping to bowl the man over with the force from her running start should he attempt to step into her path. The man didn't get in the way at all, though, instead turning sideways as if to let her pass. Just as she came level with him, his arm shot out with unnatural speed and grabbed her wrist in a vice grip, yanking her shoulder back and stopping her in her tracks.

Nora screeched in his grasp, trying to stay on her feet instead of collapsing to her knees in pain. His hand was scorching hot, tight, and burned into her skin. Thankfully, he threw her backwards almost immediately, releasing his hold on her as she tripped and fell onto her back where she'd started.

"That is no way to treat somebody who has waited so long to make your acquaintance," the man said, stepping forward so now he did loom over her where she was sprawled on the ground. As he came closer, the scant light from the lamps illuminating the underground street filtering through the pillars finally revealed his face to her. The hairs on the back of her neck prickled at the sight.

It was Leo, but somehow, not Leo at all. His skin was too smooth, and his eyes were a piercing blue where Leo's had always been dull. Leo's face looked as if somebody had read a description of what he looked like and had built it to those exact specifications with no thought for realism. Everything about the man was so perfectly human shaped that she could tell instantly that he could not possibly be one at all. This was an agent of the Shadow.

"I forgot to mention earlier," the agent said as he picked an invisible piece of lint off his immaculate suit. "I didn't tie you up because I don't need to. "

"You're— you're dead, though..."

He tilted his head. "It's true that Leo died, but I'm not really Leo. I have become more than human. I simply killed the humanity that was left, and now my...transformation is complete."

"Transformation?"

Leo held up one too-perfectly manicured hand and examined it. "As you can tell, I'm no longer really the Leo you knew. His jealousy and self-loathing were easy to twist. Manipulating him into poisoning you was child's play. Leo is now nothing more than a ball of his most negative emotions. It fuels me, and I simply wear him as a skin."

The agent paused as Nora gagged in horror.

"You know," he continued as if he were commenting on the weather, "it's so much more fun when I wear the skin of a close friend instead of an enemy. Betrayal is so much sweeter when it comes from somebody we care about. But alas, I was in a hurry, and it is much harder to corrupt those who don't already harbor some amount of hatred. So, I will have to wear the face of your rival while we have our little chat."

"What do you want to talk about?" Nora asked. If she could stall him for long enough, maybe the attack team could still track her here.

"Whatever you want to know."

"Whatever I want to know?" The agent's answer caught her by surprise. In her mind, it was going to be easy to get him to start grandstanding like a stereotypical movie villain, then she would just have to avoid being poisoned by his propaganda while she waited for her friends.

"Of course, as the guest, you get to dictate the conversation." The agent's reply was casual as he leaned up against a pillar once more in a movement so practiced that Nora would have laughed if she weren't somehow horrified by the gesture.

"Why did you fake your own death?"

"Oh, that stunt at the gala? I just knew that you would jump to sacrifice yourself once it was clear that people were going to die if you didn't do something, and it was fun to watch you be so self-sacrificial for somebody you didn't even like. So terribly in character. I'd have to be an idiot to not suspect a move like that from you, Nora."

"You know me?"

"Of course I know you." The agent sounded as if he was explaining something very simple to a small child. "How could I not know you? I've been after you for a long time."

Nora worked to put the puzzle together in her mind. "Right, since the Shadow poisoned me, you've been drawn to me."

The agent let out a sharp bark of laughter that made Nora physically recoil.

"Oh, that's the tale they fed you, is it? I'll give them points for creativity."

"Why else would you attack me?" Nora started to ask before catching herself. "They aren't lying to me. You're just trying to turn me against them."

"Suit yourself." The agent began inspecting his unnervingly uniform fingernails as he asked, "Tell me, how did they convince you to let them train you as a Warrior? It seems like a lot of work for you to volunteer for."

"It was practical. I could gain important historical knowledge, and if I learned to defend myself, I wouldn't have to have a guard follow me around forever."

"They weren't completely wrong. You do need to be able to defend yourself." The agent tilted his head thoughtfully. "Although, scaring you into thinking you need to become a weapon for them is rich, considering how they preach to fight against fear."

"They aren't using me as a weapon, they are teaching me to defend myself so I can be safe from the likes of you," Nora spat back.

"Oh, you're right." The agent shot her a pitying look. "They aren't using you as a weapon, they are using you as bait."

Nora spluttered in indignation at how he was turning her every argument against her. "I was not used as bait. I volunteered because I care about them."

"Let me guess... You think they care about you too?" The agent's perfect face contorted itself into some semblance of sympathy.

Nora ground her heels in stubbornly. "I know they care about me."

"Adam gives you one little kiss and you've convinced yourself that he has feelings for you. Funny that he's known you for months, but it wasn't until he was sending you to your death that he decided to really show his interest. If it had been the desperate kiss of not wanting to lose you, you would have expected him to be a bit more passionate about it, don't you think?"

Nora frowned. "He said he meant to kiss me at the gala, but he ended up having to leave. And he was being a gentleman about it."

"Oh right, he was going to kiss you at the gala, but he ran off to plan how to best send you into danger as soon as you gave him what he wanted by volunteering. And as for it being so long since his last kiss, I wonder why that is? He's been around for thousands of years, and he's only had the one wife. He's an attractive and smart man. Surely, it's not for lack of opportunity, so it must be due to lack of desire. You can't really think that you are enough to inspire him to end his self-chosen dry spell? In the thousands of years he's walked the earth, he has to have seen the most beautiful and most intelligent women the world has to offer, and you are nothing in comparison."

The agent was really picking up steam now, and Nora could

only shake her head and splutter. "How would you know all of this? It's not true."

"Oh, but you know it's true—that's how I know it all." The agent cracked a smile now. "I can read the doubts right out of your head. I'm just telling you the very things you are afraid to admit in your conscious mind. You aren't special enough to interest an immortal sorcerer who has seen the world; he's just using you. Why do you think he even talked to you in the first place? Coincidence isn't real. It's because you had something he wanted."

Nora grabbed on to that thought, knowing she could refute it. "You're wrong. He didn't want the weapons at all. I asked him if he wanted them back and he told me I could keep them, that he liked them in the museum."

The agent's smile got wider, revealing stark white canines that were too long to fit with the rest of his teeth.

"Oh, it's not the weapons he wanted from you. It's your abilities. It's been hundreds of years since the Eteria has found somebody capable of wielding the Light, but they found you. They tracked you down and lied to you so they could mold you into the perfect weapon to fight for them without you even knowing it. And they're so set on lying to you about the fact that they know of your abilities that they didn't even teach you to use them before sending you to face your foe."

Nora's heart hammered in her chest. By now, the agent was looming over her so intently that he eclipsed the entirety of her vision.

"But... I can't. I can't use the Light. That's totally impossible. People haven't been born with a connection to the Light since the Defeat."

"Then why can I feel the Light within you? If it wasn't burning inside you, you wouldn't have been able to survive my touch at all. And I guarantee you that your friends at the Eteria can feel it too." He spat out the word *friends* as if it were a vile curse. "They want you for the same reason I do; I'm just being honest about it. It's because your ability makes you powerful. Why else would a society that has kept themselves secluded for millenia so willingly accept you into their fold? Adam may have made you think he was interested, but after years of putting on different faces, he is a master of manipulation. He knows that your affections were the key to getting you to stick around."

Nora's head spun so fast her vision nearly blurred. Adam wouldn't use her like that, would he? He was so earnest—or at least he seemed to be, but after thousands of years of lying about his identity, he could probably act however he wanted. She struggled to hang on to her convictions.

"Adam told me you would try to poison me against my friends. He told me not to listen to you," she said, her voice coming out weaker than before.

"Hmm I wonder why he would have told you that? Maybe so you wouldn't listen to me since he knew I would try to tell you the truth." The agent's voice had taken on a distinctly gloating tone, knowing that he had finally backed Nora into a corner with his argument.

She could barely see or think straight, and she struggled to hold on to the memory of the things that had led her here. She remembered the Sanctuary, Thad's laughter, Adam's dancing, but it was all tainted now that she didn't know if any of it was what it seemed.

She did know one thing, though. Even if her friends were using her, the agent in front of her was using her too.

She clung to this thought as she hunched in on herself and let a sob rack through her, letting the agent think he had broken her spirit. As she did, she used her bent posture to hide the motion of her hand as she reached into her jacket pocket and eased the knife out of its sheath.

Distracted by his apparent victory, the agent continued triumphantly.

"See, now you know who the true enemy is. Don't let them use you. Show them that you are the master of your own destiny. Use your power to fight back."

Nora adjusted the knife in her grip and said, "You're right. I won't ever let myself be used again."

At that moment, she straightened up and flung the knife out in front of her as hard as she could. Luckily for her, the agent had come very close to her during his speech, and her throw managed to hit him squarely in the face.

The agent let out a scream that was decidedly no longer human as it began to claw at its face where the dagger had sunk in. Where Nora had expected there to be blood, though, the face that had once belonged to Leo begun to simply peel away to reveal a mass of twisting darkness underneath.

Nora shot to her feet as the last of the human visage fell away to reveal a creature of pure blackness. It looked like the Shadows she had encountered at the museum, except it was much larger and denser. The heat coming off it in rolling waves was enough to make her gag.

The Shadow continued to convulse around the knife imbedded where a face should be. Taking advantage of its distraction, Nora pulled one knee into her chest before straightening her leg out with all her might and delivering a solid kick that would make Ezra proud.

The bottom of her boot melted instantly with the contact, but the creature fell back. She didn't hesitate. She dashed around its heaving form and through the opening behind it into the tunneled road beyond. She ran without direction, dodging cars, her only thought to put distance between herself and the creature behind her. As a car honked at her, she caught sight of a ramp leading back up to street level and dashed towards it.

She emerged into the night air on Michigan Avenue. The melted sole of Nora's boot cooled in the November air and stuck to the sidewalk, causing her to trip and sprawl across the pavement.

She tried to get to her feet to continue her escape, but the adrenaline that had fueled her this far rapidly faded from her bloodstream. She only made it a few stumbling steps before tripping and collapsing to her knees once more.

People were beginning to stare and mutter, but Nora didn't care. This was Chicago, and they had probably seen far stranger things on the streets here. She could barely hear the voices around her over the rushing of blood in her ears. The sidewalk in front of her was starting to blur.

Now that she had gotten away, the Agent's words were coming back to her. Used. Manipulated. She knew he was trying to turn her against her friends, but she couldn't get his mocking tone out of her head.

Her thoughts were interrupted by the voices around her erupting into shouts, and a herd of footsteps thundered towards her.

"Nora! Nora, what happened?" Adam's voice came from nearby to her right, and a hand landed on her shoulder.

"Don't touch me," she spat, jerking away involuntarily.

"Nora, are you hurt? Where is it?" Adam sounded concerned, and Nora lurched away and to her feet before he could touch her again.

She winced as her weight came down on her foot, realizing only now that the adrenaline had worn off that the bottom of her foot was scorched. A hand reached out to steady her, but she pulled away again.

She was surrounded by a sea of concerned faces. Instead of feeling comforted by the faces of Antony, Thad, and Ezra, though, she grew angrier.

"I'm fine, no thanks to you guys. And I don't know where he is anymore," Nora spat with vehemence. A small part of her brain was shouting at her that these were her friends, that they would keep her safe. That part was taking a back seat to the fear and rage she had been shoving down as it all washed over her in an uncontrollable wave.

"Nora, please." Adam's voice was low and soothing to her right. She turned her head to look at him. His hair was wild, as if he had just run a very long distance, and his eyes widened as they darted over her harried appearance. "Please, just tell us what happened. We need to know so we can help you."

She also spotted Drew, standing next to Adam, which made her soften a little. At least she had one friend here.

"I need you to tell me something first," said Nora, her voice trembling but still full of anger.

"Of course," Adam said, his face wearing the earnest look that convinced her he cared about her in the first place.

"Have you been lying to me this whole time?"

There was a long stillness after Nora asked the question. In her mind, Adam was about to assure her that no, he hadn't been lying, then he would swoop in with all her friends and make everything better. Instead, Adam tensed, then his shoulders caved in as if he had just had the wind knocked out of him.

"Only because I had to," Adam said, his face crumpling. "I know it doesn't make anything better, but it was killing me not to tell you the truth."

Nora began to sway where she stood. Before she could fall, Drew's hands shot out to catch her shoulders. She was so numb that she barely felt him wrap her arm around her so he could support more of her weight.

"If you give me a chance, I can explain everything," Adam pleaded. He looked devastated but it didn't matter. He had looked trustworthy before and that had turned out to be a façade as well.

"I want to go home," was Nora's only response. She dropped her eyes to the pavement at her feet, but Adam's desperate eyes still bore into her.

Thad's voice came from somewhere in the group. "You should at least let us take you to the Sanctuary to make sure you're all right."

"I want to go home," Nora repeated more forcefully.

"I can take care of any injuries at her apartment," Drew interjected. He tightened his grasp on her as Nora began to shake. She wasn't sure if it was from the cold or the shock, but she was glad for his solid presence either way.

"What about a debriefing? We don't even know what happened down there," argued a voice Nora didn't recognize.

"For goodness's sake, can't you see that she's in shock!" Drew erupted next to her, "There's time for that later. Right now, she just needs to rest and feel safe."

"Okay." Adam was the one who responded, and Nora's head snapped up. "She can go home if she needs to." He sounded so defeated that Nora almost felt guilty, but not enough to stop her from looking back down at her feet without responding.

There was a flurry of activity that Nora didn't pay attention to, simply leaning into Drew's side and trying not to collapse. Nora was nudged forward and ushered into a cab that somebody had hailed before Drew slid in beside her. She turned and buried her face in the warm flannel of his shoulder, and it wasn't until she noticed the fabric was wet that she realized she was crying.

Drew rolled down the window and leaned out to ask somebody, "What about a guard for tonight? Will she be safe?"

Adam's sad voice drifted in through the window.

"I don't think the Shadow will come after her. Something tells me the agent got everything he wanted from her tonight."

21

"HEADS UP!" XANDER SHOUTED, EVEN AS HE RAISED HIS ARMS TO SHIELD his face from the impact of another fireball. It bounced off the ward he had created before rolling a few yards, making another black scar in the already charred earth. He winced as it hit, the bombardment of his ward jarring his bones. It was only a matter of time before the magical barrier collapsed under the strain. With no other Defenders around to help him, Xander wasn't sure he would be able to cast another one.

He glanced behind him at the rest of what was, for the moment, protected by his ward, pinned up against a large pile of rubble that blocked their rear. The seven Warriors in the bunch were all huddled together, trying to aid the two injured. Xander spotted Aediene tearing a strip off the bottom of her battle tunic and using it to tie a tourniquet around the arm of a wounded comrade. Demetrius and two of the others were taking turns reaching their spears outside the ward to shoot out shimmering beams of Light, keeping the Shadows at bay. While it kept the mass of darkness from assaulting the barrier directly, the fireballs they were launching were doing enough damage to force Xander to grit his teeth to keep the ward in place.

When Aediene finished her makeshift tourniquet, she stepped up beside Xander. For the moment, she held her helmet under one arm so she could wipe sweat away from her furrowed brow.

"How much longer can we hold out here?" she asked, taking in Xander's pale face and unsteady stance. She reached up to dab a trickle of blood on his cheek from where a stray piece of shrapnel had given him a shallow cut across his brow.

"A few more minutes," he admitted grimly, brushing her hand away. He needed to keep his focus on the situation and not get distracted by his injuries. Xander could practically see Aediene's brain whirring behind her eyes as she took in the reality of their situation.

"We need to get back to the main force then. It's the only way. We're much less effective when we're divided into small groups like this. The Healers there should be able to patch up our injured."

Xander nodded once, not wanting to waste energy on unnecessary words. Her reasoning was sound, but as he looked in the direction of the rest of the Eteria, all he could see was a solid mass of wriggling darkness, the creatures of the Shadow packed together so densely that he could not tell where one ended and the next began.

"You take the injured, offer them as much protection as you can. Demetrius and the others will cut you a path, and I'll protect you from the back." Aediene jammed her helmet back onto her head as she spoke, the bronze cheek and nose guards settling across her face, leaving only her determined eyes exposed. Despite the soot turning the usually crimson plume on the crest of her helmet a dirty charcoal and the blood and grime ground into the whirls of her bronze chest plate, she looked every inch the legendary Warrior as she stood before him.

Aediene turned to the rest of the group and relayed the plan, her sharp voice carrying clearly and evenly over the cacophony of battle surrounding them. The expressions of the Warriors mirrored her own grim features.

She looked back at Xander, hefting her spear.

"On your call, dissolve the ward and we'll make our break for it."

He nodded tightly once more and twisted his sword in his hands a few times, readying himself to use it to cut down the Shadows. Before he moved to release the wards, though, he met his wife's eyes and said quietly enough that only she could hear, "Aediene, I—"

"Whatever it is," she cut him off, "tell me when we make it out the other side." The way she said it made it sound like a promise, and his courage bolstered as he turned back to the ward.

Holding his sword at the ready, he took a deep breath to steady himself before shouting, "Now!"

The instant the ward dropped, the Warriors started running, charging into the wall of Shadows, the creatures falling like stalks of wheat before their arcing weapons. Xander didn't have time to watch for more than a second before he and the injured Warriors plunged into the fray after them and his world narrowed.

Xander's muscles took over and his arm swung without him telling it to. He slashed through tentacle like limbs and stabbed into creatures that attempted to block their path. The only thing keeping him from being reduced to an arm with a sword was the part of his brain listening for his wife's battle cries at his back. He barely heard the inhuman shrieks of each dissolving creature before he had dispatched the next one. The hot air stung his eyes and burned his skin. A metallic stink filled his nose, making him choke when he tried to gasp for breath. None of that mattered, though. All that mattered was the narrowing distance between their small band and the rest of the Eteria. Just fifty more yards and they would be free. Forty yards. Thirty.

Xander was torn from his battle haze by a very human scream. He wrenched his sword from the misshapen torso of a shadow creature and whirled around. Demetrius was frozen in place ahead of him, his eyes glazed, and it took Xander a moment to register the tentacle of blackness protruding from the center of his bronze breastplate. He watched in horror as the Shadow that had impaled Demetrius swept its arm out to the side, throwing the Warrior's limp body carelessly away to be swallowed up by the writhing ocean of darkness.

Xander was jerked back to reality by a sharp jab between his shoulder blades.

"Run!" Ordered Aediene from behind him. When he turned to look in the direction they had been headed, he saw an opening—a break in the darkness leading straight to the glittering ranks of the Eteria. Without wasting another moment, he started sprinting towards the gap. The Warriors ahead of him had reached the edge of the Shadow. His feet pounded the blood-soaked earth, and the burnt air ripped through his aching lungs. With a final surge, he hurtled out of the twisting mass of the enemy and through the gap in the ward the other Defenders had opened for them. The wall of Light fell back into place behind them as they tumbled through.

Bracing the hand not holding his sword on his knee, he struggled to catch his breath. After a moment, he twisted to find his wife, wanting to tell her what she had not let him say before they left their cover on the other side of the battlefield.

What breath he had managed to catch rushed out of him when he looked around to find she was not there. Frantic, his eyes roved over their small party, all heaving and panting behind the safety of the larger ward. A few Defenders and Healers were already rushing over to help them up. She wasn't there.

Xander looked back the way they had come, and a scream ripped its way from his throat. She was still entrenched in the Shadows, about twenty yards from the edge, but the Shadows were driving her farther back every second.

"Aediene!" He barely recognized the voice as his own as he hurled his body against the inside of the ward that now separated him from his wife. She tried to put a large chunk of rubble to her back to give her some protection, but the effort was futile. The Shadows were closing in on her, no longer allowing her to use the full slashing arcs of her spear. He could only make out the singed plumes on the top of her helmet as the Shadows began to engulf her.

Unthinking, he used his sword to slash at the ward. He put his full body weight behind the stroke, releasing an inarticulate scream of desperation. A rift formed in the transparent barrier, and he plunged through it. As he charged forward, Aediene was completely overwhelmed. Even as he hacked his way into the swirling dark, Shadows pressed tight to her body, so dense he could barely make out her form in her armor. He looked on in horror as a Shadow latched on to her face, and a sickening darkness forced its way down her throat, her eyes rolling back in her head. The sound was sucked out of the world as Xander watched Aediene slowly fold in on herself. She doubled over and swayed precariously. Xander was barely aware of the fact that he was still throwing himself against the Shadows, trying to reach her before she hit the ground.

Before he could get there, Xander's world went violently white. He threw a hand up to protect his eyes from the sudden, blinding light. He struggled to locate Aediene where she had fallen on the ground, only to grind to a halt as he located the source of the light. His wife was no longer crumpling to the ground, but upright again. Her feet were hovering several inches off the ground, and Light poured off her. Blinding beams burst from her mouth and eyes. Even her skin burned with a brilliance that hurt to look at. The Shadows that surrounded her skittered back, clawing over one another to retreat from Aediene's luminescent form, shrieking so loudly that Xander felt as if his skull was about to split open. He tried to take advantage of the open space, advancing towards her once again.

Before he could take two steps, Xander found himself forced to his knees as a wave of Light burst forth from Aediene. The surge ripped the air from his lungs and his ears filled with a roar that sounded as if the Gods themselves were screaming. Light rippled forth from Aediene, and everywhere it touched, the Shadows evaporated, leaving nothing but a slight haze in their absence. Xander struggled to stay on his knees as the wave passed over him, desperately keeping his eyes fixed on the dazzling epicenter of the Light, where he could just make out his wife's figure. He could have been there for seconds or minutes, he did not know.

The roaring dissipated as suddenly as it started, the last of the waves bursting from Aediene. The force of it blew her backwards, as if a massive hand had reached out of the sky and thrown her across the field like a ragdoll. She collided with the chunk of rubble she had been trying to use as cover earlier. Even with his ears still ringing from the roaring, Xander heard the sickening crunch from the impact.

Before Aediene hit the ground, Xander surged to his feet and dashed towards her. He skidded to his knees beside her form, his sword dropping forgotten from his grip. His heart stuttered in his chest as he saw that Aediene's eyes were closed, and there was a sizeable dent in the side of her helmet where her head had connected with the rock. Xander couldn't stop his hand from shaking as his fingers searched her throat, desperately seeking a pulse. He leaned in close, repeating his wife's name again and again. Xander prayed to any God who might be listening to let him feel her breath brush across his cheek as he listened for signs of life, but it never came.

Aediene was dead.

22

Nora woke with a stifled gasp, drenched in cold sweat. She shoved down the panic from the acute sensation of being suffocated, discovering that it had been caused by her lying face down on an overly soft pillow. Still, she shuddered in the chill air of her apartment as her dream faded. The images of perfect skin peeling back to reveal the blackness beneath melted into the familiar sight of her cramped bedroom.

At her stirring, Drew sprang up from the window seat where he had been dozing. Nora had offered to let him sleep in the bed, considering that they had shared it nightly less than a year ago, but Drew had insisted he would sit up for a while to make sure she was all right. Although she was loath to admit it, she was glad to have somebody watching over her as she slept.

"Does anything hurt?" Drew asked as he perched himself on the bedside next to her, obviously inspecting her with the keen eye of a physician looking at a patient with a head injury. She could just make out his narrowed eyes as he scrutinized her in the dim light coming through her window, signaling that sunrise was not far off.

Nora shook her head, and Drew moved to her hand. He picked

it up gingerly to check the bandage he had placed on the burn encircling her wrist.

He had tended to her wounds the night before after practically carrying her, numb and incoherent, up the stairs to her apartment on the third floor of a brownstone. She was endlessly grateful that he didn't ask her what had happened and simply let her indicate where her injuries were. Drew's presence was solid and familiar enough to be reassuring, even if she wasn't sure she wanted to be around people right now.

Drew moved to the bandage around her scorched foot to check on it as well, saying, "I'm glad your head feels okay. If you take one more blow to the skull, I may have to force you to go everywhere wearing a football helmet."

Nora smiled at him weakly, somewhat revived after a few hours of sleep, but still not up to full-on laughter.

"What woke you up? Was I snoring?" Drew asked.

Nora finally spoke, her voice a croak from the combination of sleep and the fact that she had barely spoken a word since getting in the cab with Drew last night.

"You know you don't snore. I'm just used to waking up before sunrise so I can get to work early."

Drew swung his legs onto the bed and folded them so he could sit cross-legged, facing her. "You sure that's the only thing that woke you?"

Nora only paused a moment before shaking her head, knowing it was no good to try and lie to Drew.

"Do you want to talk about it?"

"Not particularly," Nora answered, toying with a loose thread in the sleeve of her pajamas. "But I suppose you think I should."

"I think I'm a friend who's here to listen if you decide you want somebody to listen to you." Drew gave her shin a soothing rub. "I also happen to be a doctor who has seen enough patients come in after horribly traumatic experiences to know that it's perfectly valid to not want to talk about it right away."

Nora heaved a sigh, running her hands through her hair, which had become hopelessly tangled from her tossing and turning during the night.

"I do actually think it might be...cathartic to talk about it. I just don't know how to explain how unbalanced the whole thing made me. You're going to think I'm crazy for how I reacted when you found me."

"I already know you're slightly crazy and I like you anyways, so I wouldn't worry too much about that. Besides, you talking about this is for your benefit more than mine. And I'm not one to question your methods for staying sane immediately after going through something harrowing."

Nora grabbed the pillow from the spot next to her and hugged it to her chest. She looked at her own twisted thoughts and decided it might not be the worst idea to pick them apart out loud, so she dove in. Once she began to talk, it was if a faucet had been turned on, and the story poured out of her—from the moment she walked into the museum until the moment they found her on Michigan Avenue. Drew didn't interrupt her once, letting her follow her own streams of consciousness, never asking for an explanation.

When she finally fell silent, Nora felt both deflated and light, as if the weight that she had released by sharing what had happened had also been what was propping her up. She also realized that most of the blinding rage from the night before had drained away, only to be replaced by an aching deep in her chest.

Drew's only comment was, "I want you to know that you are incredibly strong for being where you are right now and making it through what you did."

Nora snorted. "I don't feel strong. I feel like a used Kleenex."

"You know what I mean," Drew said with a roll of his eyes. "Even heroes have to go home and feel like a used Kleenex sometimes."

Nora offered him a rude hand gesture in response, and the pair enjoyed a few moments of levity before growing serious again.

"So what do I do now? About everybody at the Sanctuary?" After a slight hesitation, Nora added, "About Adam?"

Drew gave her a knowing look. "Well, I think you have to decide how you feel about him first."

Nora looked down at the pillow she was still hugging to her chest.

"I think you know how I feel about him. But how can I, in good conscience, feel that way about him if he's been lying to me this whole time?"

"I'm going to tell you a few facts I think you should consider, but at the end of the day, only you can decide what you are going to do."

He didn't continue until Nora looked up and met his eyes.

"First, last night was the second time I've seen Adam react to your life being in danger, and let me tell you, this was even scarier than when he charged into my ER covered in your blood. For somebody you would think has a lot of experience being cool under pressure, he was dangerously close to a blind panic. That wasn't the type of act he would put on for my benefit.

"Second, when you asked him if he had been lying to you, Adam admitted to it immediately. Not the move you would expect from a shameless manipulator. And you didn't get any clarification from him on what he was lying about. This could all be one big misunderstanding, like the ones you always make fun of in romantic comedies.

"And last, something Thad said the other day really stuck with me. I was at the Sanctuary when Adam was getting ready to go to your gala, and he stopped by Thad's room to borrow some cuff links. He was practically bouncing out of his skin, he was so excited. When he left, Thad said, 'I haven't seen him this happy in over six-hundred years'. If you are making him that happy and he still lied to you, he must have had a damn good reason."

Nora had decided what she was going to do before Drew got to his last point, but by the time he'd finished, her heart leaped up into her throat. She wasn't surprised that her rage from the night before had faded. Nora was always quick to anger, but equally quick to calm down and resort to rationality.

What surprised her was how much Adam's feelings affected her. She knew she liked him, but she hadn't realized the extent of her own feelings until the hurt of his betrayal ripped her to shreds.

"Would you think I'm crazy if I said I want to go to the Sanctuary and talk to him now?" asked Nora.

Drew smiled. "I think you would be crazy not to."

I⊤ was almost noon by the time Nora stepped through the electric silk of the portal and onto the Sanctuary lawn. She had been anxious to head out right away after making up her mind, but Drew had insisted she take care of herself first. She was glad for his insistence now that her belly was full of greasy diner food and copious amounts of coffee.

Nora limped through the Sanctuary, avoiding putting too much pressure on her singed foot and hoped that she would find Adam in his room. When Nora poked her head around the door into Adam's room, she found that he was there, but he looked as if he'd had an even worse night than she had. He wore the same clothes from the night before, but they didn't have the distinct rumpled look of somebody who had slept in them. He was slumped in the chair in front of the fireplace, examining a small object in his hands. There was a full cup of tea sitting forgotten on the table next to him, no longer steaming.

Adam jumped to his feet as if he had been shocked when Nora cleared her throat. Seeing her, he crossed the room towards her in a few long strides before pulling up abruptly a meter from her. His body was almost vibrating with tension, and his eyes were rimmed with red.

"How are you feeling?" Adam asked, his calm voice a sharp juxtaposition to his frantic appearance.

"Tell me everything," Nora demanded. "Now."

"Okay." Adam gave a jerky nod, somehow managing to look even more tense. He gestured towards the chairs by the hearth. "You better sit down."

Nora made her way over and took a seat, but Adam remained standing. He paced in front of the fireplace, beginning to fidget with the object in his hands again. It appeared to be a small piece of jewelry, like a locket.

"I need to tell you about how my wife died," Adam blurted out.

Nora was taken aback. This was not how she had expected this story to start, but she nodded for him to continue.

He took a shaky breath before beginning. "She was an incredibly brave Warrior. We were fighting side by side at the Defeat, and things were not looking good for the Eteria. We were making our last stand when the two of us were separated. It looked like she was about to be overwhelmed when, all of a sudden, she used the Light in a way nobody had ever seen before. It was as if she were simply a vessel for it, and she burned away every last Shadow on the battlefield.

It was incredible, but the act was too much for her body, leaving it completely broken. It wasn't until later that we found out her destruction of the Shadow had also hindered our ability to use the Light."

Nora felt a pang of admiration for the woman who had given her life to protect what she loved, but she tilted her head in confusion. She couldn't follow how this was going to come back around to her.

Adam continued pacing while he talked, twisting the object in his hands unconsciously.

"When she collapsed on the battlefield, I ran to her. Seeing her dead...it left me broken. So out of my mind with grief, I tried to use my power to do the unthinkable. I tried to bring her back."

Nora gawked. She had read enough novels to know that was not a good idea.

"To everybody's surprise," Adam soldiered on. "I managed to grab on to her spirit as it was slipping away. When I went to put it back in her body, though, it was too broken to hold it. The best I managed to do was give her a tether to this earth in my own soul, and she began to slip away to find another source of life. Before her spirit escaped from my grasp, my wife's voice whispered in my head. 'Come find me.'"

Nora furrowed her brow at Adam, who had now stopped his pacing and was looking at her intently.

"So...she was reincarnated?" puzzled Nora.

Adam nodded slowly. "And she has continued to be reincarnated, again and again to this very day."

Adam stared at her as if he were waiting for her to combust on the spot. There was something about his story she was missing. The link that would explain why he was telling her this.

When it hit her, it was as if Zeus himself had struck her with one of his thunderbolts. She was glad that Adam had suggested she be seated for this conversation as she opened and shut her mouth several times like an oversized goldfish before stammering, "You can't mean *me*?"

Adam nodded again, his eyes overly bright.

"But how... Why do you think it's me?"

Adam crossed the rug and sunk to his knees in front of her. "You look the same in every life, but that wouldn't even matter. I would know your spirit even with my eyes closed. As soon as you chased after me and yelled at me to stop in that alley, I knew it was you."

Nora would have told him he was insane, but her spirit seemed to have opinions of its own and was whispering to her that he might be right. It was like when she had found it surprisingly easy to believe in the existence of a race of immortal sorcerer warriors, only magnified.

"So we've been doing this repeatedly for thousands of years?" Nora asked.

Adam flinched, still staying on his knees in front of her. "Not exactly. I haven't done a stellar job of finding you. The world is a very big place."

"How many times?"

"Three."

The single syllable hit Nora like a physical blow. Two thousand years of walking the earth, and he had only managed to run into her three times.

"We've only spent three lives together in all that time?" Her voice trembled as she said it.

Adam shook his head. "Even when I find you, it's not always simple. My feelings for you may be eternal but being together is not guaranteed. We have a choice."

"Tell me," Nora urged, needing to know.

Adam sat back on his heels but didn't move to get up from his seat in front of her.

"The first time I found you, it was a few hundred years after your death, in Egypt. I had begun to think I had imagined the voice telling me to find you altogether, when suddenly there you were. You weren't as you were when I'd lost you, though, but frail and failing with all your hair turned gray. I stayed near you for the short few years until the end of that life, trying to help you in whatever ways I could."

Nora gripped the arms of the seat so hard her knuckles cracked, but she did not interrupt.

"The next time I found you was almost five hundred years later. You were young and just as I always pictured you in my dreams, but when I followed you, trying to come up with an excuse to run into you organically, I saw you were married, and you already had three beautiful children, all with your eyes and your beautiful smile.

It was in that life that I was forced to come to terms with the fact that just because I had married you in one life did not mean I had the right to derail every other life you had. If we were going to be together, you would have to choose me all over again. It was one of the hardest realizations of my life, but you and your husband ended up being some of the best friends I ever had."

Nora was barely breathing now, but she held on.

"The last time I found you was seven hundred years ago, in France. You were in the prime of your life, a young widow. We met and had a whirlwind romance that was everything I had dreamed of. When I suggested marriage, though, you turned me down. You were managing your late husband's estate, and you knew you would lose legal ownership of the property if you were ever to marry again. Devastated by your refusal, I took a trip to the country to clear my head. I had only just left when I heard the news that the black death was spreading. I rushed back to you, but I was too late. I ended up holding you in my arms, and I vowed that I would never assume anything about our relationship again."

Adam reached down and plucked the piece of gold jewelry off the ground where it had fallen on the rug when he kneeled in front of her. He ran his thumb over the face of the round locket she had spied on his shelf weeks before.

"This is from that last life," Adam explained. "I keep it with me so I never forget, well...any of it."

He popped the locket open to reveal the picture inside, and if Nora had any doubts about Adam's honesty, it was instantly banished as a miniscule painting of her own face smiled back at her.

Tears filled her eyes as she asked, "And now?"

"And now...now you're here in front of me again. I saw the life you had built for yourself, and it made me admire you even more. I never wanted to take that life away from you. I wanted to give you the type of love you deserve in the life you chose, but then you got dragged into everything here at the Eteria, and I knew I could not keep this from you forever." A tear leaked from the corner of Adam's eye, but he didn't move to wipe it away. "I had hoped we might fall in love first, so I could tell you this without forcing you into anything. I wanted to give you the space to make your own decisions and destiny, and not feel like you owed me anything because we had once been married."

Adam scooted forward until he kneeled directly in front of Nora and put his hands on her knees. "And now I— I have spent thousands of years learning every language there is to know and reading the best work by the greatest writers of every age. Still, I have never found the proper words to express how I feel about you. Yet I can tell you this: I have seen your face every time I have closed by eyes for the past seven hundred years, and still, I never could have imagined the joy I would feel when I finally saw you again."

Nora stared into Adam's dark eyes, tears now freely streaming down his face in a mirror of her own. She knew she had a choice. She knew she could get up and walk out forever and Adam would let her do it.

Instead, she threw her arms around his neck and crushed her lips to his.

This kiss was nothing like their first. If their first kiss had been a mild summer's day, then this one was a hurricane. She poured everything his words had made her feel into the kiss, hoping he would understand what she was trying to convey. He only froze in surprise for a moment before responding in kind. He pulled her closer to him, letting the locket fall from his hands to the carpet with a dull thud. She knelt with him as his hands wandered all over her. They trailed through her tousled hair before coming to cup her face briefly, then wandered down her back, as if they had to touch every part of her to make sure she was really there.

Nora's hands began to explore just as much as she tilted her head to kiss him more deeply, the kiss morphing into exploring tongue and nipping teeth. He tasted like the spiciness of the chai tea he preferred mixed with the saltiness of their combined tears. Her hands began tugging at the buttons of his shirt, but he stilled them.

"I've thought about this reunion for the last seven hundred years," Adam said as he looked through his lashes at her. "I won't let this be some frantic romp on the floor. I'm going to savor every moment of this, take my time to relearn every inch of you."

Nora swallowed and couldn't repress the shiver Adam's words sent up her spine. Instead, she looked down at the white fur beneath her knees and joked, "Yeah, I don't think a bearskin rug in front of the fireplace is quite your style."

"I refuse to be that cliché." Adam stood before scooping her up off the carpet and depositing her on the enormous bed. He crawled on top of her and kept to his promise, their next kiss slower and more intentional. His lips didn't leave hers until she was shaking like a leaf in the stiff Chicago winds.

His hands and mouth began to explore her body at a torturous pace, divesting her of her clothing piece by piece. His lips mapped behind her ear and the hollow of her throat, painting her skin with the affection he had carried for so long. His breath ghosted over her breasts before teasing them with the flat of his tongue. If Adam noticed Nora's fingernails digging into his shoulders, he gave no indication but to lavish even more attention on every inch of her. She yearned to urge him on faster, but she bit her lip to control herself, wanting this moment to be everything he had promised.

Then his mouth came to land between her legs, and she lost all ability for coherent thought. If Adam had seemed intent on his task before, it was nothing compared to how he took her apart now. Nora could only rock up into him, one hand coming to cover her mouth and contain the sounds now forcing their way past her lips. Adam reached up and pulled her wrist away from her face, and when she glanced down, his eyes were desperate, as if being deprived of the noises coming from her physically hurt him. So instead, Nora dug her fingers into his hair and let him have every groan and whimper she had to offer as curling fingers joined his artful tongue at her center.

Once Nora was hoarse, she pulled Adam back and flipped them

over so he lay on his back and she was able to hover over him. She felt like she might shatter at any moment, but she was determined to hold out until she could be joined with Adam fully. He made a slight noise of protest, but a small smirk and a glint in his eye told her he was far from unhappy with her enthusiasm. His lips glistened from her, and Nora ran her thumb over them, only for Adam to dart his tongue out and make sure he had licked her there too.

She removed his clothing with much more haste than he had hers, knocking his glasses off as she ripped his sweater over his head. Once he was bare, though, she did pause to take him in, wanting to seal the way he looked in her mind, from the length emerging from the curls between his legs to the ruined look in his eyes. He humored her for a moment before it was his turn to get impatient and he pulled her down to kiss him again.

She didn't make him wait, and when he slid inside her, Nora nearly cried with the satisfaction of it. She was reduced to a bundle of sensations—Adam's hands on her hips, his breath on her neck, and the slight scratch of his stubble against her cheek. Their bodies fit together like they had been made to do so, which didn't seem so farfetched anymore. Nora shuddered as her muscles were overcome with the pleasure of it all, but Adam took matters into his own hands. He flipped them over and drove into her, chasing after what they both needed.

As Nora's back arched and she fell apart in Adam's arms, she found the words to say what she had been trying to this whole time.

"I love you."

"I love you, too," Adam said, breathless but without hesitation, as if it were as necessary for him to tell her this as it was to breathe. As if he burned with it.

Much later, when they were content and breathless in each other's arms, Nora had the fleeting thought before she was claimed by sleep that this was worth waiting seven hundred years for.

23

Nora was delighted to find that Adam snored. It was not a heavy sound that would keep her awake, but a soft fluttering that somehow managed to be endearing. She woke before him and spent several minutes listening to him, smiling to herself all the while, knowing that she would enjoy teasing him about it. It was the sort of intimate detail that seemed fitting to know about somebody she felt so strongly for.

After a few moments of admiring how Adam's messy curls fell across his forehead, Nora determined that she was going to have to get herself dressed and head to work. She was just debating whether to wake Adam or to leave him a note when her conundrum was solved for her by a quiet knock on the bedroom door.

The sound roused Adam, and he was fully awakened by Nora pulling the star-embroidered comforter off the bed to wrap around her still naked body as she padded across the room.

Cracking the door, she was relieved to see Drew's face peeking in instead of somebody who might be more scandalized by her state of undress. Then again, the Greeks ran naked in the original Olympics, so maybe they wouldn't even notice.

"Good morning."

"Good morning," Drew said, taking her disheveled appearance in stride. "I was just stopping in to see how everything went yesterday, but it seems like I shouldn't have worried."

Nora felt as though she should blush, but when she glanced over her shoulder. Adam was sitting up and rubbing sleep from his eyes, and she could not bring herself to feel any embarrassment. Instead, her face split in a broad grin.

Turning back to Drew, she said, "I have so much to tell you, but unfortunately, I have to get going to work right now."

"That's the other thing I stopped by to tell you. You don't have to go to work today. The whole city is shut down for a blizzard."

"A blizzard?" Nora almost dropped her blanket in shock and was forced to readjust. "But it's barely November, and it wasn't on the radar, was it?"

Drew shook his head. "No, but you know Chicago weather, and Odelle is always complaining about how the meteorologists at work make everything up anyways."

It still seemed rather odd to Nora, but she brushed it off, saying, "Thanks for coming to tell me. Let me get dressed and then we can have breakfast or something."

"Don't worry about it." Drew shook his head, eyes glinting mischievously. "You look rather busy, and I'm going to see Thad right now anyway. We can meet up for lunch."

Nora winked at him before shutting the door and turning back to Adam. He was sitting up with the sheets draped low around his hips, looking transcendent in the morning sun that streamed through the skylight. His tanned skin glowed, and Nora noted with pride several marks across his neck and chest that were clearly shaped like her teeth.

She wasted no time climbing back into bed with him.

"I have the day off," she murmured against his lips after giving him a good morning kiss.

"Good," Adam growled, pulling her with him so they were both lying down again. "We still have a lot of catching up to do."

"Mmhmm," Nora responded absently, kissing her way down his neck.

"I'm sure you have a lot of questions." Adam's hands carded gently through her hair. "And I want to make sure you have all the answers you need to be comfortable with this."

Nora responded by showing him that now was not the time for questioning by doing something very different with her mouth. His hands shifted from caressing her hair to fisting it desperately, and it was a long time before they picked up the threads of their conversation again. After all, Adam insisted on returning the favor, and Nora was of no mind to object.

ALTHOUGH ADAM AND NORA DIDN'T GET OUT OF THE BED FOR THE majority of the morning, she did end up asking him all sorts of questions to satisfy her endless curiosity.

She was lying on her side, pulled tightly to Adam's chest with her head tucked under his chin, when the gold ring on the hand intertwined with hers caught her eye. She had noticed his habit of fidgeting with it when he was anxious but had never gotten around to asking about it.

"Where is your ring from?" Nora inquired, lifting their hands to her eyes to get a closer look. Now, she could see that there were tiny stars made of sparkling stones set around the gold band.

"Oh." Adam pressed a kiss to the top of her head as he paused. "That's my wedding ring."

Nora jumped slightly before melting back into his body once more. "Then why do you wear it on your right hand?"

Adam shifted behind her. "Well, I'm not married anymore. I'm technically a widower, but I can't bring myself to not wear it at all. Besides, if I ever did find you, I didn't want you to see it and think I was unavailable."

"Not to mention you wouldn't want to give other women the

wrong impression," Nora tried to joke, but the end of her sentence rose as if she were asking a question. She would be lying if she said she didn't want to know if there was more to his romantic history than her.

Adam was silent for a moment.

"There have been a few other women," he finally admitted. "Does that bother you?"

"I honestly would find it a bit weird if there weren't," Nora snorted, but she squeezed his hand to reassure him and returned to inspecting the ring.

"We really had a thing for the star motif, didn't we?" she commented, thinking of the silver constellations emblazoned on the canopy over their heads, as well as the tattoo of stars encircling his bicep that she had traced with her fingers and lips last night.

Adam's warm breath stirred her hair as he nodded against the back of her head.

"It was sort of a theme in our relationship. We loved stargazing together. That's why my sword has that inscription on it. You gave it to me as a gift."

"We owe a lot to those weapons."

Adam kissed her neck and murmured against her skin in agreement. "You know, stars turned out to be the perfect symbol for our love, even now. The stars give their light to the earth even though they have long since burnt out. That was you for me. You were the light that guided me through the dark parts of my life, even long after you had died."

Nora turned in his arms and found his eyes as bright as her own. She raised his hand to her lips and kissed his knuckles in acknowledgement.

"So will you start wearing your ring on your left hand again?"

"No." Adam paused, considering. "Not yet anyways. I want to do this whole thing right. Give you the relationship and romance you deserve, not just rush through it because you know the truth now. I want to get to know every bit of who you are now, your past, and what makes you so intoxicatingly special."

"Maybe this whole reincarnation thing is a blessing," she mused. "How beautiful is it that we get to fall in love over and over again? We get so many first kisses, so many chances to remember what makes us so right for each other. Falling for you... I'm glad I get to do it more than once."

"I could fall in love with you forever," Adam vowed.

"Tell me about the first life we spent together."

"Well, I know I was hopelessly in love with you when I watched you temporarily blind a guy in the courtyard for being an ass."

LEAVING THE SUNLIGHT DRENCHED SANCTUARY AND WALKING through the portal back into the city shouldn't have been a shock, considering Nora had been forewarned of the raging blizzard. Still, her body immediately tensed up at the frigid wind whipping at her hair and tugging her scarf from her face. Adam put his arm around her shoulders and pulled her to his side to share his body heat. She turned to look up at him with a smile, and the swirling snowflakes caught in her upturned eyelashes.

They stepped out from under the Bean to catch the bus back to her apartment. She had known that she could not stay in the happy bubble of the Sanctuary forever, and tomorrow she would go back to the mundanity of her day-to-day life. When Adam had offered to come back to her apartment with her, she had been grateful, as if she were able to bring some of the magic from the Sanctuary back to her home life with her.

She was strangely nervous to have Adam in her space for the first time. Her chest warmed, thinking about him among all her books and art and favorite belongings. The butterflies in the pit of her stomach reminded her that their relationship was still in its infancy despite all they had been through.

As she began to think about picking up some tea to keep at her apartment, her phone buzzed in her pocket. Fishing it out, she struggled to unlock the screen in her chunky mittens.

She frowned at the screen when she finally got it open.

"What is it?" Adam inquired, spotting the furrow between her brows.

"I have two voicemails from Odelle. I hate that I don't get service in the Sanctuary. We're supposed to have dinner tonight, and I hope she isn't cancelling. I was going to tell her everything, and well, after this, that seems like something that should be done sooner rather than later."

Adam nodded, stepping to the side so Nora could pause while she opened her voicemail. Her heart quickened inexplicably under her coat, wondering what was important enough that Odelle would have called multiple times.

As she got the voicemails open and raised the phone to her ear, she froze. She felt as cold as the ice under her feet as she listened through both messages. Adam's voice asking her what was wrong sounded distant as the phone slipped from her numb fingers and fell to the pavement below.

24

NORA SIPPED AT THE CUP OF TEA IN HER HANDS. SHE BARELY TASTED it, even as the steam thawed her still-chilled cheeks. Her eyes stared unseeingly at the phone sitting in the center of the table in front of her, now with a cracked screen from being dropped on the frozen pavement.

It played the messages from Odelle for the third time in a row as the worried faces of Drew and the Eteria members looked on. Drew sat next to Thad, and Nora was grateful that he was still there, concern on his normally calm face. Everybody snuck glances out of the corners of their eyes at Nora, as if they thought she might implode at any moment. Nora thought they probably weren't that far off base.

The first message from Odelle started again, the panic and confusion in her voice apparent even on the low quality microphone.

"Nora, I need your help. I was at work reporting on the blizzard when a huge sheet of ice fell from a building, and now I'm trapped in an alley. I can't climb out. The ice is too slick and I'm wearing my work legs."

A staticky shuffling noise came across the receiver before Odelle's voice returned.

"Nora, there's something happening. I don't know—"

There was a sharp crack as if the phone had been dropped on the ground, followed by the beginning of a shriek before the message cut out.

The cheerful automated voice that recited the options to delete the message or save it was jarring after the horror in Odelle's scream. Antony reached out and hit the option to play the next message, cutting the recording off.

It wasn't the first time Nora had heard the message, but it still made her heart freeze in her chest.

"You're a tricky one to scare, Nora Zvezda."

Nora would recognize the disturbingly articulated voice of the agent anywhere, but hearing it on a voicemail left by Odelle's phone was something she had not imagined even in her nightmares.

"I think I figured out the right tactic this time, though. Why don't you come find your sister while she's still in one piece? Don't even think about bringing along those friends of yours if you don't want to make things worse for her. I look forward to having another chat with you."

Antony reached out again to stop the phone from playing the message a fourth time.

"You're sure it's him—the agent?" Ezra asked, his fists tight under his folded arms.

Nora nodded. She had barely spoken since hearing the voicemails for the first time, but her mind whirled a mile a minute. This was all her fault. She hadn't come clean to Odelle about what was happening soon enough, and now she was paying the price. Odelle wouldn't even know what the Shadow was, leaving her completely vulnerable to its manipulation. Nora's stomach felt like a lump of coal.

"Do you have any idea where he might have taken her?" Thad probed gently.

"None," Nora said. "I don't know how he expects me to come find them. Maybe he's just taunting me. Giving me false hope that she's still alive."

Adam reached out and put a hand on Nora's shoulder, making her jump. "I'm sure she's all right. Remember the Shadow's game is fear and manipulation. He wouldn't give up a piece like Odelle that quickly if he's trying to get to you. We've seen this before."

Drew ran a hand through his hair with a scowl. "If you've seen it before, why does the Shadow keep doing it?"

"Just because we know what it's doing, doesn't make it less effective," Antony said. "We know it's a trap, but that doesn't make us care about the bait any less."

Nora nodded, although the thought of Odelle being alive in the clutches of the agent wasn't particularly reassuring either.

"Then what are we waiting for? I have to go find her."

"*We* have to go find her," Antony amended, giving Nora a pointed look that she didn't quite understand.

"You heard what he said," Nora argued "I have to come alone or—"

"He's the bad guy. Of course that's what he said," Adam reasoned, doing his best to sound reassuring but not totally hiding his concern. "He's messing with you, trying to separate you from your support system."

Nora knew this was the part of the story when the hero would run off, reckless and alone, to save the damsel in distress, and Nora would bang her head against the wall in frustration at them for being so incredibly dense. Still, her sister's panicked voice played on repeat in her head. Maybe it was Nora's turn to be incredibly dense.

"You're right." Nora leaned into Adam's hand on her shoulder. "Thanks for wanting to help. We need a plan, though."

Adam looked relieved and turned to the rest of the group to

start throwing out ideas on how to find Odelle. Nora wasn't paying attention, though. Her mind was too busy with her own plan, which she had to come up with before Adam finished outlining his. She caught Antony still staring at her with unnerving perception, but she quickly looked away.

As Thad chimed in with some information about combing the city in a grid pattern, Nora leaned over to murmur in Adam's ear. "If we're going to go on a manhunt, I'm going to need to rest for a bit. This has all been...a lot to process. Do you mind if I go lay down while you guys comb out the details?"

Adam looked at her with furrowed brows.

"Do you need me to come with you?"

"No." She shook her head. "I think I'd rather be alone. I need a minute to think."

Adam continued to appear worried, but he agreed.

"Ok, go ahead and use my room. I'll come fill you in when we're finished here."

Nora nodded gratefully and did her best to look worn out as she made her way out of the courtyard. As she passed Antony, he looked up and met her eyes. She looked down at the ground quickly, as if he might spy her intentions in her face. Her whole plan would be for nothing if he guessed it too soon.

When as she was out of sight of the group, Nora quickened her pace, striding purposefully through the halls towards the main entrance. She hadn't made it fifty feet when she stopped in her tracks and doubled back in the other direction. Just because she was being reckless didn't mean that she had to be completely unprepared.

Nora was pleased to find that she was able to remember her way through the labyrinthian hallways back to the armory. She pushed open the heavy wooden doors as quietly as possible before slipping inside, leaving the door ajar to light her way.

She looked over the racks of weapons only for a moment before heading to the same case that had caught her attention the last time she was in this room. Now standing in front of the case with the Warrior's armor, she understood why she felt so drawn to it.

It was hers.

She fumbled with the latch for only a moment before getting the case open. As she went about taking the breastplate off the wooden form, she thanked her profession for making her well versed in dressing and undressing mannequins in ancient armor. She never would have guessed such a skill had applications outside of working in a museum.

She finished buckling the breastplate to herself before deciding to add the grieves for good measure. She got the impression they were not designed to go over skinny jeans, but she made do.

Nora looked longingly at the helmet with its impressive plumage but decided it was best to forgo it. She was already making quite the fashion statement with the bronze armor over her jeans and sweater.

Just as Nora was closing the case again, the room got dimmer, as if the light coming from the cracked door had been blocked.

"I see you figured out who the armor belonged to."

Nora whirled around so fast that she almost toppled over with the new weight now attached to her body. When she had found her footing, she looked up to see Seraphina standing in the doorway. The woman's arms were crossed over her chest, and her chin was raised at an angle which suggested she was accustomed to wearing a crown.

"It took you longer than I expected for somebody who so obviously enjoys sticking her nose in other people's business," Seraphina continued.

"I'm a historian," Nora snapped, unable to stop herself. "Other people's stuff is my job."

Seraphina acted as if she hadn't spoken.

"I heard what happened to your sister." The way she said it was a simple statement, holding neither comfort nor judgement.

"And I suppose you're here to tell me what I'm doing is incredibly stupid?"

"No. I knew you before and criticizing you when you were doing something rash was never an effective way of dissuading you from anything." Seraphina's tone left Nora with no doubt she had disliked her former self as much as Nora's current incarnation.

"Then why are you here?" Nora huffed, getting impatient with the conversation. She had wasted too much time already.

Seraphina walked into the room until she stood only a foot in front of Nora. "I came to tell you that you buckled this on all wrong."

She reached down and tugged a few of the straps around Nora's midsection, none too gently, while Nora looked on with her mouth hanging open.

"You're...helping me?" she asked, dumbfounded.

Seraphina did not look up from her work. "Surprisingly, yes."

"Why?"

At this, Seraphina did pause and met Nora's gaze. Her typical haughty expression was still firmly in place, but Nora caught a hint of something softer in the woman's pale blue eyes.

"I guess because everybody deserves a chance to save the people they love."

As Seraphina looked down to finish her adjustments, Nora remembered what Adam had told her about Seraphina's husband. He had died in the Defeat, just as she had. Adam and Nora had gotten a second chance at their love. Seraphina hadn't.

"I hope I'm not doing all this work for you to go out and waste it all by getting killed in seconds," Seraphina commented as she finished up. "Please tell me you have some sort of plan besides charging blindly into a trap?"

Nora chewed her lip for a second.

"I need you to do me a favor."

Seraphina raised a brow. "Another favor? Will the wonders never cease?"

Nora ignored the dig.

"I need you to give Adam a message for me."

NORA WALKED THROUGH THE MUSEUM AFTER HOURS FOR THE SECOND time in three days as she mentally berated herself. A few months ago, she had felt nervous bringing Adam down to the office when it wasn't strictly allowed. Now she had made a habit of breaking into the museum and was planning to steal from her job. Although, she could argue that this no longer counted as stealing considering she had recently found out that the spear in the museum had once belonged to her former incarnation.

She might have been afraid as she walked through the darkened hall to the arms and armaments exhibit, considering what had happened last time she was alone in this museum. But some voice in her gut told her that the Shadow would not touch her while she was here. The agent was waiting to spring his trap for her.

Not to mention that Nora was too angry to be afraid right now. The icy numbness that filled her when she first heard the fear in Odelle's voice had gradually melted into a simmering rage that boiled through her veins. Nora had never let anybody bully Odelle about her legs on the playground as a child, and she was not about to let anybody bully her now.

The only feeling that managed to cut through the anger was a shred of guilt in the back of her mind. She tried not to envision Adam coming after her and what he might be doing, knowing her plan would never work if she thought about him like that.

Nora reached the case with the spear and slowly opened it with the key she had grabbed from the downstairs office. She had already deactivated the alarms using the system they used when they took artifacts out to clean them, so all she had to do was reach in and grab the spear from its plinth. Her hands immediately slid into the worn handholds comfortably, like walking back into her apartment after a long vacation. Nora loved having her wooden practice spear in her hands, but it was nothing compared to this. Armed with this spear, she would be a force to be reckoned with, and the agent had better be careful who he tried to catch in his snare.

25

As Nora made her way through the streets of Chicago, she suddenly understood the practice of warriors wearing capes on a new level. She had tried to put on her puffy winter jacket over her clothes and armor, and it had turned out to be obnoxiously bulky and restrictive. She was unable to zip her coat over the added bulk of the breastplate, so she was forced to use one hand to hold it around her as the other carried her spear.

The storm had intensified even further since she and Adam had exited the portal the first time. Nora bowed her head and pressed forward into the frigid wind, which threated to tug the edges of her coat from her numb fingers yet again. This blizzard was of epic proportions for it not being fully winter yet, but Nora could sense the malice in the wind that told her this was not a natural storm.

Knowing the Shadow would want Nora's journey to Odelle to be as hard and demoralizing as possible, Nora turned and walked directly into the wind, towards where the air seemed the coldest and the swirling snow felt the densest.

So far, it had led her away from the lakefront and among the towering skyscrapers of the loop. Nora had hoped the shelter of the buildings would give her some relief from the biting wind, but it only served to tunnel the air, whistling through the streets so loudly that Nora could hear little else. There wasn't much to hear anyway, with the streets as empty as Nora had ever seen them, the only cars in sight blanketed in snow.

Nora tried to think positively as the last of the feeling left her frigid face. At least the abandoned streets meant there would be minimal collateral damage from the coming confrontation.

As Nora approached the L tracks, any ability to think positively was lost as the howling wind became impossibly loud. The snowfall was so dense that Nora had to squint to make out the poles holding up the tracks for the elevated train.

The howling of the wind began to take on a groaning quality, and Nora paused before she realized it was not the wind at all, but a voice. She followed the sound towards one of the square metal poles buried in the street.

Through the haze of snow, Nora could just make out a huddled form propped up against the painted yellow column. She did her best to run towards it, slipping on the accumulating snow and gritting her teeth against the stinging in her still tender foot until she skidded to a halt in front of the bundled figure and clattered to her knees.

As she had suspected, the figure was Odelle. Nora was relieved to find her still bundled in the excessively large puffer jacket with the fur lined hood that the newscasters were issued when they broadcasted in extreme weather. Odelle herself appeared to not be aware of Nora's approach, masked by the whistling of the wind. Odelle buried her face in her coat so that it was completely obscured, and a fresh rush of rage filled her blood as she saw that one of her hands was bound to the pole at her back. The rage almost immediately gave way to puzzlement when she saw that one of Odelle's prosthetic legs was no longer strapped on, but instead clutched tightly in her free hand.

Nora touched Odelle's shoulder, and her sister flinched away as she pulled her head out of her coat. Her eyes widened before becoming narrow and hard.

"You." Odelle's voice was as angry as it was broken. "This is all your fault."

The words twisted like a knife in Nora's heart even though they were an exact echo of what Nora had thought when she'd heard Odelle's capture. Just a few more hours and Nora would have been at dinner with Odelle, telling her the truth about everything. Now Odelle had had the truth thrust upon her in the cruelest way possible.

Nora distracted herself from the pain by reaching for Odelle's still bound hand to untie her.

"I know, *zaika*, and you can be mad at me once we get you out of here," Nora said, struggling with her numb fingers to untie the cord that held Odelle's wrist. She did her best to hurry when Odelle shivered violently against her arm.

She didn't manage to loosen the knot at all before a voice colder than the raging storm sounded behind her.

"I would call this a touching family reunion, but I think you are the last person Odelle wants to see right now."

Nora whirled around and jumped to her feet in the same motion, snatching up her spear as she rose.

"Not after I've told her how you lied to her," the Agent continued, unperturbed by Nora being substantially more well-armed than she had been at their last meeting. He looked exactly the same as he had then, dressed in an impeccable suit without a coat, despite the temperature. He still bore Leo's face, but Nora knew that Leo was gone, and this twisted creature of darkness wore him like a mask by his own admission.

"You need to work on your human disguise," Nora spat at him. "Normal people need to wear winter coats in a blizzard."

He cocked his head and looked down at his clothing. The snow around his feet melted from the heat that she knew radiated from his body. Her foot still ached slightly from kicking him a few days ago.

"I was human once, you know," the agent said in a tone that would have been conversational had his voice been capable of any sort of warmth. "I haven't missed the condition."

"Then why don't you just show yourself as the monster you really are?" The feelings from Nora's last meeting with the Agent crept up her spine and she gripped her spear tighter until her fingers ached. She couldn't let him keep talking and get inside her head again, as much as she needed to buy more time. She would rather goad him into a fair fight. Running him through with her spear felt like a fantastic idea when she thought about the pain in Odelle's eyes.

"If memory serves, taking a human form hasn't stopped me from being a monster before," the agent continued with a shrug. "In fact, I think I do some of my best work when I wear a human face."

Nora responded by tugging off her bulky winter coat. "You aren't going to do any more work at all if I have anything to say about it."

"Fiesty after our last meeting, aren't we? I must say, I'm surprised that you and Adam reconciled so quickly. Shame that you abandoned him so soon after reuniting. I can feel the guilt rolling off you for running away without explanation."

Nora tried desperately not to worry about where Adam might be at that moment, only sparing the barest thought to hope that Seraphina had given him her message. Then she distracted herself by swinging her spear into its ready position. Held in her left hand with her arm bent, the long blade pointed to the ground to her left and the butt pointed up behind her right shoulder.

The agent smiled at her unspoken challenge, but the smile grew and grew like a rip across his face to reveal the fiery blackness beneath. His skin continued to peel back as it had last time, his form growing until it was a seven-foot monster of darkness with whip like arms and red coals where eyes should be. When the gash where the mouth should be parted, Nora saw the harsh glow of white fire within and the heat of it scraped across her numbed cheeks. Odelle began whimpering behind her, but Nora didn't spare her a look, keeping the whole of her focus on the adversary before her.

Nora swung her spear first, and the force when the Shadow blocked it with one of its arms was enough to make her eyeballs hurt. As they began exchanging blows, Nora became grateful that her spear was longer than her usual practice weapon. The extra reach allowed her to stay away from the Shadow's disproportionately long arms, which swung out faster than her eyes could follow. Still, Ezra's training had managed to work its way under her skin, and she blocked a blow without having to give it conscious thought.

As the Shadow feinted one way, Nora fell for its maneuver and was forced to dodge narrowly as it swerved the other direction, ducking into a quick roll. She was suddenly much more grateful for the afternoon she had spent collecting bruises while practicing rolling with a weapon as she managed to regain her feet without impaling herself.

Hoping to catch the Shadow off guard, she stayed low and stepped out into a lunge, swinging her spear in a sweeping arc to knock the creature's legs out from under it. The blow connected but the Shadow managed to keep its footing, its unnaturally shaped legs bending in a way that looked wrong to absorb the impact.

Now it was the Shadow's turn to catch Nora off guard, locking its arm against her blade and pulling in so close that Nora's breastplate heated rapidly against her body. Its face loomed over her, and the mouth split in the parody of a grin, opening wide enough to swallow her whole. Just as the Shadow began to lower its head as if it were about to do exactly that, a shuffle behind Nora made it pause for a moment.

A split second was all Nora needed to free her blade from the lock and execute a quick spin, catching the Shadow in the chest with the spike on the butt of her spear. As the Shadow stumbled back with a shriek, there was a whoosh and a metallic thud.

Nora looked towards the far side of the elevated train track just in time to see Ezra drop from above and land on one knee in a dramatic pose that Nora would have to tease him for if she managed to make it out of this encounter. Still, she sent a silent thanks to Seraphina for successfully delivering her message.

The Shadow spun towards the fully armed Warrior in surprise, and Nora took the moment of distraction to glance at the commotion behind her. Pounding down the street towards her were Adam, Thad, and Drew.

"Odelle!" was all she could yell to them before turning her attention back to the fight. Thankfully, Adam understood her meaning and tugged the group over to where Odelle was still huddled a few meters away.

The Shadow and Ezra circled each other, the Shadow sporting a gash in the blackness of its chest, showing the same white fire that filled its mouth.

"How?" it hissed in a voice that had lost all its unnatural polish. "I could feel your guilt in abandoning them."

"I needed you to feel that, but my friends were with me all along," was the only gloating that Nora allowed herself before she and Ezra lunged at the Shadow together.

Now that there were two of them, the pace of the battle was nearly blinding. Bronze spears and black arms swung so fast that they blurred into colored arcs against the stark white backdrop of the snow. The Shadow fought more viciously now, growing so hot that Nora dripped sweat from the proximity, despite the cold of the surrounding air.

Still, the Shadow began blocking more than it was swinging under their coordinated attacks. Ezra and Nora both swung their spears in sharp downward cuts at the same moment, and the Shadow caught both blows on one long arm. The pair of Warriors bore down together, and the Shadow folded under the weight. Just as Nora thought she could taste victory, the Shadow's mouth spread into a smile once more.

Nora watched in horror as the Shadow's free arm snaked out towards where Odelle was huddled, surrounded by Adam, Thad, and Drew. A scream tore from her throat but was powerless to stop anything as the whip-like limb tore a huge icicle from the train tracks above Odelle's head.

Everything happened slowly as the icicle hurtled towards where Odelle was on the ground. Just before it made impact, a dark figure ploughed into her and knocked her out of the way. Instead of Odelle lying on the churned snow, impaled by a spear of ice as long as Nora's arm, it was Adam. The icicle had pierced the right side of his chest, pinning him to the ground like a butterfly in a glass case.

Time stood still for a moment, and even the snow seemed to stop its flurrying in midair. If the wind was still howling, Nora didn't hear it as she stared at Adam, lying injured on the ground.

All at once, the sound rushed back in and time picked up again at double speed. Nora whirled back towards the Shadow and swung her spear in a savage arc at its face. It managed to block in time, but just barely. Undeterred, Nora hacked doggedly at it without form or finesse. She let out a broken cry as the Shadow was forced to stumble back. She pursued it relentlessly. This creature had made this happen, and she would swing at it until it was reduced to nothing. She felt hot all over now, as if she herself may burst into flames. Wisps of smoke drifted off her shirt and her hair as her blows grew in strength.

As she raised her spear in both hands for one final stroke through the Shadow's chest, a hoarse shout sounded behind her. The voice was thin, but it stopped her in her tracks.

"Nora."

When Nora turned her head back towards where Adam lay, his head was lifted. Drew knelt next to him, holding a bloody icicle in his hand, but all Nora saw was Adam's face, looking pale but alive. The emotion in his eyes made Nora think of the message she had left for him with Seraphina to let him know that she was not really abandoning him.

Through the darkest night.

Adam knew her well enough to know what she intended from just those four words, following her and setting up a trap for the Shadow that Nora wouldn't give away in her feelings. He loved her enough that he was willing to die to save her family. He loved her through the darkest night.

That's when Nora felt it. The rage that had fueled her rampage against the Shadow had dissipated, and instead a small golden kernel of something calm sprouted in her chest. She reached for that something inside her, and her consciousness brushed against it, a pleasant warmth like the sun caressing her face.

The warmth felt like the love she carried for Odelle and Drew and Adam, and the golden kernel grew until she was full to brimming. Her vision was white, and she sensed she was going to dissolve into Light. Nora threw out her hands in front of her wildly and recognized the Light tearing through her, filling up and ravaging her insides as it went.

It was over as quickly as it had started, and Nora opened her eyes to find herself on her knees in the snow. Where the Agent had once been lingered the last wisps of smoke, and when Nora looked down at her hands, the faintest glimmers of gold danced between her fingers.

Whatever she had just done, she had destroyed the Agent.

Drew's gruff string of expletives behind her shocked her from her amazed stupor. Remembering Adam's injury, she scrabbled to her feet and rushed to his side. Drew had already peeled back Adam's shirt to reveal the wound. The icicle had pierced him a few fingerbreadths below his collarbone, just to the right of his breastbone, leaving a hole as big as a quarter

"It missed his major blood vessels," Drew said, digging a pair of blue nitrile gloves from his bag and tossing a pair to Thad. Thad put them on, looking as if he would roll his eyes at the gesture had the situation not been so dire.

"He shouldn't bleed out, but it managed to puncture a lung," Drew continued, pulling more supplies out of his pouch. "We need to cover the wound and get him to a hospital, stat."

From the amount of red on the surrounding snow, it still seemed like Adam had lost a lot of blood, but she trusted Drew's judgement. Nora looked up at Adam's face to find that he was taking quick, shallow breathes. The edges of his lips had turned a dusty shade of blue, but it was hard to say if it was from the cold or a lack of oxygen.

"I wouldn't recommend this," Adam said through gritted teeth. "It's making me very dizzy."

"Dizzy?" Drew paused in his work, hands hovering over where he had been taping a square of gauze over the hole in Adam's chest.

"Yeah," Adam managed to wheeze between breaths. "I'm very lightheaded."

Drew reached up and ran his fingers deftly over Adam's throat. It looked to Nora as if his Adam's apple had pushed off to the left side.

"Shit," Drew plunged his hands back into the supply kit, searching frantically for something. "His lung is completely collapsed from the air getting in. It's shifted his lungs off to the side and it's compressing his heart."

Now that Nora looked, Adam's exposed chest was only expanding on one side with each of his labored breaths, and his normally bronze skin had taken on a ghostly quality.

"A tension pneumothorax," Thad said, nodding quickly.

Drew paused for the barest of moments and looked up from the supplies he was organizing on Adam's stomach in surprise.

"I did read the modern emergency medicine books you brought me you know," Thad retorted.

"Then you can help me with the needle decompression. We need to puncture the chest to let the air out."

Nora picked up Adam's hand from where it rested in the snow next to her and squeezed tightly.

"Will he be okay?"

It was Odelle who asked the question everybody had been thinking. She had managed to scoot over from where she was seated in the snow and now came up next to Nora.

Drew nodded, busily palpating the location of Adam's ribs before wiping his chest with alcohol wipes.

"If we let the air out, the lung should re-expand, and he should stabilize. Then we can get him to a hospital and put a proper chest tube in."

Drew nodded to Thad, who put one hand on Adam's shoulders and the other on his hip to keep him still.

"I suspect I'm not going to like this," Adam panted, staring apprehensively at the excessively long needle that Drew had just unsheathed.

"Probably not," Drew admitted. "But you'll like being alive to tell the story."

Nora gripped Adam's hand tightly in both of hers. Odelle put an arm around Nora comfortingly, and Nora leaned into it. It was a far cry from her younger sister's earlier hostility, but Nora wasn't going to question it at a time like this.

Carefully, Drew inserted the needle between Adam's ribs. Adam hissed in pain and jolted, but Thad's firm hands kept him steady until the needle was fully inserted, and the small red stopper on the end of it was pressed against his chest.

There was a quiet rush of air like a small pressure valve being released, and Drew relaxed next to her.

"I got it," he murmured, sounding relieved. "It's been a while since I've done one of these in the field."

Within moments, Adam's chest began to expand more evenly again, and the labored sounds of his breathing decreased. The color started returning to his cheeks and Nora almost threw herself across him to hug him in relief, but she stopped herself when she realized it probably wasn't a good idea to jostle him just yet.

Instead, she contented herself with giving Adam a watery smile and holding his hand to her still armored chest. Drew was now moving over to Odelle to help her re-strap her prosthetic leg and make sure she wasn't too banged up. Nora stayed where she was, knowing Odelle was in good hands.

The snow was now drifting down slowly, and it would have been almost a serene picture if not for the blood staining the snow beneath Adam. He smiled back at her and she knew from just that look that he was proud of what she had accomplished today. Through their love, they had managed to push the Shadow back and claim a victory for the Light.

Adam's face began to blur before her eyes, and she frowned. She was finding it hard to stay upright on her knees. It was the feeling of when the danger has passed and the adrenaline drains from your system, only magnified a thousand times.

Nora's ears rang, but large hands grasped her shoulders even as Odelle's worried voice repeated her name.

"She'll be fine; she's just exhausted," came Ezra's voice from very far away. "She's never used the Light before. It's taken a lot out of her."

"The what now?" she heard Odelle ask before she didn't hear anything else.

26

NORA TOOK A SIP OF HER BLACK COFFEE AND GRIMACED AS IT BURNT her tongue. When she was nervous, she had no patience to wait for it to cool.

As she looked up from her steaming mug, the reason for her nervousness walked in the café door. Odelle spotted Nora sitting at the quiet corner table and signaled that she was going to order a drink before coming to join her.

Nora went over exactly what she was going to tell Odelle about what had happened over the last few months for the dozenth time since she had gotten her sister's text message earlier in the afternoon. Nora had woken up in her own apartment, thoroughly confused and disoriented. For a moment, Nora had thought that the entirety of the fight with the Shadow had been some sort of vivid fever dream, but the pieces of armor piled at the foot of her bed told a different story.

There had been a series of messages from Odelle, telling her that she had brought her home to sleep off her magic-induced hangover in her own bed. However, Odelle hadn't foreseen Nora sleeping for over twenty-four hours and had eventually had to leave to go to work.

Odelle made it very clear in her messages that saving her life in such a spectacular fashion as to be unconscious for over a day in no way got her off the hook and that she still owed her an explanation.

There were also several messages from Drew and Adam, assuring Nora that Adam's condition was improving, although he was still in the hospital for monitoring.

So, Nora had peeled herself out of her bed, her mouth as dry as sandpaper, feeling as though she had drunk more than she ever had in college. She called Odelle to set up this coffee date, then made a quick stop by the hospital to see Adam on the way over. When Nora had expressed her nerves about telling her sister the whole truth to Adam, his answer had been simple.

"I guarantee you I was just as nervous when I had to tell you the whole truth. I had been imagining all the ways that moment could go for seven hundred years, and I felt like my heart was going to explode. But in the end, the truth is always the right answer. Look how wonderfully it turned out for us."

The wisdom of Adam's words was somewhat diminished by the fact that he was gesticulating with a spoon full of Jello in an over-sized hospital gown.

Now, as Odelle slipped into the seat across from Nora, she hoped that her good luck when it came to the truth would continue to hold. Nora opened her mouth to start with an apology, but it snapped shut when Odelle started speaking first.

"I have to come clean. Drew filled me in on most of what's been happening." Odelle took a sip of her cappuccino and licked the line of foam off her upper lip. "I was too impatient to wait for you to wake up, and you know me—it wasn't hard to pry the important parts of the story from Drew."

"And you believe it?"

Odelle snorted into her foam. "After everything I saw, I think I have to. Otherwise, that would mean I need you to take me to the mental hospital, like, yesterday."

"I guess that makes my job a little easier then." Nora sighed in relief.

Odelle shook her head.

"Don't think this gets you off the hook. I want to hear your side of the story. I need to know why you didn't tell me about all this sooner, and I need to know what's going on with you and Adam."

Nora knew she owed the whole truth to her sister, as long a story as it was to tell. She took one more sip of her coffee and then launched into the tale, starting from her first meeting with Adam. Odelle was a perfect listener, as always, nodding along and asking incisive questions in that way that made her an excellent reporter.

When Nora got to the point in her story where she could have told Odelle the truth, she paused, trying to get her thoughts straight.

"I wish I had a better reason for not telling you, but I guess I was just scared," Nora admitted. "It was all so new to me, and the thought of there being something so terrible coming after me...it felt like if I told you, then it would be after you too."

Odelle looked at her quizzically. "It looks like not telling me made me more of a target."

Nora winced. "I know, but you're my little sister. You're so aggressively capable that I have to keep you safe from yourself. You hear about something dangerous and you run towards it instead of away, looking for the next great story. It makes you a great journalist, but it's bad for my blood pressure."

"Okay," Odelle snorted. "First, hello pot, it's kettle. You are one of the most reckless people I know, so don't give me that 'you run into danger' nonsense. And second, you shouldn't worry about my journalistic instincts. Trying to make a story out of a secret society of immortal sorcerers on the news sounds like a great way to ruin my credibility forever."

"Fair enough."

Nora continued with her story, through the part where Adam told her the truth about her past lives. Odelle grew quiet and Nora was unable to gauge her reaction. She soldiered on, recounting how she had found Odelle's voicemail and set off to save her, explaining how she had left Adam a message so that he would know to come after her, but she wouldn't know what his plan was so she wouldn't give their presence away to the Shadow.

Reaching the part where she found Odelle under the train tracks, she finished lamely, "And, well, you know the rest."

There was a long silence before Odelle responded. "Maybe it's a blessing in disguise that you didn't tell me all of this until now, because I definitely wouldn't have believed it unless I'd seen it with my own eyes."

Nora was taken aback at Odelle's forgiveness in the face of her protracted lying.

"You're taking this awfully well," she ventured carefully, "Especially since the last time I saw you, the Shadow had you convinced everything was my fault."

It was Odelle's turn to look like she was grasping for the proper words to explain herself.

"I will admit, I was furious," Odelle began. "But it was Adam who changed my mind in the end. I was convinced that you had chosen this crazy band of sorcerers over your own sister, but when he threw himself in front of me to save my life, I was forced to see things differently. If he loves you enough to give his life for me, even though he'd barely met me... Well, that really says something, I guess. It's hard to feel betrayed when a stranger is willing to die for you."

There wasn't much Nora could say to that, so she reached across the table and took Odelle's hand in her own.

"So, you really love him?" Odelle asked.

"I really do."

Odelle's smile turned wicked.

"Well then, I gotta know, does two thousand years of wisdom pay off between the sheets?"

Nora wished she could say she contained the urge to stick her tongue out at her sister as if she were a child, but she had no such luck.

Nora batted Adam's hand away from where he was fiddling with his sling, and he took the opportunity to put his free arm around her shoulders and pull her close.

He had been discharged from the hospital a week earlier, the arm on his injured side still immobilized. He made no secret of how glad he was to be free of the place. Being immune to most diseases kept Adam from consuming much modern healthcare, and it turned out he wasn't a fan of the institution. Nora could still hear him complaining about how there were too many tubes involved in his treatment. He had tried to convince Thad to take him back to the Sanctuary for treatment. Thad, however, was fascinated by the chest tube that had been inserted to treat Adam's collapsed lung and insisted that he stay under Drew's care. It was Thad's reasoning that Drew would be able to offer superior care, considering that his quick thinking had been what saved Adam in the first place.

Now, Adam and Nora walked together through the crowded streets of the West Loop. It seemed odd to be heading to a bar to meet a band of immortal warriors, but Thad had insisted that it would be good for the group to get out into the world more. Odelle jumped to suggest a place while Thad led a shopping expedition for appropriate clothes.

Nora and Adam were the last to arrive, and Thad made sure that drinks were pressed into their hands as quickly as possible. Once everybody had an adequate libation, Odelle clambered onto a chair, commanding the group's attention.

"This just in, my sources have alerted me that Nora has, at long last, received her promotion to department head at the museum."

Nora's cheeks heated even as she grinned so hard her face hurt.

She hadn't wanted to brag about her own promotion, feeling like it was a small victory after the battle that had just been won, but she couldn't help laughing as everybody raised their glasses to her and Odelle let out a whoop.

"To Nora, who can carbon date a spear as well as she can gut you with it!"

The group laughed as they drank, eventually dispersing into smaller conversations throughout the room.

As Nora settled herself onto a stool, she looked out at the group and marveled at how well the different facets of her life mixed. As Nora watched, Thad slid into a booth next to Drew and stole a sip of his craft beer. Across from Drew sat Ezra, who was trying to understand Drew's explanation of American football. He was all about the tackling each other part, but he did not understand why grown men would chase after a ball instead of simply fighting each other with real weapons.

In the corner by the window, Nora spotted Odelle talking to Antony. She was radiant and sporting a new pair of legs the Smith had built for her. Odelle had been dismayed to find that her one prosthetic had been hopelessly damaged by her use of it as a club to keep the Agent at bay. Antony had immediately risen to the occasion and offered to Smith her a new set of legs that would be far more durable, even if she did choose to use them as projectiles from time to time.

What Antony didn't mention in advance was that he'd managed to fulfill Odelle's dream of having sparkling prosthetics. At first glance, they looked to be flesh colored, but as she moved, iridescent threads running through them caught the light and sparkled with all the colors of the rainbow.

When Antony had presented Odelle with the legs, she had squealed with glee and promptly thrown her arms around his neck, pressing a quick kiss to his cheek. At her reaction, Antony's eyes had taken on an even dreamier cast than usual.

Nora was drawn from her reverie by Adam, sliding next to her and echoing her earlier thoughts. "Everybody blends together better than they have any right to."

Nora agreed, pressing an absent kiss to Adam's cheek.

"You know," Adam continued, obviously trying to sound offhand and not quite succeeding. "I think our lives would blend together pretty well, too, if we lived together."

Nora paused with her glass halfway to her lips.

"Are you saying...you want to move in?"

"Only if you want to."

"Where would we live?" Nora asked. "The Sanctuary? My apartment or yours?"

"Either. Both." Adam shrugged. "We don't have to, though, only if you're ready. I'm determined to do all of this right. Not skip anything."

"Hmm," Nora teased. "Well I think I'll have to make you a set of keys then and take you home to meet Irina this Christmas. Make you wear an ugly holiday sweater for good measure while she stuffs you full of pirozhki."

"Meeting the parents, huh? Make sure she breaks out the vodka," Adam teased.

Nora chuckled in response before fishing her phone, which had begun to buzz, out of her pocket.

"You've got to be kidding me," she groaned. "It's Mandy, and she's saying that the humidity alarms in the new display case are going off. Somebody has to go check on them."

Adam looked at her quizzically. "Nora, a few weeks ago, you dragged that spear unprotected through a blizzard. I doubt a small percentage change in humidity is going to hurt it."

Nora was already starting to locate her purse and her coat. "Yeah, but they don't know that. I should at least put on a good show of going and checking on it. I can't start off on the wrong foot in my new position of power."

It was only a couple minutes before Nora and Adam were out on the street, waiting for a cab. A few flurries of snow were just beginning to flutter down through the air as they waited, and Nora sighed heavily.

"Somehow, I thought things were going to be less crazy now that we had defeated the Agent. But I guess I didn't consider that all the demands of my job weren't going to go away that easily, and here I am running out on parties again to go check on ancient weapons."

Adam huffed a small chuckle, his breath clouding the air in front of him. "Nora, I think you're always going to pick ancient weapons over parties. Now you just know how to fight with them as well as restore them."

She shrugged. "I like to be thorough in my expertise. And at least this time you won't be there trying to steal the museum's artifacts."

Adam held up his hands defensively. "Hey, I told you before that I was there trying to protect the weapons. And if I hadn't broken in, we might not have ended up meeting so soon."

It was Nora's turn to chuckle. "I know. I would just rather have you coming in the front door with me than me chasing you through the loading docks."

They fell silent for a few moments as they searched the passing cabs for one that was unoccupied.

"It's not really over, is it?"

Adam shook his head, continuing to look at the street ahead of them.

"No, it's not. We won a battle, but the war isn't over."

Nora shoved her mitten-clad hands in her pockets.

"At least we've got plenty to be fighting for."

At that moment, a taxi spied them on the curb and pulled over. Adam opened the door for Nora and let her slide inside before slipping in and directing the driver to the museum. Nora held Adam's hand as she watched the glittering buildings go by, his grip firm as they sped towards the challenges ahead.

Thank you for reading! Did you enjoy? Please add your review because nothing helps an author more and encourages readers to take a chance on a book than a review.

And don't miss book two of *Defenders of Light* series, CHAOS AND CROWNS, available now. Turn the page for a sneak peek!

You can also sign up for the City Owl Press newsletter to receive notice of all book releases!

SNEAK PEEK OF CHAOS AND CROWNS

The paper coffee cup in Odelle's hand creaked in protest as her long nails dug into the cardboard sleeve. She forced herself to relax her grip before cappuccino exploded onto her new blazer.

"A talk show host?" Odelle asked her producer, trying not to let her anger creep into her voice. She partially succeeded.

"It would be a great gig," Ernie insisted. "A charismatic woman like you—you'd get to cover all the fun special interest pieces, instead of all the bleak news the rest of us are stuck with. You would be a household name!"

Odelle resisted the urge to douse Ernie's encouraging smile in hot coffee. Instead, she did her best to keep her tone cool as she responded, "Plenty of journalists become household names without having to resort to being the background noise in doctors' office waiting rooms. I mean look at Amy Biderman. National News America wouldn't be the same without her as their anchor."

Her boss's smile remained plastered to his face, taking on a condescending edge.

Odelle pressed on. "What about covering some of the gun violence in the city—I could work on covering that. There's been so many shootings recently, I'm sure we need more people in the field to do more eyewitness interviews. Or maybe the upcoming mayoral elections—"

Ernie waved a dismissive hand. "You don't want to cover that. Hardcore journalism can be so messy. It's easy to think the next story could be your big break, but who knows if it will work out?

With a talk show, you can use that captivating reporting style of yours without having to do any of the leg work."

"You think I'm not willing to put in the work for serious stories? I didn't bust my butt to get this far, only to be relegated to interviewing the internet celebrity of the week."

Her boss appeared humbled, but he didn't back down completely.

"Just think about it. It could be a step up from your current beat."

"Yeah, I'll think about it," Odelle conceded. "I've gotta go for now. I need to check something for the election story I'm reporting on tomorrow before I leave."

Odelle strutted from the room, pointedly avoiding thinking about how wonderful it might be to host her own morning talk show. She had become a reporter because she was committed to delivering the truth to those who deserved to know it, and she wasn't about to give that up now. Instead, she focused on how to find her own big break, to show him just how capable of a journalist she was. After all, reporting was a world she understood.

Odelle laid her head on the granite countertop of her sister's kitchen island with a groan. The coolness of the surface against her forehead grounded her even as she vented to Nora.

The clink of glass against stone made Odelle look up to find the stem of a wine glass inches from her face. She sat up, plucking it from the counter and taking an appreciative sip of the rosé within.

"You've gotten out of being pigeonholed before," Nora pointed out as she picked up the two other glasses of wine she had poured, bringing them over to the couch where Adam sat.

"Yeah, but a morning talk show is harder to get out of than sports reporting. They may have wanted to put the cute blonde on the sidelines of the football game, but the truth is I know nothing about sports."

"You know more than you let them know." Nora collapsed onto the couch next to Adam, casually throwing her legs over his lap.

He absently stroked Nora's shin and offered her a smitten smile as he accepted the wine from her. Odelle's heart squeezed painfully at the exchange, but she shoved the feeling down to get back to the matter at hand.

"Maybe, but it's getting harder to put Ernie off. I haven't done any really great reporting in the field since the blizzard a few months ago. I need to nab something big, cover something so impactful they won't be able to ignore me anymore."

"Knowing you, you already have something in mind," Adam observed.

"There are a few things coming up. The Mayoral election is at the end of next month, and coverage is really ramping up. In fact, I managed to score an invite to Charles Gainey's fundraiser this weekend. Getting a few good quotes from him—it could give me an edge in getting assigned to more election coverage."

"You always did know how to work a party to your advantage, and you're at your best in heels." Nora paused before asking in a tone of forced nonchalance, "Are you bringing a date to the fundraiser?"

Odelle examined her fingernails instead of looking at Adam and Nora, frowning at a chip in the trendy greige polish.

"I wasn't going to. I didn't want people to think that I wasn't focused while I was there," Odelle explained with a shrug. She glanced up and saw Nora and Adam exchange a knowing look. Odelle felt scrutinized, and it was unbalancing for somebody who was used to being the one asking the questions.

"That's not like you," Nora commented. "You've always liked having some 'arm candy' as you like to call it. Didn't you literally once call a date the most enviable accessory?"

Odelle snorted lightly. She supposed she had said that in explanation of why she was bringing a fitness model to a charity auction.

"I just haven't met anybody interesting recently, I guess."

It was Nora's turn to snort. "I literally introduced you to a secret society of immortal sorcerers a few months ago. If that doesn't count as interesting, I'm not sure I really want to know what interests you."

Odelle waved her off even as Nora's words struck a nerve.

"The Eteria aren't interesting in a way they can really talk about in public. And you guys normally keep to yourselves—except of course you, Adam."

Adam nodded in acknowledgement even as he pressed her. "Yeah, but since we left the Sanctuary in the fall to help Nora, some others have been thinking it might be nice to reintegrate into the world a bit more. Antony asks a lot of questions about modern technology. He might like to see some in person."

At the mention of Antony, Odelle took a sizable gulp of wine.

"I doubt kissing ass at a political fundraiser is what he had in mind," Odelle said in a voice that she hoped sounded casual.

Adam opened his mouth as if to argue, but Nora put a hand on his arm.

"You'll call us right away if you need anything while we're gone right?" Nora changed the subject and Odelle sighed inwardly at the temporary reprieve.

"I absolutely will not," Odelle retorted. "I refuse to interrupt you when you finally decided to use up the vacation days that you've been collecting for years, *zolotse*"

Odelle considered it a personal victory that Nora had finally gotten it through her head to enjoy her life a little. She refused to be the reason that her older sister put fun on hold.

Nora's brows creased.

"That's sweet, but the Shadow has been bold these past few months. Ever since—well..."

"Ever since it captured me and you saved me in a daring rescue, yes, yes," Odelle brushed away her older sister's concern. "I know what I'm up against now though, and I'll be careful. Besides, something tells me you two are going to be...otherwise occupied...on this getaway of yours."

Spots of color bloomed high on Nora's cheeks, but the sidelong smile she shared with Adam spoke volumes. Nora and Adam had a lot of lost time to make up for. After all, in a prior life, Nora had been a Warrior for the Eteria, fighting the evil Shadow in an ageless war. Her former incarnation had given her life to save what was left of the Eteria from the Shadow, and her husband had managed to pull her soul into a cycle of reincarnation. She and Adam had found each other again in this life, and Odelle had never seen Nora happier. Seeing Nora having found her niche made Odelle's heart warm, even as she itched beneath her skin. Nora now had a whole different side to her life with the Eteria that Odelle wasn't a part of—wasn't sure she *could* be a part of. Having spent her whole life showing the world how capable she was and building an armor of self-confidence, discovering a world where she might be unable to pull her weight made her grind her teeth.

Odelle looked away from the couple's shared moment and took another sip of her drink, refusing to let her melancholy musings dull her happiness for her sister.

"Still, you shouldn't face the Shadow on your own," Nora said, "None of us should. We'll come back if anything comes up."

"Why does everybody seem to think I can't handle things recently?" Odelle snapped back, trying to swallow the words back as soon as they were out of her mouth. Nora was the last person who deserved to be on the receiving end of her frustration. She opened her mouth to apologize, but Nora took the comment in stride.

"Odelle, fighting the literal physical incarnation of fear isn't something anyone should have to do alone. I'm not your boss. I know you can handle yourself and your job just fine—better than fine, actually."

"Thanks." Odelle nodded. "I'm just a little on edge from stuff at work."

And only stuff at work she added silently, trying to convince herself.

"Then you blow off some steam schmoozing and dazzling at the fundraiser this weekend. I'll be enjoying a pina colada on a beach and not worrying about you."

"Because there is nothing to worry about," Odelle agreed as she put on her coat and scarf, bracing herself for the biting winds of a Chicago winter. In truth, Odelle was looking forward to a little time away from Nora and Adam's scrutiny. Nora glowed with happiness since having found her home with Adam and the rest of the Eteria. Odelle refused to ruin it by complaining about her own childish grievances with the group of immortal sorcerers—or one sorcerer in particular.

***

Don't stop now. Keep reading with your copy of CHAOS AND CROWNS available now.

Don't miss book two of the *Defenders of Light* series, CHAOS AND CROWNS, available now. And find more from S. C. Grayson at www.scgrayson.com

As a television reporter and double amputee, Odelle is used to having to prove herself. But fighting against the physical incarnation of evil for the fate of the world certainly raises the stakes.

When a magical, ancient crown surfaces in Chicago, Odelle joins forces with the Eteria, a secret society of immortal sorcerers from the Greek empire, to keep it from falling into the clutches of the evil Shadow. Odelle's sister, Nora, has been fighting alongside the Eteria as a Warrior, but Odelle has avoided the sorcerers after one of their number hurt her pride by rejecting her romantic advances. However, Antony the Smith, the very sorcerer who spurned her despite his gentle disposition, is the one she's stuck with.

As the Shadow threatens the city she loves, Odelle is determined to show that she can contribute to the fight, despite her inability to use the magical Light. When she sets out to prove to Antony he was wrong to reject her, and to herself that she has a place in this magical new world, the hunt for the crown heats up.

If Odelle and Antony can't set aside their need to prove themselves and work together, the Shadow will gain the power to engulf all they love.

Please sign up for the City Owl Press newsletter for chances to win special subscriber-only contests and giveaways as well as receiving information on upcoming releases and special excerpts.

All reviews are **welcome** and **appreciated**. Please consider leaving one on your favorite social media and book buying sites.

Escape Your World. Get Lost in Ours! City Owl Press at www.cityowlpress.com.

ACKNOWLEDGMENTS

I thought that after writing an entire book, writing the acknowledgements would be easy. I was wrong. It's unspeakably hard to hold a dream come true in your hands and somehow thank everybody that got you here in a few short pages. So before I start, know that whatever thanks are here, they can't possibly be enough.

That being said, I'd like to thank Lisa and the entire team at City Owl Press for making this dream a reality. This story wouldn't exist in its current form without them, and I am eternally grateful for this unreal opportunity.

Thanks to my husband, Rhys, for his endless support and supplying cereal treats during long days of editing. This book wouldn't exist if I didn't have the best life partner I could ever ask for. Amanda also deserves an extra special round of applause for being my alpha reader, my beta reader, and the one I trust to give me honest opinions on things I'm afraid to let other people read. I don't think I would have even attempted to write a book if she hadn't introduced me to fantasy novels from the day I could read and continued to never get tired of talking books with me to this very day.

Of course, my parents deserve a standing ovation for making me feel like I could do anything I set my mind to and giving me the skills to see it through. They've stuck with me through every crazy plot twist I've thrown at them (and there have been a lot) and for that I'm eternally grateful. To every family member and friend that has ever asked me about my book and told me *"That's so cool"*, you've given me more encouragement than you could ever imagine.

My lovely cats, Will and Jessie also deserve a shoutout. Not because they helped with this book (quite the opposite in fact), but just because they're awesome.

And lastly, I'd like to thank you. Yes *you*! If you're reading this book, you're part of the story too. A book is more than just words on paper, but it takes on a life of its own in the mind of the reader. So, thank you for giving my story and my characters life. I know they are in good hands.

ABOUT THE AUTHOR

S. C. GRAYSON has been reading fantasy novels since she was a little girl stealing books from her older sister's shelves, and that has developed into a love of writing and storytelling. Her writing is currently focused on fantasy and paranormal romance. When she is not sitting in a local coffee shop writing and consuming an iced americano, Grayson is a nurse working towards a PhD in nursing with a focus on breast cancer genetics. She lives in Pittsburgh with her loving husband and their two cats, who enjoy contributing to her work by walking across her keyboard at inopportune moments (the cats, not the husband).

www.scgrayson.com

ABOUT THE PUBLISHER

City Owl Press is a cutting edge indie publishing company, bringing the world of romance and speculative fiction to discerning readers.

Escape Your World. Get Lost in Ours!

www.cityowlpress.com

facebook.com/YourCityOwlPress

twitter.com/cityowlpress

instagram.com/cityowlbooks

pinterest.com/cityowlpress

Made in the USA
Las Vegas, NV
27 July 2023